Legend
of the
Young Gun

DeAunte Anderson

Liliam,
Thank you for support. I hope
you enjoy the book.

ISBN 13: 978-0-9899868-4-7

Author: DeAunte Anderson

1

Junnie sat in the passenger seat, his eyes red and low as he held his gaze on the building across the street. The blunt in his hand was burning slowly as he kept his focus on his main goal. Two hours passed since they had been waiting, and he intended to wait two more if need be.

"We've been sitting here for about three fucking hours. You sure this nigga in there?" Harlem asked impatiently.

He was sitting in the backseat, chain smoking cigarettes and getting more and more impatient. This was the sixth time he'd asked in the past ten minutes.

"It's only been two hours, and yes, I'm sure he's in there," Junnie answered easily, finally taking another hit from the blunt. "Be patient."

"Being patient and being stupid are two different things," Harlem shot back. "We could just be sitting out here while this muthafucka is across town, at home in the bed."

"I don't know, I'm kinda with Harlem on this one," Allah chimed in, from behind the driver seat.

He was smoking his own blunt and was a lot closer to finishing his off than Junnie was.

"Two hours is a long time to be out here posted up. You sure Chino knew what he was talking about?"

Junnie shook his head slightly.

"Y'all gotta chill. Just take my word for it, he's in there."

Being the level-headed one out of his crew was stressful at times, but it was a position Junnie played well. The three had been a unit for years and friends even longer. Each was a soldier in their own way, but when it came to leadership, the title had been bestowed upon Junnie.

Two weeks earlier, Junnie had been at the bar having a quick drink before he headed home. While he was there, he ran into an old associate who went by the name of Sammy.

Sammy was a notorious loud mouth who loved putting on a show for people, and making a spectacle of himself. Usually, Junnie didn't associate with those types of dudes but he had known Sammy for years and tolerated him to a certain degree.

While they were there, they got a few drinks and watched a little of the game that was on. The Oakland Raiders were playing, and naturally, Junnie voiced his opinion on how his team was going to take the win, even though they were two touchdowns down.

Sammy, being the knucklehead he was, disagreed with Junnie and that started the bidding war. By halftime, they had put five hundred on the line and had everyone in the bar watching in anticipation.

When the game ended, the Raiders had come out victorious with the win, ultimately the underdogs. Sammy told Junnie to wait while he went to his car to grab his extra stash.

Junnie knew Sammy heard how he operated and knew the consequences for trying to cross him, so he allowed him to go outside to grab his money.

Sammy never came back. Not only had Sammy skipped out on paying Junnie, he had dropped off the radar for the past couple weeks. This was why Junnie and his boys were sitting outside the strip club on a stakeout. It was through an associate named Chino that Junnie had gained the location of Sammy's whereabouts.

Junnie wasn't worried about the cash. He would never be strapped for such a small amount of money. It was the fact that Sammy had the nerve to play him like he didn't know what would happen.

"Listen, I'm about to go inside and scope the place out. It's hot as hell in this damn car, and my patience is thin," Harlem complained, flicking his cigarette butt out of the cracked window.

"You can't go in there because he knows who you are," Junnie pointed out. "He will know what time it is as soon as he spots you and we can't have him ducking off before I get my chance to talk to him."

"Then let's run in there and drag his ass out. Anything is better than sitting here," Harlem grumbled as he sparked another cigarette. "At least turn the radio up. I ain't trying to sit here and listen to you muthafuckas breathe."

Allah turned and gave Harlem a look. "I'm getting tired of you crying about every little thing. You're blowing my high."

"Do something about it," Harlem challenged, returning Allah's glare.

"Y'all be easy," Junnie warned, seeing the fire building in Allah's eyes. He knew how far the two would be willing to take it if he let them. "I know we been here a minute but it's about to pay off."

"How is smacking up this nigga Sammy going to 'pay off'?" Harlem questioned.

"Because Sammy isn't here just to look at some ass and toss cash out." Junnie informed them, nodding towards the strip club. "He's meeting his connect here and apparently doing a pick up. So he's going to pay up one way or another."

"And Chino told you all this?" Harlem shook his head. "This could be a set up. He could have tipped this nigga Sammy off and they on their way out here right now to blow our heads off."

"They could try," Allah snickered, shifting the 9mm he had in his lap. He had started loading it once when they had first parked the car.

"I trust Chino." Junnie replied easily, taking a long drag from his blunt. Suddenly, he sat up in his seat. "And for good reason. Look who it is."

Allah and Harlem both looked towards the entrance, and saw three men stepping out. The one in the front was Sammy. He was laughing with his boys, unaware that he was being watched.

"This fool got the nerve to be walking around with a smile on his face, having a grand ol' time," Harlem shook his head in disgust as he pulled his gun from his jeans. "I'ma be the one to split his wig. I don't like shit about this nigga."

"Chill out, bruh. I'm going out here on some diplomatic shit. No shooting." Junnie told him.

He was nowhere near a saint but, he didn't feel like killing someone when a simple ass whooping would suffice.

Harlem looked at Junnie in disbelief. "Nah, fuck that. Y'all had me sitting in this hot ass car all night, the least you can do is let me shoot off some steam."

"No killing." Junnie replied firmly. Harlem glared at him before sitting back in his seat. "Fuck that, you two go holler at ol' boy then. Don't make sense for all of us to get out the car if all you want to do is shake hands with the nigga."

Allah shook his head. "Don't you ever get tired of being a pain in the ass?"

"Nope." Harlem smirked, raising his feet up on the seat as he smoked his cigarette. "And leave the keys in the car so I can bump some Jeezy."

Junnie shook his head and turned his attention back to Sammy who was moving across the parking lot. Making sure he had his gun on his hip Junnie nodded at Allah and they exited the car.

****

Sammy walked from the bar feeling like a million dollars. The day had been filled with nothing but positives and the night wasn't over yet. For years, Sammy had been a part of the Bay Area underworld, working as a dealer until he could venture out on his own and start his own crew.

Tonight, his boss had trusted him with the assignment of picking up their next shipment from their connect. When Sammy had come to the strip club to meet the cocky Dominican kid who had the delivery, Sammy was shocked. He had never seen so many bundles of coke in his life. Once he paid the Dominican kid, Sammy left the club much to his crew's disappointment. They had been planning on staying and enjoying the show but Sammy wasn't trying to kick it while he had bricks on him. Besides, he had a nice piece of ass waiting in his bed, right where he left her.

"You know you off that bullshit," one of Sammy's boys, Randy spoke up as they walked across the parking lot. "You didn't see ol' girl who was about to go on stage next? Ass fatter than a chubby boy's lunch bag."

"That same bitch will be here tomorrow night when we don't have a duffel bag full of dope," Sammy replied, taking a cautious look around.

"Sam's right," Wick chimed in.

He was a tall kid who rarely spoke, but his attention had peaked at all the scattered ass that had been inside the club.

"Those hoes were nice but they aren't nowhere near bad enough to get booked over."

"Yeah, y'all right," Randy agreed. "Still, I wouldn't mind taking one of those bitches home. All you would have to do is offer them a little change and they'll be ready to fuck."

"Back in my day, we would take ladies out for a dinner and a movie before we tried to get the panties off."

Sammy and his crew jumped in surprise as they turned around simultaneously. Junnie was standing a few feet away with his hands shoved in his jacket pockets.

There was a small of smirk on his face as he came into view. Stepping out beside him, Allah took a toke from his blunt, his red eyes focused on Sammy as if he were a T-bone steak.

Sammy couldn't help but smile as he realized what was about to go down.

"June the Goon, what you doing on this side of town?" Sammy asked adjusting the duffel bag on his shoulder. He stepped forward and held his hand out in greeting.

"Just out enjoying a nice walk." Junnie looked at Sammy's hand but didn't bother to shake it. "It's been awhile, my nigga."

"Yeah, I've been meaning to catch up with you." Sammy put his hand down. "I just been out here making moves, trying to catch up on some shit and what not. Plus, there's been a lot of heat on the streets, so I've been laying low. You know how it is."

"Indeed," Junnie nodded slowly. "But seeing how we happened to be here now, you got that bread for me?"

Sammy snapped his fingers. "You know what? I don't but, meet me over on East Avenue tomorrow and I'll be able to drop that change off for you."

"See, the thing with that is I feel like you've been dodging me for the past few weeks so I'd rather collect it now that I'm here." Junnie retorted.

"Dodging you? Course not. I've just been busy. The fact that I owed you some change is a coincidence," he stated grinning.

"There are no coincidences, just the illusion of coincidences. As much work as you put in on the streets, I'm sure you can pay me what you owe."

Even though Junnie wasn't speaking with hostility, Sammy didn't appreciate being confronted in front of his team.

Sammy knew exactly who Junnie was and how he gave it up, but he wouldn't be swayed. In his mind, he was just as brutal as the young man in front of him.

"Yo, check this shit out, bruh. I told you, I don't have it right now. If you want to meet me tomorrow like I said, then you might get this bubblegum money you're bitching about. If not, then I don't know what to tell you. Holla at me later."

Junnie's eyebrows raised in slight surprised at Sammy's words. He turned to Allah who looked just as shocked as he did.

"Okay Sam, you're right." Junnie nodded in agreement. His face was surprisingly calm. "We can just meet up tomorrow. What time?"

Sammy was stunned that he had got away with talking to Junnie the way he had. Sammy opened his mouth to come up with a lie he was going to tell Junnie but the words never left his mouth. Before he could say anything Junnie's fist had connected with his jaw.

The punch rocked Sammy as he flew back into a parked car. He didn't have time to collect himself before Junnie had let off another swing that busted his nose wide open. Wick and Randy ran forward but Allah raised his gun making them freeze with fear.

"Don't risk it," Allah cautioned them.

Junnie leaned over Sammy, who was sprawled on the concrete, and lifted him up by the front of his shirt.

"Who the fuck you think you talking to?" Junnie demanded, slapping Sammy with his free hand. "Don't ever try to play me, nigga."

In one motion Junnie ripped the duffel bag from his shoulder without even tearing the strap.

"Hold up, I can't let you take that," Sammy mumbled groggily.

He might have been dazed but he had enough sense to know that he couldn't let Junnie walk off with his bag. Inside was all the drugs his boss had sent him to get and if he lost it he was as good as dead. Sammy stretched his hand out but Junnie kicked it away.

"Everybody wants to be a tough guy." Junnie tossed the duffel bag over his shoulder. "Should've just payed what you owed. Now you're assed out. You gentlemen have a fine night."

Junnie turned to leave while Allah continued to aim his gun at the three men. He gave them a wink as he walked backwards to the car, following closely behind Junnie. They reached the car and hopped inside, where music was blasting, and smoke filled the inside.

Harlem was watching them with a look of amusement as Allah started the car.

"So how'd it go?" Harlem laughed.

Before the two could respond, a gunshot rang out. They all turned around in time to see Wick and Randy running into the street, the muzzle of their guns flashing as they fired shot after shot.

Allah revved the engine and sped away from the curb, swerving to avoid hitting a parked car. The back window shattered spraying Harlem with glass.

"Ahh, fuck that, no shooting shit."

Aiming out of the broken window, Harlem began to fire back at the two men, causing them to take cover. Allah slammed his foot down on the peddle and they sped off into the night.

2

The sun had set a few hours earlier, but the day was just starting for Calvin Cole. He sat in front of the giant picture window in his hotel room and stared out into the city's skyline.

Whenever he got a room at The Hilton, he enjoyed looking out at the city he had laid claim to years earlier. Taking a sip from the glass of whiskey he had in his hand, Calvin glanced at his watch before continuing his stare at the tall buildings and lights of his town.

Calvin Cole was a twenty-eight-year-old, who had decided at a young age that he was born to be a king and it was a belief that had followed him to his adulthood. True, he wasn't ruling a country or reigning over a nation, but he had seized control of the entire Bay Area some years prior and in his mind, that was good enough.

A tall man, with his hair neatly braided into two twisted cornrows, and a goatee trimmed to perfection, Calvin Cole was as handsome as he was charismatic. He had a certain charm about himself that drew people to him and just made them want to be in his presence.

When he was only twelve years old, Calvin's uncle showed him the ropes of the drug game and gave him his first dime bag of weed to sell. Through some of the hardest work and determination, Calvin managed to build his legacy and empire from that one bag of herb. With his best friend, Johnny Welcome, the two gained power over their city and then spread to the surrounding areas.

Calvin disposed of the necessary people he had to in order to get to the top, but other than that, he gave everyone a fair shake. It was pretty simple; either join him and his squad or get killed or shut down. A lot of people chose the first option, but for those that didn't their story was cut short.

There was a knock on the door before it opened. The man that stepped inside wore a scowl etched across his face, which was a common thing for him. He was a light skinned cat with his hair pulled back in a bushy ponytail and cold black eyes. A deep scar ran from his eyebrow across his cheek where one of his enemies had gotten the better of him. Though Johnny received a scar from the encounter, the man who had given it to him was never seen again.

Johnny Welcome had been Calvin's right hand man since he had begun his rise to becoming the king. For the entire journey, his loyalty had never wavered once. In his twenty something years of being alive, Johnny Welcome had been in countless street wars and was still around to talk about them.

"How's the city looking?" Johnny asked, closing the door behind him.

"Like it's a product of what I always wanted it to be," Calvin replied, drinking the rest of the whiskey. "Did you find him?"

"Yeah, Polo is bringing him up now. It took a while to find him, but Wolf tracked him down in San Jose."

Calvin nodded. "That's why we pay Wolf the big bucks."

"Not to mention, he almost beat the kid to death."

Calvin wasn't too surprised to hear this information. Wolf wasn't exactly known for his verbal skills. He was more about action. At that moment, there was another knock on the door, this one a lot harder than Johnny's had been. Johnny opened the door and a man came crashing inside, falling to the floor.

Polo stepped in next, looking down at the man he had just pushed in disgust. "Fucking rat," he mumbled. Polo walked around the man on the floor and went to give Calvin dap. "What's up big homie?"

"Not much. Glad to see you brought me my package."

Polo was a young boy that Calvin and Johnny had found a few years prior living on the streets and getting into more trouble than he could handle. Calvin took a liking to the kid and brought in him to assist with the empire. Polo turned out to be an efficient soldier and was always more than willing to do whatever his two mentors asked of him.

"Yeah, Wolf brought him to the warehouse earlier." Polo looked back down at the man in disgust. "This piece of shit had the nerve to be at a motel with some bitch, laid up chilling like he had the right to be."

Calvin took a good look at the man. Usually, he didn't meet with any of the soldiers he had working for him. That was Johnny's job, and sometimes Polo, but this meeting was necessary. Calvin leaned over the man.

"What's your name, youngsta?" he asked softly.

"Jonah," the young man answered weakly.

Besides a few scrapes and a busted lip, he appeared to be okay. Just terrified. He knew exactly who Calvin was but the man was like a phantom. No one he knew had ever met the drug lord personally.

"Jonah," Calvin repeated. "Do you know why you're here, Jonah?"

At first Jonah thought about lying, but one glance at the harsh look on Johnny Welcome's face caused him to change his mind.

"I've been having money missing," he told Calvin, who was watching him with a calm face.

"And why is that?"

"I've gotten robbed twice and the third time the cops ran up on me. They knew I was selling so they emptied my pockets and took all my shit. I swear." Calvin nodded slowly.

"You haven't been stealing, have you?"

Jonah's eyes got wide. "No, I swear Calvin! I would never steal from you!"

"You still lying nigga?" Johnny kicked Jonah in his face, causing him to yell out in pain. Jonah's nose immediately began to gush blood.

Calvin gave Johnny a look. "Polo go get me some napkins from the kitchen." Polo rushed and grabbed a few napkins from the counter. He handed them to Calvin who reached down and passed them to Jonah. "Wipe yourself off, homie." He instructed.

Jonah hesitated slightly as if it might be a trick, but he finally accepted the napkins and held them to his nose. "Now, you can understand why my associates might be a little in disbelief. You've been robbed three times, once by cops, and no one else can confirm that. It's looking pretty bad for you, my nigga."

"You gotta believe me, Calvin. I wouldn't do that. You're the reason I'm able to feed my family. You gave me a job when I didn't have shit, I would never steal from you!" Jonah cried, trying his best to control his bowels.

Calvin rubbed his beard as he stared deep into Jonah's terrified eyes. After a few seconds he nodded. "Get up," he said. Jonah uneasily climbed to his feet, keeping his eyes on Calvin. He wasn't sure if he was about to die or not, and the unknowing was the worst part.

"I believe you, all right? I'ma let you get out of here." Calvin patted his shoulder. "From now on, I want you working with someone so you don't have to worry about getting robbed anymore, cool?"

Jonah nodded, not trusting himself to speak. He continued waiting for Calvin to strike him, or for Johnny to pull out his gun, but neither happened.

"But let me tell you," Jonah winced as Calvin applied pressure to his shoulder. A cold look crossed over Calvin's face. "If I find out you're lying to me, I'm going to have Johnny here kill you, but that's only after I send Wolf over on Lennox Avenue and have him torture your momma, Ms. Sherryl. I've heard she's a nice lady so I would hate to have my boy slit her throat while she sleeps, do you understand?"

Jonah's eyes were wide open in horror. It was true what everyone said. Calvin knew everything he ever needed to know. Once he had mentioned his mother and where she lived, it put a whole new fear in Jonah's heart. Again, he just nodded.

"Good." A smile spread across Calvin's face. "Now get outta here and be safe out there."

Jonah turned and slowly walked to the front door, still expecting to hear gunfire. When he made it out of the room he ran down the hallway and took the stairs instead of wasting time with the elevator.

Once the door closed behind Jonah, Johnny and Polo both turned to Calvin. Polo's face was surprise; Johnny wore one of anger.

"What the fuck was that?" Johnny asked frowning. "Why you just let that nigga go?"

"Because neither one of you have proof that he did anything wrong." Calvin said simply, walking to the kitchen to pour himself another glass of whiskey.

"So you believe that shit about him getting robbed three times in one month?"

"Not exactly, but I'm not going to murder the little dude just because of suspicion. How would you feel if you were truly innocent and some niggas tried to kill you?"

"I would never be mistaken for being a rat ass muthafucka so I can't put myself in that position," Johnny responded coolly.

"Yeah, you might have made a mistake on that one, big homie," Polo chimed in, helping himself to a glass of the whiskey. He wasn't even of legal drinking age yet and had already put in more work than men twice his age. "This nigga Jonah has always been questionable. I don't like his vibe."

"I usually only take lives from people I know actually did something. Bring me proof and my next meeting with this nigga will be different. Until then, just keep an eye on him."

Calvin's phone vibrated as he got a text. As he read and replied to the message Johnny looked at him. They had become friends back when they were just youngsters, pitching dime bags on the corner and robbing kids from the neighborhood for their sneakers. Back then, Calvin was a heartless goon who didn't have a problem letting his gun spark for the smallest offense but since he had become the king of the region, he had become a lot more diplomatic. In all honesty, he ran his dynasty the way it should be ran.

He was fair and all around pretty kind when it came to giving people a fair shot. They hadn't been in too many street wars, but every once in a while, Johnny had to make sure he put a few people in check.

Even though Calvin had calmed down a lot in their adult years, Johnny had no problem still sharing his bullets with anyone who deserved them.

"So, beside that shit with Jonah, how has everything else been going?" Calvin asked, typing away on his phone.

"Same ol', same ol'. I went to meet up with Santana earlier today and he was telling me about a business opportunity with some new dudes out in San Jose."

"Santana always has something going on," Calvin shook his head. "You think it's a good prospect?"

Johnny shrugged. "I would have to check them out first. They're from Washington and I'm not too familiar with how niggas up there operate."

"Sounds reasonable." Calvin nodded.

"Aye, how'd shit go with shorty from the club the other night?" Polo asked, taking a seat in the armchair.

The night before, Polo had talked Calvin into going to the club. Since his rise to power Calvin had calmed down a bit on kicking it in public settings. True, a lot of people had love for him in the hood but he knew from experience that there was always at least one hater creeping in the shadows.

Calvin leaned against the wall and rubbed his chin. "She was cool," he answered after pondering the question for a moment.

Polo gave him a look. "Just 'cool', huh?"

"I mean, don't get me wrong, shorty was bad. Pussy was some of the best I done had in a minute."

"But?"

Calvin shrugged. "The chick was dumb as hell. We couldn't even hold a basic conversation. You might find it hard to believe but all that body she had didn't really amount to shit because it had no substance."

Polo shook his head in disappointment.

"Big homie, you missing the point. Who cares if she was dumber than a stick of butter? You ain't supposed to be out here loving these hoes anyway. All that ass she had should have made up for her lack of IQ."

Calvin looked at the seriousness on his protégés face and couldn't help but smile. "You're still young, Po. I wouldn't expect you to understand," he told him simply. "But I'm good off the club for a minute."

"Yeah, while y'all were out getting your party on, I was conducting business." Johnny told them, arms folded over his chest.

Polo stared at him. "I should've took you instead of Cal. You always angry. We gotta get you some pussy."

Johnny smirked. "I've been putting pussies to sleep since you were a little nigga collecting Pokemon cards."

"Yeah, I bet."

"Listen," Calvin said, setting his glass down. "We've been taking care of business a lot better than usual and I'm proud of you guys. Calvin Cole wouldn't be anywhere as successful as he is without you two. J, we started this shit together so I'll be glad when you stop running around busting your gun like you're a soldier, instead of sitting at top like the general you are."

"There's no doubt about my position of power," Johnny clarified. "But I'm a killer. Always have been, and it won't stop now."

Calvin understood what he meant. Since they were younger, Johnny had always had a knack for murder and the older they got the more he liked to quench his thirst for blood.

"Well, in any case, things are sailing smooth as of now, and I'm proud about it." Calvin filled three glasses of whiskey and passed them out. He held his up in salute. Johnny and Polo followed suit. "To the, Family."

3

The sun's rays managed to peek through the blinds and shine directly into Junnie's face. Slowly opening his eyes, Junnie shielded his face from the harsh sunlight.

He sat up in the bed and glanced at the clock on the nightstand. It didn't surprise him that he had ended up sleeping most of the morning away. The previous night had been a wild one. From somewhere on the other end of the bedroom door he could hear Essence singing loudly to her music, and from the sound of it, she was in the kitchen putting in work.

Swinging his legs over the side of the bed, Junnie got up and went into the bathroom. Earlier the day before, he had taken his braids out and his long mane of hair was now running wild all over his head. Looking at his reflection in the mirror, Junnie rubbed his face trying to get rid of the grogginess.

Dark toned, with a muscular build and a handsome face, Junnie never had a problem gaining the attention of women. Even though his charming feature is what drew the females in, it was his pale gray eyes that kept them captivated.

They glowed like jewels against his dark skin and had a way of seemingly peering through someone's soul. It was the only trait that he had inherited from his father, Rodney, but it was one he cherished.

Rodney had been an animal during his reign in the streets, putting fear in the most respected hood officials as well as law enforcement, which is probably what led to his untimely death. His life ended in a hail of bullets in the middle of the street, leaving behind a distraught girlfriend, and two sons.

Junnie only vaguely remembered his father, so his younger brother Seven had no memories of the man at all, which was crazy seeing how he turned out to be exactly like him. Junnie was well known throughout the streets as a wild card but Seven was on another level.

Turning on the hot water, Junnie splashed some on his face before leaving the bathroom. Walking into the living room he found the television on BET, music blasting, and the welcoming aroma of bacon drifting through the air.

Junnie stood in the doorway of the kitchen and watched Essence as she moved around the kitchen fixing their breakfast. Even with sweatpants and a scarf on, she was beautiful. She was a gorgeous golden skinned girl, with oval hazel eyes, and full lips. When her long brown hair wasn't tied up, it fell past her shoulders in long swift curls.

She was so wrapped up in her singing and stirring the pancake batter, she didn't notice him at first, but when she did finally look up and find him standing there, a smile crossed her face.

"Oh, about time you decided to wake up. Smelled that good cooking, huh?" Essence walked over and gave Junnie a quick kiss on the lips before going back to work.

"Yeah, the smell of burnt eggs usually pulls me out of the bed," Junnie teased, taking a seat on the stool. "Why you up so early?" he asked, grabbing a magazine that was sitting on the counter and flipping through it.

Essence gave him a look. "Early? It's one in the afternoon. I was going to wake you up but you looked so peaceful I decided to let you keep going."

"Thanks for having mercy on me. I needed the sleep."

"Where were you last night? I didn't hear you come in."

"Just went to take care of some business with Allah and Harlem," Junnie said simply.

Essence turned and stared at him for a second before going back to scramble the eggs.

Back when Junnie was nothing more than a nappy headed teen, standing on the corner trying his best to look hard he had the fortune of running into Essence. He had been coming from a house party one night which had ended after some joker had decided to start shooting at a rival gang.

Junnie stepped off of the bus, still slightly tipsy from the party, but that didn't stop him from noticing the pretty girl sitting at the bus stop.

Even though it was near two in the morning, the girl didn't have a jacket on, but the telltale sign that something was wrong was due to her crying softly and staring into the distance. Junnie looked towards his house, then back at the girl before deciding to approach her.

Once he got closer, he noticed her busted lip and swollen cheek. He asked the girl if she was alright and she ignored him at first, but after a little more prodding, he finally managed to get her to respond.

She told him her name was Essence and she was having a rough night. She didn't seem to want to talk about it but that didn't stop Junnie from sitting next to her and making small talk anyway. They sat there for about half an hour before

Essence finally began to warm up to him, and her responses turned into complete sentences.

It took about another hour before Junnie convinced her to come to his house. At first, she was apprehensive but when he had asked if she really wanted to stay at the chilly bus stop for the night, as opposed to a warm house, Essence agreed.

When they got to his house, Junnie gave her some sweatpants and a T-shirt and allowed her to take his bed, while he settled in his armchair. Even though it was extremely late, neither were ready to sleep yet and they stayed up talking for the rest of the night.

It was during that time that Essence told Junnie about her father and how he loved making her his punching bag. She shared her life story, and in return, Junnie opened up about his own life which was something he'd never done.

By the time the sun had peeked over the horizon, Essence was curled beneath the blankets, snoring softly, but Junnie couldn't sleep. He stayed up thinking about the feelings he had caught for this girl he had only known for a few hours.

Junnie would never admit it, but he knew he was in love from that first night. From that time on, Essence would come visit Junnie whenever things were bad at her house and for the first month, the sleeping arrangements stayed the same, until one night when Junnie decided to ease under the blankets with her.

After that, it was never announced aloud that they were together but it didn't need to be. That had been three years ago and their relationship was just as solid now as it had been back then.

Even though Essence understood Junnie's love for the streets, sometimes it would interfere with their relationship.

She understood that it was genuinely a part of who he was, but the constant stress of having to worry about him put a strain on her. Essence grew up on the same streets Junnie had, so even though she wasn't running through them she still knew what was going on.

More than a few times she had heard talk about people wanting to hurt Junnie, and it didn't get any easier hearing about it. He always assured he would leave the streets for good, but he would never give a specific date or time.

"You work today?" Junnie asked mostly to avoid her questioning about last night's events.

"Yeah, I'm leaving here around two. We have some type of promotional sale going on at the store and I have to get there a little earlier. I probably won't get off at my scheduled time either. They have this new girl closing who doesn't have a clue to what the hell she's doing."

"That's crazy." Junnie tossed the magazine back down and went into the living room. "When you going to quit fucking around and just become a manager?" he called out, plopping on the sofa and grabbing the remote. "You've been there for the past year and a half."

"I'm just waiting for them to raise my pay. I was supposed to get a raise a few months ago and never did. Plus, that's a lot of extra stress, you know?"

"True," Junnie mumbled, flipping through the channels.

He wanted to get to ESPN to see who had won the game but something caught his eye. He went back to the previous channel and his eyes narrowed as he listened to the newscast.

They were going over a story covering a shooting the night before outside of a strip club. No one had been injured but people reported that the series of gunshots that had went off sounded like firecrackers.

There were no suspects so far, but the police chief promised he would get down to the bottom of it. He vowed that he wouldn't let common street punks terrorize his city. Junnie couldn't help but chuckle as he watched the grumpy old man give his speech. There was a knock at the front door just as the chief was finishing his speech.

Junnie turned it to cartoons so Essence wouldn't see the story, before getting up to see who it was. Peeking out the peephole he unbolted the door and swung it open. Allah stepped inside, dreads swinging and smelling like weed.

"What's good with you, J Boogie?" he drawled, giving Junnie dap.

"Just woke up, waiting for Essence to finish this food."

"Yeah, it does smell like Denny's in here. What's up with you Essence?" Allah called as he walked past the kitchen.

"Nah, we're not on good terms right now, Lah," she told him, giving a stern look. Allah raised his hands in surrender.

"What I do?" he asked innocently.

"You had my man out all night, doing God knows what, instead of being home where he needs to be."

"Aye, this a grown ass man right here. He makes his own moves. Does this mean I don't get a plate?" Allah leaned in the kitchen to get a look at what Essence was fixing.

"Boy, bye," Essence laughed.

"I'll take that as a yes." Allah winked before going to join Junnie in the living room. "What you watching?" he asked seating in the recliner. Junnie nodded towards the screen, placing his feet on the coffee table.

"Just watching the clips from last night's game."

"Oh yeah, I heard it was a good one."

"Yeah, that's what they're saying. Where you coming from?"

"I spent the night at Monique's house after we took care of that thing. She was giving me the same shit I'm guessing Essence gave you." Allah grinned knowingly.

"She must be tired of not having her man at home either when he should be," Essence joined in from the kitchen.

"I'm pretty sure Michelle don't give Barack any shit when he's out taking care of business," Junnie said without taking his eyes from the television.

Essence came out of the kitchen on that one. "Well I'm not the first lady, and you damn sure ain't running this country so try another one."

"Y'all crazy as hell." Allah chuckled.

He checked to make sure Essence was back in the kitchen before speaking again. "You hear anything about that situation?" he asked in a hush tone.

"Yep, the story was just on channel five." Junnie turned it back to the news just as the chief of police was wrapping up his speech on cracking down on the growing violence of the city. Allah shook his head, staring at the screen with his red slanted eyes.

"When do you think Sammy's going to come through and try to flex?" he asked.

Junnie made a look of disbelief. "That nigga knows better than that."

"You think he's just going to count his losses."

"No, but I hope he does. He already proved he was an idiot once and we see how that worked out for him. It's best he just goes about his life."

"You ain't never lie. But shit, at least we stars for the moment," Allah nodded towards the television where the news reporter was finishing the story by asking anyone with information to come forward

"The foods ready. Come and get it while it's hot!" Essence called out.

The two men stood up and went to get their plates, crowding in the small kitchen with Essence. Once everyone was situated with their food they went into the living room and turned it back to BET.

They watched the music videos top countdown, and discussed the state of the current hip hop scene. Junnie had never really been into the rapping phase but Allah had always been pretty nice with his wordplay.

If they weren't in the streets as heavy as they were, he might have had a chance at a career, but all of their current focus was on getting enough money to leave the hood. Within ten minutes all of their plates were clean, finishing off the pancakes, bacon and eggs Essence had put together. Junnie grabbed his cigarettes off the coffee table and leaned back on the couch cushions.

"You put your foot in that, baby," he told Essence, patting his sweatpants for a lighter. "You need to start cooking like that every morning."

"If you're never around for dinner then you don't get the privilege of breakfast." Essence grabbed his cigarettes from him. She gave him a kiss and stood up.

"I'm going to get in the shower so I can get ready for work. You guys need anything?"

"Nah we're straight. Go do your thing ma." Junnie reached for his cigarettes but Essence smacked his hand away before heading to the back room.

"When you going to quit fucking around and just marry that girl?" Allah asked, pulling a swisher from behind his ear and leaning over the table.

"When the times right, my brother. I need to hurry up and make a few million first so we can get the fuck out of here before I start making any marriage proposals."

"You know Essence doesn't care anything about you having any millions. She's been with your ass since we was little niggas still hustling dimes on the block. You better hurry up and propose before she realize you ain't shit," Allah cracked, pulling a bag of weed from his pocket.

Junnie laughed. "Fuck out of here, nigga. I don't see you getting down on your knee to grab Monique's hand."

Allah shrugged as he began to roll a fresh blunt. "That's because that girls crazy as hell. I thought that bi-polar disease was just an excuse for females to act like psychos, but after dealing with Monique, I think that shit might be legit. This girl be bugging out. Besides, we're not like you two. You two are like a Disney movie or something. You see Aladdin? Beauty and the Beast?"

"Shut up." Junnie pulled his lighter from his pocket. "Let me get a cigarette."

As Allah was digging for his cigarettes, Junnie's cell phone began to ring. He got up and went to retrieve it from the kitchen counter. "What's good?" he answered.

"Rise and shine, my nigga." Harlem's gruff voice came through the speaker. "What you up to?"

"Just sitting up here shooting the breeze with Lah. Where you at?" Junnie asked, not recognizing the number.

"Over here at Lee John's, breaking these old timers for their pensions. When you and Lah get done bullshitting, come swing through and get a nigga."

"Why don't you just come over here?"

"I ain't whipping today. I told you fools last night that I had to take my car to the shop."

Junnie sighed as he accepted the cigarette that Allah was holding out. "Alright, we'll be on our way over there in a little bit."

"No doubt. Hurry up too. I got something to lay on you."

"Bet." Junnie ended the call and tossed the phone on the sofa.

"What's up?" Allah asked, concentrating on the blunt he was rolling.

"That was Harlem. He wants us to meet him at Lee John's in a few."

"That nigga," Allah shook his head. He checked to make sure Essence wasn't around before lowering his voice. "You know what we're about to do with the yayo?"

"Yeah, I know a cat who might be willing to buy the duffel bag off us."

Allah raised his eyebrows in surprise. "Right at the door? Who you know that got bank like that?"

"Just a cat I met when I got locked up a few months ago. He's one of the few people that don't get his drugs from Santana out here."

"That's what's up. You going to call him?"

"Already did. Last night. He's waiting for us to get over there. I'ma get dressed. Don't spark that shit until I come back." Junnie headed to the bedroom, pulling off his t-shirt as he went.

He went to the closet to pick out his attire for the day. Since it was a hot day, Junnie didn't bother with anything fancy. He selected a solid black T-shirt, his black Dickies, and all black Air Forces.

Once he had buckled his pants, Junnie strapped his bulletproof vest on, adjusting it to look natural. It was a gift he had received from an old comrade, months ago, but he had only recently taken to wearing it.

His T-shirt fit a little snug over the vest, but you couldn't tell he was wearing one. Junnie was just tucking his .40 caliber in his jeans when Essence stepped from out the bathroom. Her hair was pinned up, and she was wrapped in her bath towel. She stopped to look at Junnie fully dressed and gave him a dark look.

"Where you running off to?" she asked suspiciously, drying her hair.

"I'm about to go pick up Harlem from the west side, then we have some business to take care of." Junnie grabbed his wooden rosary from the dresser and draped it around his neck. He looked up to find Essence still staring at him. "What's wrong with you?"

"Did you even remember that we're supposed to be having dinner tonight at the Cheesecake Factory?"

Junnie gave her a look. "You don't give me any credit huh? Of course I remember, Essence. I said I was going to pick up Harlem, not running off to Mexico. I'll be back before you even get here."

Essence gave him a disbelieving glare. "Yeah, I would hope so."

Junnie stopped adjusting his shirt and walked over to her. Essence had her back to him so he eased his hands around her waist and pulled her closer.

She closed her eyes in pleasure as he planted a tender kiss on her neck. "I'm not going to miss our night for anything. I'm thinking we should catch a movie afterwards, what you think?"

"Yeah, me and Vivica was just talking about that new Denzel movie that came out last week. She said it was crazy."

"Well, we can be the judge of that tonight." Junnie turned her around and gave her a deep kiss, which she gladly returned, wrapping her arms around his neck. They embraced for a moment before Junnie broke away. "Call me when you go on your lunch break," he told her, smacking her behind before heading for the door. He had just grabbed the handle when Essence stopped him.

"I love you, baby." She told him.

"I love you to, ma." Giving her a smile and a wink Junnie walked out the room and shut the door behind him.

****

The sound of the blaring alarm jarred Bobbi from her sleep. She grumbled before slamming her hand on the button shutting it off. Yawning, she sat up in bed and looked around. It was already warm in her room indicating that it would be a nice day. Feeling good about her weather predictions she jumped out of the bed.

Bobbi ruffled her hair as she made her way to the full length mirror hanging behind her bedroom door.

Everyone at school had referred to her as the baddest redbone on two feet, something she had inherited from her black mother and Hispanic father. Her long brown hair was wild at the moment, and covered her beautiful face, but she simply brushed it to the side and examined her eyes.

They were their usual brown again, but last night they had been extremely red and low. Smoking with her best friend, Tavae, usually had that effect.

Bobbi was a head strong girl, who grew up believing nothing was impossible. It was something her parents had both instilled in her at a young age and it was something that Bobbi had stuck with.

She received top grades in school, was captain of her debate team in her sophomore year, and had even played on the junior varsity basketball team.

There was no one on earth who could tell her she wasn't the greatest at what she did, but her best attribute was her attitude. She wasn't cocky or stuck up like most girls who only had half of her talents.

She never kicked it around the "popular" girls or treated anyone with disrespect, which is why she was usually liked by everyone. But being liked also brought her a lot of haters, which Bobbi could care less about.

Her mother, Charity, was her role model, and best friend. Charity had only been fifteen when she had Bobbi, so the fact that she was so young helped her relate to Bobbi as she got older.

Bobbi never felt she had to keep anything from her mother, and she never did. From the time she stole a designer bag from Macy's at the mall and had to outrun the police, to the time she lost her virginity.

Charity was understanding but that didn't stop her from getting in Bobbi's ass whenever the occasion was needed.

For as close as Bobbi was with her mother, she simply praised her father Anthony. He had been a young smooth talking Hispanic boy who had been born and raised in the Bay Area. He did his dirt but he never caused trouble for anyone.

Bobbi used to remember him coming home late at night, and bring her special toys and candies when she was in bed. It was his signature move to lift her shirt and blow on her stomach until she went into a laughing frenzy. He loved her more than anything in the world, and worshipped Charity. He was very near perfect.

One night, they had all been home watching television when Anthony's best friend called and asked Anthony to meet him. Charity complained about Anthony leaving but he told her he would be right back.

Giving her a kiss on the forehead, Anthony came over to Bobbi and told her he loved her. She was pouting because he promised he would stay home and watch Lion King with her, but once he lifted her shirt and blew on her stomach, she laughed until she forgave him. When he walked out the front door to leave, Bobbi rushed to the window and watched him get in the car. It would be the last time she saw him alive.

Charity and Bobbi were awakened the next morning by a grim faced police officer who informed them that Anthony had been found dead in his car, half of his head blown off. The news sent Charity into a near nervous breakdown, and left young Bobbi scarred for life. Without her dad around, Bobbi and Charity hung on to each other throughout the years. Even though it had been thirteen years ago, Bobbi knew that Charity hadn't fully gotten over the death of her lover.

Taking a quick shower, Bobbi laid out her outfit for the day. Deciding on something simple, she picked a pink tank top, with her white short shorts and pink sandals. She had just gotten her nails and feet done so she came out looking correct. Once dressed, she headed downstairs.

Charity was seated on the couch, with a plate of food watching the news. She looked up when Bobbi entered the room. If you ever saw them together and didn't know better, you would think that you were looking at twin sisters.

Charity was a slightly older version than Bobbi, with a body to match. Bobbi found it hilarious when they would be at the store and the young boys would break their necks to get a peek at Charity's rump roast.

"Well, Sleeping Beauty," Charity started, looking Bobbi up and down. "You graduate high school and think you can sleep all day and night, huh?"

"Correction, I sleep all day, but be up all night," Bobbi told her smiling. "Besides, it's only eleven."

"Yeah, yeah, I was about to come in there with a cold jug of water to toss on yo' ass." Charity went back to her plate and watching the news. "Did you know this boy?" she asked, referring to the news story.

Bobbi looked. They were going over the death of a young man who had been gunned down in his apartment building the previous night.

"Nope, didn't know him." Bobbi went into the kitchen, and her mouth dropped open. The only thing on the stove was empty pots and pans. "Aye, Aunt Jemima. Where's my plate at?"

"You were asleep so I didn't know if you were hungry or not."

Bobbi nodded with a smirk. "Oh okay. I can't wait until Mother Day swings back around. Hope you like boxes of Kleenex." Going to the cabinet Bobbi grabbed a box of Cinnamon Toast Crunch and a bowl.

"See this why I don't like you being out at all times of the night." Charity called to her, still wrapped up in the news story. "They found this boy in his own apartment, shot in the head. It isn't safe anywhere."

"Momma, you don't know what that nigga could have done. He looked like a shady dude to me."

"It don't matter. Taking black lives is taking black lives, no matter the circumstances. But these young niggas out here don't see it that way. They don't see that their doing the Klan's work for them. Why would the white man need to kill us when we out here doing it to ourselves?"

"Whoa, calm down Sista Soulja. What got you so riled up this morning?" Bobbi walked in the living room and plopped in the armchair across from Charity with her cereal.

"This is why I don't watch the news," Charity shook her head.

Switching through the channels, she landed on Jerry Springer and sat the remote down. Bobbi looked at her and laughed.

"So, this is your alternative? This shows nothing but garbage and filth, and doesn't do anything but show how dysfunctional relationships are."

"Yeah, that's why I won't be surprised when I see you and that li'l nappy headed boy on here." Charity said slyly.

Bobbi sighed. "Momma, we ain't getting into this this morning. My head hurts."

For the past year, Bobbi had been in a relationship with a cat named Xavier. A few years older than Bobbi, Xavier was known in the streets for his antics and wildness but he wasn't that way with Bobbi when they first met.

She had been attracted to him, and him to her, but after the first few months he changed into an entirely different person. Charity always took credit for saying she predicted what kind of man Xavier was, and even though she had been right, Bobbi was never going to readily admit it. There was a knock at the door that made them both look up.

"That better not be that little nigga now," Charity warned. "He know I don't like him anywhere near my house.

Before Bobbi could respond the front door opened and Tavae came strolling in, with a smile stretched across her face.

"Party people," she greeted.

"Ho, how you just gonna knock then come strolling in?" Bobbi asked laughing.

Tavae shrugged. "The doors to keep strangers out. I'm family. Better question is why is the front door unlocked?"

"Momma probably left it open for the mailman to come through," Bobbi joked, and both girls laughed. Charity threw her hands up.

"I say he looked nice in his shorts one time, and now I can't live it down," she said.

"It's good, we know you're a cougar in her prime," Tavae said, coming to sit on the couch.

Bobbi and Tavae had been friends since elementary school and had been hanging tough ever since.

She was a pretty light skinned girl, who was rather on the small side, but had an ass that would make the hustlers on the block always take a second peek.

Whereas Bobbi was usually chill and laid back, Tavae was riled up and always ready for a good showdown. She had made a name for herself throughout the hood for being nice with her hands, and even for her small stature, females hesitated in approaching her.

"That's where you're wrong. I'm nowhere near a cougar. I'm only twenty-seven," Charity told them. The girls both laughed.

"I already knew you be out here false advertising to them young boys," Bobbi giggled.

"Maybe, maybe not. You'll never know. What are you two getting into today?"

Bobbi shrugged. "It's going to be nice all week, so I figured we'll go downtown or something. See what's popping off."

"Yeah, you know it's always packed down there every weekend." Tavae said.

"You two better be out here acting right because I will go out here acting a fool if I hear any more stories about y'all." Charity got up from the couch and took her plate into the kitchen.

"You got the two best daughters in town, Momma," Bobbi assured her.

"Girl please, don't act like I didn't hear about what you and Tavae did last week. Always out here fighting and carrying on. Every time I hear a story its either Bobbi slapped a girl or Tavae was kicking some little girl in the head."

"Bitches be having it coming," Bobbi laughed.

"Damn straight." Tavae said, exchanging high fives.

"Watch your mouth!" Charity called from the kitchen.

"Anyway," Bobbi whispered. "What you end up doing last night?"

"I just ended up going home after we left the restaurant." Tavae said easily. Bobbi gave her a look of disbelief.

"Bitch, who do you think you're talking to? So you mean to tell me you and Dewayne's fine ass went out and you didn't do anything else that night?"

"Alright, let me rephrase that statement; we ended up going home after we left the restaurant," Tavae said licking her lips.

"Ooooh Momma, Tavae out here being a ho!" Bobbi called into the kitchen.

"Snitch."

"Y'all better chill out!" Charity called.

"C'mon, let's get out of here. It's hot as hell and I'm ready to get into the action." Bobbi stood and tugged on the bottom of her shorts. "We'll be back later Momma. I want my dinner ready when I get home too, women!"

A water bottle came sailing from the kitchen and whizzed past Bobbi's head. Laughing, the two girls ran to the front door just as Charity came from the kitchen, another water bottle in her hand, ready to throw.

"I'ma hit you in your smart ass mouth with the next one," she threatened as Bobbi slammed the front door before she could make good on her promise.

4

Lee John's was a hole in the wall bar that was well known by everyone, but only few went to. It served as a front for many things that only a select few knew about. If you were in that particular set of lucky people then on any given night you could come and purchase anything from weapons, to drugs, and even a woman if you wanted to.

Junnie didn't usually hang around Lee John's too often, but it was one of Harlem's favorite spots. It didn't take long for Allah to get them to the bar. When they arrived, Harlem was posted outside, apparently arguing with a group of older men. When they got out of the car, Harlem stopped in mid-sentence and walked over to his brothers.

"My niggas," he greeted, showing off his gold teeth.

Harlem was the type of dude who whole appearance screamed trouble. He was on the stocky side, with muscular arms that were covered with countless tattoos. His hair was cut low, complete with thick sideburns that trailed his face. The constant smirk he wore was crooked and always gave the impression that he knew something that you didn't, which was usually the case.

Harlem was born and raised in his namesake, complete with the brazen attitude that most East coasters had. He had moved to California five years earlier and had immediately made a name for himself as being a troublemaker. At the tender age of fourteen, he got into an altercation with a well-known drug dealer by the name of Rahmel. Rahmel had made the mistake of loud talking the youngster and Harlem ended up knocking out most of his teeth. After that, people in the hood decided to approach with caution.

Junnie and Allah ran into Harlem outside of a nightclub where they had all been laying low waiting to rob people coming out after the party ended. While they waited, a blunt was sparked and they struck up a conversation with the shit talking New York kid and realized he was good people. The three of them robbed a group of men that night and a bond was formed.

"Why the hell you always over here?" Junnie asked, giving Harlem their signature handshake.

"You know me; I'm out here getting it." Harlem grinned, shaking the dice in his hand. "I was just in there breaking that old nigga Mike for all his pension. You know these old ass dudes don't know when to call it quits."

"And your young ass don't know how to shoot craps!" One of the old men yelled. He was clearly drunk and missing most of his teeth.

"Shut yo ass up," Harlem yelled back playfully. "Quit trying to roll dice when you know you have arthritis."

The old man stuck up his middle finger before turning back to his group of friends.

Allah snickered. "This who you kick it with when you aren't with us?"

"Only when I'm not busy with your girl." Harlem cracked. Allah gave him a hard shove, to which Harlem just laughed.

"Enough fucking around, what is so urgent that you had us rushing over here?" Junnie asked, leaning back against the car.

"A'ight, check it. So I was out with this little bitch I met the other night, right, and we stop by Jack in the Box before we head to her house. We get up in there and it's packed because the club up the street had just let out. I'm ordering my food when this nigga Rowdy walks up to me with some of his people."

"Rowdy?" Junnie quickly scrolled through his mental Rolodex. Rowdy was a wild card from around the way that was known for letting his gun bust. He was feared by many for his willingness to always take a situation to the next level. "What the hell did he want?"

"He said his boy Ace Boon wanted to meet with us about some business." Junnie had only ever heard of Rowdy but Ace Boon was someone that he had actually crossed paths with occasionally.

Unlike his partner Rowdy, Ace wasn't known for his killing capabilities, but he was no doubt one of the most well-known hustlers in the game. He had been putting in work for quite some time and had a reputation of getting money.

Junnie had met him a couple times before but had yet to make a decision about him. He didn't like nor dislike the man, but he could never see them being friends.

"What the hell they want to meet with us about?" Allah questioned suspiciously. Harlem shrugged. "Dude wouldn't say. He just told me that Ace wanted to meet up with us tomorrow night over at Oscars, and to let him know if we're interested."

"Nah, I don't like that shit." Allah shook his head as he reached behind his ear and lit the blunt he had tucked away. "Why he want to do business with us? I know who that nigga Rowdy is and he has no problem putting somebody to sleep himself, so if they're reaching out to us for some business, that means whoever they want knocked off is going to be a risk."

"Yeah, that's true, but that's usually the case when people come to us about business," Junnie responded.

It wasn't new for someone to reach out to they're group when they needed help getting rid of a "problem". If the cash was right the three of them would make sure your problem was solved and could never come back. It was a risky business however. You never knew who was trying to set you up, or who was working for the feds, so it took a lot of precaution.

"How was Rowdy acting?" Junnie asked thoughtfully.

"It was my first time meeting the nigga and to be honest, I wasn't impressed." Harlem fanned his shirt from the heat. "Kid looked zoned out like he was tweaking and shit."

"See?" Allah said as if that confirmed his suspicions. "These niggas are weirdos bruh. I ain't fucking with them."

"Just because the nigga was thizzing doesn't mean it's not a reliable deal." Junnie stroked his beard as he thought it over. He wasn't too familiar with Ace personally so he would have to check out what the guy was talking about. "We can go check it out and see what's going on."

"That's what I was thinking." Harlem agreed. "I want to see what these soft ass niggas could possibly want us to do for them."

"You two are wildin'. If you go in this meeting and it's a set up, then what?"

"Then I kill every muthafucka in the building." Harlem said seriously. "But I don't think them niggas are built like that."

"I actually agree with Harlem on this one." Junnie spoke up. "The only hitter on their squad is Rowdy and from what

I've always heard about him, if they had a problem with us then Rowdy and Harlem would've had a shootout instead of a conversation. I'm more willing to believe that Ace really has a business deal for us than the thought of him trying to set us up. We should check it out."

"Whatever y'all say. Just remember I said it was a bad idea when it comes down to it." Allah said.

"Shut your negative ass up," Harlem laughed. "Aye, so anybody heard from Sammy's punk ass?"

"We just robbed that nigga for his whole work supply. I don't think he's going to necessarily be in a talking mood afterward." Junnie said.

"Yeah, he better not be. Speaking of which, you two have any plans on what you wanna do with all that shit? We can't hold on to it for too long. Once Sammy tell whoever he works for what happened they're going to come wanting it back."

Junnie shrugged. "Let them come, but we already have plans on getting it off. That's actually going to be our next stop. You trying to roll, or are you trying to see how much beer money you can win out of these old folks?"

Harlem waved his hand. "Nah, I'm gonna let them live for now, but Gerald better have my money ready next time I come up here!" he yelled out loudly to the group of old men.

"Fuck you!" One of them yelled.

Harlem smirked as he followed Junnie back to the car. "Gotta love them old niggas."

5

It was early in the morning, so there weren't many people out looking to purchase drugs, but that didn't stop two young dealers from standing in their usual spot, aiming to catch the few early fiends.

One was a short, chubby cat who rocked his hair in short nappy braids. He leaned against the wall of the corner store, while his partner sat on an overturned milk crate, counting a roll of bills he had had stuffed in his pocket.

The partner was a light skinned kid, with acne so bad, it scarred his face. Neither were handsome in the looks department but they were vicious youths who had just been recruited to work on the block.

"Nigga, its 'bout to be a hundred today, and you wearing that hoodie like it's the thing to do," the one with the nappy braids said, looking at his friend's sweatshirt.

"See, that's what's wrong with you, my dude," the one with acne said, smirking. "While you're sitting up here worried about my fucking hoodie, I'm worried about this gwap we out here stacking." He held up the thick stack of bills in his hand. His friend just snickered.

"Cool, that's enough to pay the taxi when I gotta take your ass to the clinic for heat stroke," he laughed.

The two of them exchanged words, joking and making time passed by. A few minutes later their attention turned to a Buick Regal which pulled in front of the store.

The driver sat in the car for a second before opening the door and sliding out. He was a man of medium build with charcoal skin and menacing eyes.

He was smoking a Black 'N' Mild and watching the two boys as he adjusted his jacket and zipped it up. They both stopped talking as they returned the man's glare. He sneered at their attempted mean mugs and headed in their direction.

"What's good with you, niggas?" the man asked innocently. "It's a little hot to just be sitting out here posted up, ain't it?"

"Nah, it's a little hot to just be walking around here asking questions, homie." short braids said harshly.

"Yeah my nigga. You know where you at?" Acne asked, nodding towards the street sign above their heads. The man didn't even bother to check.

"Yeah I do," the man nodded. "Especially since this my niggas turf that you busters call yourself hustling on. Who gave you pass to move anything on this street?"

The two men shared looks of confusion before busting out laughing.

"Nigga, what?" Short Braids asked. He took a step towards the man. "You know who the fuck—"

The slap came so quickly the boy hadn't even realized he had been hit until the second one came, which sent him flying back into the wall. His friend tried to get off the crate to help but he was in a bad position. Before he could get to his feet, the man had delivered a vicious hook to his skull, knocking him out instantly.

Short Braids tried to recollect himself but by the time he did, the man had shoved a pistol in his face and had one hand wrapped around his throat.

"What was you saying, nigga?" the man breathed into his ear. "Talk that tough shit now, partna."

"Come on, fam. Be easy," Short Braids said, all the bark gone from his voice.

"Be easy, huh?" The man looked him directly in his eye. "You know who the fuck I am, little homie?" The boy shook his head. "I'm the voice out here for Ace Bone. They call me West, don't forget the shit. Tell all your buddies and whoever the fuck you work for that this shit is shutdown, you understand me?" The boy nodded weakly and West slapped him with the gun. "I said, do you understand me muthafucka?"

"Yes!" short braids cried, holding his bleeding mouth.

"Good." West turned to leave but stopped short. "Matter of fact, run everything you got on you," he ordered raising the gun again.

With shaking hands, the boy emptied his pockets and West snatched everything in the boy's hands from money to his cell phone.

"Now pick this pussy up and get the fuck off my street."

Without waiting to see if the boy was complying, West turned around and headed back to his Buick. Hopping behind the driver's wheel, he tucked his gun underneath his seat.

"You was right, these niggas were out there holding," he told the passenger who had been watching the scene from behind the cars tinted windows.

Ace nodded slowly as West passed him the zip-lock bag he had snatched from the boy. It was filled with smaller baggies that were packed with green buds.

"Yeah, I figured they were," Ace replied smoothly, examining the zip-lock bag. "These rookies stick out like sore thumbs."

"I was so preoccupied with putting the hurt on these niggas, I didn't even bother to ask who had them out here," West said, lighting the blunt he had left in the ashtray when he went to check the dealers.

"No need. I know who it is." Ace dug in the bag and pulled out one of the small baggies. He held it up for West to see. "This is Mickey's calling card," he said referring to the Ying Yang sign printed on the bag.

West frowned. "That bitch ass nigga," he said snatching the bag. "I told you months ago we would have to wet that nigga sooner or later. He was always selling dreams too big for his head, but this time he crossed the line. I'ma go over there and body every one of those pussies he got with him."

"Slow down, West," Ace cautioned. "You know checking this nigga isn't going to be as simple as that."

"And why not?" West asked heatedly, even though he already knew the answer.

Ace Bone was well known in his city and West was just as notorious. The two had joined forces many years ago and had been making moves ever since.

Through many methods of bullying, murder and extortion they had managed to set up a pretty established operation that had exceeded those of most regular gang's business.

Ace was more along the lines of a diplomat among the duo. He usually made sure his way was seen through smooth talking and tricky wordplay, while West served as the enforcer and regulator.

If anything ever went wrong, West was the one that was sent out to put it right again. Together, the two were a perfect combination for trouble.

A few months back one of their associates, Mickey, had decided that he was tired of working underneath the pair, saying that he deserved a bigger portion than what he was receiving.

Pretty soon work of his was turning up missing and the corner Mickey was in charge of had gotten robbed twice in one week. West had urged Ace to let him kill Mickey and replace him with one of the youngsters that was dying to take his spot, but Ace objected.

Not too many knew it, but Mickey was the only son of Ace's uncle, Charlie. Instead of killing his cousin, Ace decided to just exile him from their crew. A few weeks went past without anyone hearing from Mickey but when he resurfaced, he had pulled the impossible.

Not only did he have his own crew but he had been employed by one of the biggest gangs in the bay; Calvin Cole's Family. No one was exactly sure how he pulled it off, but the move left a lot of people in awe. Especially Ace.

"Be easy, cuddy. You know if we touch this nigga Mickey it'll be a direct slight at Calvin Cole and once that happens, we'll have a lot more on our plate to worry about than a bitch-ass, wannabe, drug dealer," Ace warned.

Looking down at the baggies in his lap, he racked his brain to come up with a plan to solve the current problem they had just accumulated. "We're going to have to see Calvin about this."

"What you mean?" West asked, not liking the way this sounded.

"I mean, if we want to touch Mickey, we have to get at Calvin about it," Ace clarified. "If not it's going to be looked at as disrespect. You can't just go in a man's yard and kill one of his dogs without asking permission. Even if the dog is a fucking poodle."

West stared at him in disbelief. "Am I listening to you right? You want to go ask this nigga Calvin permission before we check Mickey on trying to snatch our block?"

"Yes," Ace answered simply. West just continued to stare at him so Ace explained. "A'ight, let's say somebody came through and put the heat to one of our people. What would you do?"

"Probably kill him and the bitch who birthed him," West answered seriously.

"Exactly, and though Calvin Coles not as demented as you, I'm pretty sure he would feel some type of way about us killing Mickey. Not only would that mess up any connect we could form with The Family, but he'll more than likely send a death squad out here to wipe us out. All of that can be avoided by simply showing the proper etiquette, feel me?"

"Man, fuck all that," West mumbled, hitting the blunt and focusing out the window.

"Don't worry my nigga, you'll be able to let your thing bust soon enough." Ace assured as he stuck the zip-lock bag in the glove department. "Have you talked to Rowdy?"

"Yeah, he called last night."

"Did he take care of what I asked him to?"

"He said he seen that nigga Harlem but Junnie wasn't there. Obviously, he calls the shots because he said he would talk to him about it and get up with us later with a response."

Ace nodded slowly. "Good, then that means our problems going to be getting solved real soon," he said grinning wickedly.

West turned to face his friend and frowned. "What you mean?"

"C'mon West, you know me better than that. You really think I didn't know Mickey was the one out here trying to muscle us? I recognize this shit-bird's MO from a mile away. Whether it's to try and throw dirt on us, or simply because he really thinks he can take our shit over, I can't say for sure. All I know is Mickey's been on my radar for the past few weeks."

"What's that got to do with this nigga, Junnie?"

Ace accepted the blunt from West, and took his time responding, mostly to build suspense.

"Cuddy, everyone out here knows how Junnie and his people get down. There like fucking wolves. Give them a bone and they'll hunt and kill for you. Now why would I jeopardize one of my people getting killed for mopping Mickey, when I can just get someone else to do it?"

Slowly a grin began to spread across West's face. It looked as if it was his face first time ever forming one.

"I like that shit. Untraceable back to us. How you know he'll do it though?"

"Like I said, throw a wolf a bone he'll kill for you."

At that moment his phone vibrated in his pocket. Pulling it out, he looked down at the text he had just received. "And, today just keeps getting better."

"Who's that?" West asked curiously.

"Remember that bitch, Jaleesa, that was at the Chocolate Bar last week?"

West thought about it. "Shorty with the heart tattoo on her titties?"

"Nah, her friend. The Puerto Rican bitch with the red hair."

"Ah yeah." West remembered the thick Puerto Rican who had been the main attraction at the bar that night.

Every man in the place had aimed to snag her, but there was only one who eventually managed to rope her in.

"You dug those out?"

"Nah, I just been giving her the run around for a few days. Shorty is wild as fuck," Ace laughed as he responded to the text. "I'm about to go see if she ready for the life, but before I do, ride over to Grant real quick."

"Fuck you want to go over there for?" West asked as he started the car and pulled away from the curb.

Grant Ridge was a rundown apartment complex that was considered the projects of the hood. The rule was if you weren't from Grant Ridge, you stayed out of Grant Ridge.

"I wanna have one last talk with my cousin before his funeral," Ace replied, his attention focused on the pic Jaleesa had just sent him in her panties.

6

The breeze was welcoming as they cruised through the hood, bumping one of Mac Dre's early hits.

Allah and Harlem were in the front seat having a debate about something over the music, while Junnie sat in the back staring out the window.

He watched the scenery, and looked at all the faces blurring past as Allah whipped the vehicle like a true professional.

Days like this, Junnie loved being out and about in the thick of things. It was as if the summer brought out everyone you didn't see during winter.

Allah turned onto 74th and Gerald and kept heading east. With the expert speed control and maneuvering, they arrived at their destination ten minutes earlier than MapQuest would have estimated.

Stopping in front of a shabby looking house on a dead end street, Junnie was satisfied when he saw the jet black Jeep letting him know that the person he had come to see was home.

Two young Mexican cats he didn't know were posted in front of the gate, passing a cigarette back and forth and watching the Monte Carlo suspiciously. Junnie adjusted the 9mm hugging against his hip before reaching down and grabbing the duffel bag.

"Look I'm about to run in here real quick and I'll be back out," he said, turning to the front seat. "I don't want to overwhelm the homie by bringing all of us up there with some hot shit. Y'all gonna be straight?"

Harlem turned around and gave him a look.

"You know who the fuck you talking to, B?"

"My bad, guess I forgot," Junnie grinned before slipping out of the car.

The two Mexicans continued to stare as Junnie made his way up the path to the gate. He nodded at the two men, but they just looked without returning the gesture. Snickering Junnie walked past them, brushing shoulders with the bigger one as he went.

"Something funny, homie?" the big one asked, with a hint of threat in his voice.

Junnie turned as he continued walking. "Yeah, I usually laugh at jokes," he said smoothly.

The men both muttered responses but Junnie didn't pay them any mind. Jogging up the steps to the porch, he knocked on the screen door and waited patiently.

A few seconds went by before the scraping of the chain could be heard, the turn of the lock, and the door swung open.

A short light skinned man with his shirt off stood in the doorway with a scowl on his face. He wore his hair in a low fade, and tattoos covered almost every inch of his torso.

His tan Dickies hung low, showing his briefs and the gun he had tucked in the waistline. His mouth fixed to bark at whoever had interrupted what he had going on, but he paused when he saw who it was. A broad smile filled his face as he pushed open the screen door.

"Awe shit, what's good with you June the Goon?" Charlie greeted warmly, stepping forward and embracing Junnie. "I wasn't expecting to see you around here anytime soon, homie."

"I told you I'd be around the way every once in a while. Today is one of those whiles," Junnie told him.

"Sooners always better than later," Charlie told him. "Come in family, come in." Moving to the side Charlie allowed Junnie to pass by before shutting the front door.

The televisions volume was on high, while music boomed from somewhere in the back room. The room was set up decoratively, as if by a women's touch, but the presence of Charlie couldn't be ignored.

Situated around the room was an arsenal of different firearms, ranging from rifles to handguns. On the table were thick bundles of white powder, packaged and ready for distribution.

Next to them was the largest pile of weed Junnie had ever laid eyes on in real life. The stench was overwhelming but that didn't stop Junnie from inhaling the aroma. Charlie looked back at him and grinned.

"Best stink you ever smelled right?" he asked proudly. He waved his hand towards the pile of green and purple buds. "I had my uncle Cervantes send me a little bit right after I got home. What you're looking at is premium diesel, straight from my homelands garden. Tell me, do you know what they call munchies where I'm from?"

"I can't say that I do," Junnie admitted.

"Neither can I," Charlie shrugged, "I'm not too good with Spanish, my nigg, but this shit will get you hungry enough to chomp through the cabinet door. I haven't put any of this on the streets yet but when I do, I guarantee that Taco Bell is going to owe me some royalties for all the customers they're going to have in line."

"That's what's up, it sounds like I came at the right time," Junnie nodded. "I remember you saying how you only dealt with the realest of piff and from the way it looks and definitely smells, you weren't exaggerating."

Charlie's face turned serious. "One thing I never do is exaggerate homie. However I say it is, is how it really is. As should hold true for every man's word, I also remember telling you that once we were both free, I would look out for you the way you looked out for me, and you best believe I hold true to that word just as tight as the day I gave it to you." Charlie gave him a small salute.

Just a short time ago, Junnie had got booked over a fight in the street where the dude was sent to the hospital with a concussion.

Instead of wasting money on bail, Junnie just decided to sit tight until his court date. He already knew most of the convicts in the correctional facility so it was more like a reunion then serving time.

A few days into it, Charlie had gotten brought in on grand theft auto charges. Being the only Hispanic in a tank full of rowdy, wild blacks, he was immediately identified as a target.

It was highly anticipated that something would pop off with the quiet Mexican and sure enough it did.

One day while they were in the yard, three large brutes had rushed Charlie in an effort to get his shoes. Everyone expected the small Mexican boy to roll over and play dead, but instead he knocked one out with a single blow, and stood toe to toe with the other two.

Even though he had heart it was a handicap match, and Charlie soon found himself on the losing end. They would have finished him off if it wasn't for Junnie who intervened. He had never been able to stand someone getting jumped, plus he respected the Mexican for standing his ground. They fought side by side until the officers came pepper spraying, and grabbing everyone in a jumpsuit.

"It was nothing," Junnie said modestly. "Real niggas are hard to find so we have to stick together once we find one."

"Too true," Charlie nodded. "I had enemies on the inside but the outsides just as rough. It seems like the last few deaths I've encountered were because some bitch ass fool they knew was hating off them and wanted them bodied. Shit's getting real out here. That's why I got my boys out front waiting to tune some busters up."

"Yeah, I met them."

"They didn't get crazy with you did they?" Charlie asked hurriedly, frowning.

"Nah, they cool. Just doing their job." Junnie tossed the duffel bag on the floor and unzipped it. Charlie looked down at what was inside and whistled.

"Talk about a Merry Christmas," he said, rubbing his hands together. Leaning down he picked up one of the bundles of coke. "Who said it doesn't snow in Cali?"

"Somebody who isn't hip to this coke game." Junnie nodded down at the duffel bag. "That's ten bricks right here."

Charlie grinned as he looked at Junnie. "I'm guessing you ain't going to tell me where you copped this shit from, huh?"

"You guessed right, amigo."

Charlie nodded. "Figured as much." Flicking out a pocket knife he cut a slit into the package and snorted the tip of the knife. He instantly sneezed and made a face of surprise and satisfaction. "This shit ain't no joke, homie."

"You thought I would waste time bringing you some bullshit?"

"Nah, of course not but I haven't had a hit like that since I went to Puerto Rico with my uncle."

Nodding, Charlie closed his knife. "This is better than I expected though, I won't lie. I wasn't really looking for such a large shipment before your call last night, but this shit is too good to pass up on. What you looking to get?"

Junnie considered it. "You know I'm not really a drug dealer like that, but I still know my way around how these prices go around. You my people so I'll let you cop it for fifteen a key."

"Fifteen thousand huh?" Charlie rubbed his chin as he thought it over. "That's pretty steep for something right at the door."

"C'mon Charlie, you know if I drop it any lower than that I'm letting you rob me without a gun."

Charlie laughed. "This guy Junnie," he shook his head. "Marisol!"

A pretty faced young Hispanic chick came to the door, holding a baby in one arm and a bottle in the other. Charlie said something to her in Spanish and she nodded before heading back in the kitchen. A moment later she came back, with a brown paper bag. When she set it on the table stacks of cash spilled out and landed on the table top.

Junnie smirked at the money. "That's all mine?"

"I think so."

"So you just knew I was going to say fifteen thousand?"

"Well, I took a good guess, but just in case I put sixteen in there. Do you care to count it?"

"Nah, you have a trustworthy face." Junnie shook Charlie's hand, before grabbing the large paper bag. "Your just about to earn some of it back anyway. You know I'm not leaving without purchasing some of this fine herbal you have sitting out here."

Charlie smiled. "How much you looking for?"

"I was just trying to see what was up with the eighth..."

Before Junnie had finished his sentence Charlie had grabbed a zip-lock bag from the table and began to stuff handful of the weed in it. Once it was filled, he zipped the pouch and tossed it to Junnie.

"That should be about a zip," he said, waving his hand. "Take that, and once you let your homies hit it, tell them who they need to be buying they shit from now on."

"Bet." Junnie gave him dap and a half hug. "I'm not gonna forget this, C. Good looking out."

"Nah, you good looking out. Thanks again, June. Next time you're on this side make sure you stop by. We can go get a few beers or something. Go chase some of these sheep, know what I mean."

"Nah, I'm more about chasing a dollar these days, compadre. Plus, I'm married, so that would complicate things with the sheep. But I'll stop back by so we can get active. Trust me."

"Fasho, stay safe out here homie," Charlie waved as Junnie shut the front door behind him.

He walked off the porch and back down the stairs. The two men were still posted at the gate but there was another one that had joined them. They all looked at Junnie as he got closer and the big one from before spoke to him.

"Aye, your name Junnie?" he asked curiously.

"Depends on who wants to know?" Junnie asked, looking between the trio.

"Me." The big one stepped forward and stuck his hand out. "I heard what you did for my cousin when he was booked with you, and you got my respect. Sorry about earlier, but you can't be too safe, you know?"

Junnie looked at the hand for a second before deciding to shake it. "Yeah, I live that way every day of my life, fam."

"All day every day," the big one replied, while his friend nodded.

Returning the gesture Junnie continued down the driveway and to the car where his friends were waiting.

"What were they crying about?' Harlem asked, his gun placed on his lap ready to bust out the window at the slightest sign of trouble.

"Nothing, just giving credit for some past shit," Junnie said simply. Once in the car he tossed the bag full of weed to Harlem. "You still got that swisher I seen you with earlier?"

"Oh shit, you know it?" Harlem stuck his nose in the bag and inhaled deeply. "Damn, nigga, this shit smells like unicorn pussy. Where he cop this shit from?"

"Unicorn pussy?" Allah raised his eyebrow as he pulled away from the curb.

"I guess his uncle sent it to him." Junnie shrugged, leaning back in the seat and pulling his phone out.

Essence had sent him a text saying she loved him with a smiley face, just as she usually did on her lunch break.

"Aye, my bitch Charise just told me there's a party on the east side tonight," Harlem announced to everyone in the vehicle. "Y'all trying to roll through?"

"Shit I'm down," Allah said, staring out the window at a group of thugs on the corner.

"Not me, I'm having dinner with Essence." Junnie said, not looking up from his phone. Harlem stopped rolling the blunt to look back at him.

"Having dinner?" he asked as if he had never heard of such a thing. "You two live together. Don't you have dinner every fucking night?"

"No, we're going out to dinner, dumbass."

Harlem shook his head and resumed his task. "I'll never understand that marriage shit," he mumbled

"That won't be a problem seeing how no one would marry yo' crusty ass anyway," Allah cracked, whipping the car clean through traffic.

They all talked shit, while Harlem finished rolling one of his signature blunts. Once it was sparked and being passed in rotation he started kicking a freestyle over a Young Jeezy song that was playing.

Junnie nodded his head to the beat, taking a deep pull from the blunt just as Allah started kicking some of his complicated lyrics on the next song that played.

By the time they reached In'N'Out burgers the car was filled with smoke, and Harlem was telling Allah how they should go pursuit a record deal. Junnie led the way inside the restaurant while the two of them discussed plans on how to get it started.

In'N'Out Burger was as packed as usual in the afternoon, and since school was out there was even more customers. Junnie and his crew maneuvered through the loud crowd of teenagers and went to the front to place their orders.

Junnie got his receipt and stood to the side. He pulled his phone out and continued his text to Essence. He was halfway through typing when he felt a pair of eyes on him. Looking up, he instantly spotted who the eyes belonged to. She was a pretty brown girl, with just the right amount of makeup that let you know she was a professional at applying it.

Her blonde hair traveled in curls down her back, and her full lips were glossy. She was wearing a tank top, a pair of ripped jeans, and red pumps. A group of young boys standing behind her stared at her ass with wide eyes, and gave each other dap as they quietly discussed the size of it.

Once Junnie made eye contact with the girl, she smiled and made her way over to him, drawing the stares of every man in the restaurant as she moved. She removed her sunglasses as she stopped in front of Junnie, showing off her stunning brown eyes.

"Well, well," she said, showing off her pearly whites. "Long time no see, Mr. Junnie."

"What's up with it, Asia," Junnie greeted unenthusiastically.

Years ago, before he had met Essence he and Asia had messed around for a while. She had always been a pretty girl, but her attitude made her very unlikeable. Most dudes would put up with her trash mouth just because of her looks but not Junnie. That was one of the reasons Asia was so attracted to him.

Once he had gotten with Essence, he had cut Asia off completely and he hadn't heard from her in a while. Word was, she had moved to Miami to pursue a modeling career. Looking at her now, Junnie could see that the years had been good to her.

"Geez, I wasn't planning on seeing you here," Asia said smiling coyly. She licked her lips as she looked him up and down. "If I had known I would have actually fixed myself up."

"I wasn't expecting to see you either. I heard you only eat in the best of circles. What you doing eating in the slums with us normal folks?" Junnie swept his hand through the air.

"Well, I just flew back from Atlanta, you know, had a photo shoot out there. And I was out in Miami for a little while to be in the homeboy's video, now I'm back home for a minute to visit my auntie. Down-south food is good, but they don't have burgers like the west coast, feel me?"

"Yeah, I bet they don't." Junnie agreed. "Well, you look good."

Asia's smile grew wider. "Why, thank you. I was just thinking the same thing about you. You still with what's her name?"

"Essence, and yeah I am."

A look of disappointment flashed across Asia's face for a brief second. "Damn, you're practically a married man now, huh?" she asked, her smile forming again.

Before Junnie could answer Allah and Harlem came over. Allah looked mildly surprised to see Asia, but Harlem didn't bother to hide his reaction. He looked Asia up and down as he drew closer and let out a loud "damn" as he got a good look at her booty.

"I know that ain't Asia," he said, standing next to Junnie.

Asia looked at Harlem and her attitude switched to disgusted. "What's up Harlem?" she asked rudely. "Still alive, I see."

"Did you have any doubt?" Harlem asked, staring openly at her breast.

"A little."

The cashier called out a number, and one of Asia's friends signaled for her to come over.

"I guess that's my order." Digging in her pocket book, Asia pulled out a business card and handed it to Junnie. "I'ma be in town for a few days before I leave again, so make sure you call me. We can catch up on old times."

"We'll see what happens," Junnie said politely, accepting the card.

Asia smiled at him seductively before waving at Allah, giving Harlem a stink face, and walking away.

Junnie watched her ass switch in the jeans for a minute before shaking his head to get rid of the thoughts that had temporarily crossed his mind.

Allah was giving him a suspicious look.

"Fuck you looking at?" he asked, turning to the line to see if they were close to calling his order.

"Let me find out you're thinking about creeping with an old piece," Harlem said, nudging his arm.

"Fuck no, you know that's a closed case." Junnie waved his hand, dismissing Allah's comments.

"Shit nigga, you might want to think about re-opening that muthafucka." Harlem said, still peeking through the crowd to try and get a look at Asia and her friend. He turned to Junnie, a smile stretching across his face. "You see that ass? Bitch looked like she could take a good dick."

Junnie shook his head. "You just say whatever comes to your head, don't you?"

"Yeah, mostly." Harlem shrugged.

"Didn't anyone teach you it's not polite to call a lady a bitch?"

They looked up to find a young boy walking up to them. He was dark skinned, with a wild afro and a perfect line up. His face was as smooth as a baby, void of any facial hair, but the hard look on his face gave him an older appearance.

His gray eyes were sparkling with humor as he walked up to them. His right hand man Angel followed closely behind, quietly surveying their surroundings. Junnie smiled when he seen his little brother come through the crowd.

"If it isn't One Eight Seven," he said, giving his miniature version a handshake. "What you doing up in here?"

"Grabbing something to eat just like you squares," Seven said, giving Allah dap.

"About to eat good, huh? What you do, snatch some ladies purse?" Harlem asked.

"Been awhile since I snatched a purse, ugly." Seven pulled out a wad of money and began to flip through the bills. "Here, I know your ass out here struggling. By yourself a decent meal," he peeled the only dollar bill he had in the stack and held it out for Harlem.

"Good, run that shit little nigga." Harlem snatched the dollar from him.

Junnie just looked at Seven. "You think it's smart to just be pulling out stacks like that?" he asked, nodding towards the money in Seven's hand. Seven gave him a look as if he couldn't have asked a dumber question.

"C'mon bro, niggas know how I give it up here," he said loud enough for everyone standing around to hear.

He lifted up his shirt, showing the butt of a gun as if there weren't dozens of people inside of the restaurant. "They should be more worried about me." Pulling his shirt down Seven pulled out his receipt to check his number. "These niggas take all night calling a fucking number, don't they?"

"Where you in a rush to?" Junnie asked.

"Me and my nigga got a party to get it to in the east."

"You little niggas are going to that?" Harlem asked, rubbing his hands together. "I didn't know you even liked going to functions."

"I don't, I like robbing niggas at functions." Seven replied nonchalantly.

"You always on some hot shit, huh?" Allah asked, looking in respect at the youngster.

"Nah, I'm always on some making money shit," Seven replied. He looked down at Allah's Jordans. "Oh shit cuddy, where you cop them from?" he asked, examining the shoe closely.

As Allah told him where he could find them, Junnie studied his little brother. Seven might have resembled their mother in looks, but his characteristics were more of Rodney.

Seven had no memory of the man, yet, he still inherited their father's fierce temper and knack for running the streets.

Some people just summed it up as being a teenage phase for a boy in the ghetto but Junnie knew the rebellious spirit was in Seven's blood and he would probably have it forever.

"Where you niggas heading after you leave here?" Seven asked.

Angel tapped his arm and nodding at something across the restaurant. Seven looked to where he was pointing and his face soundly shifted from friendly to its usual scowl.

"These two are heading to the party and I'm going back to the house. If y'all are heading to the west, you can ride with us." Junnie offered.

"Nah, we're straight," Seven replied distracted.

His attention was still focused across the room. Mumbling to himself he turned to Junnie.

"I'ma catch up with you fools later. Keep it G." bucking at Harlem. Seven went to get his food.

"That little niggas off the chain." Allah laughed

"I just hope he makes it to see twenty-one." Junnie walked to the counter as they called his number.

Grabbing his bag, he looked through it to make sure they got the order right. Walking over to the condiment station, Junnie grabbed some ketchup packets just as his phone vibrated.

"Speak on it." he answered.

"There's my baby," Essence's voice came through the receiver.

"What's up ma? I was just texting you back. You still on break?"

"No, it was going pretty slow today so Janice just let me off early. I'm just picking up a few things right now then I'm going straight to the house. What time do you think you're going to be there?"

"We're across town right now, but we'll be on our way back over that way in a little bit. By the time you get there I'll be coming up the stairs."

"Okay baby, I love you."

Junnie looked up as Asia was walking out the front door. She turned back and gave him a finger wave, which he returned with a head nod.

"I love you too," he said sincerely.

"Awe, how cute," Harlem snickered, stuffing French fries in his mouth.

"Time to get you home, Love Jones?" Allah asked, causing Harlem to laugh as if it was the funniest thing he had ever heard.

"Fucking comedians," Junnie shook his head. "Grab your shit, Chris Tucker and let's go."

As they were walking towards the exit there was a commotion from across the restaurant. The crowd started shouting and moving out of the way as there seemed to be some sort of altercation.

Suddenly, one of the tables flipped over as a large kid was punched and went flying into it. Seven hopped over the fallen kid and began to rain vicious blows to his exposed face. The kid's friends tried to help and Angel came from the crowd and hit the first one with a stool, opening a gash across his head and knocking him out instantly.

Together Seven and Angel put the hurt on the group of boys until one of the dudes pulled a gun out and fired into the air. The restaurant was sent into pandemonium as everyone stampeded towards the exit.

Through the commotion, Junnie spotted Seven and Angel ducking out of the emergency exit and disappearing into the night. Shaking his head at his younger brother's antics Junnie allowed himself to be carried through the crowd of terrified customers.

7

Grant Ridge projects looked as rundown as you would expect the projects to look in the hood. It seemed that the tenants could care less about picking up all the trash that surrounded the area, or cleaning the graffiti off of the side of the building.

If the outside was bad, the people that occupied the apartments were even worse. Grant Ridge provided shelter to the grimiest of drug dealers, killers, and fugitives. The young boys ran wild, causing as much mayhem as they wanted, with only one person who controlled them.

He was a tall, lanky man with wild dreads and large droopy eyes. The tattoos on his face gave him a sinister appearance, especially for those who understood what they meant.

Mickey had been born in Grant Ridge and had never lived anywhere other than behind its infested walls.

Once Mickey's father had been killed in a drug deal that took a wrong turn, Mickey decided it was up to him to stand up and lead his people. That's why he was more than willing to put his alliance with Calvin Cole.

The drug lord knew of his track record and had offered to give him full power over Grant Ridge, with the assistance of The Family. Mickey had accepted, gladly paying the percentage that Calvin had asked for in return. It was good business.

By noon, the sun was high in the sky, burning down on the civilians of the streets. Mickey was sitting on the trunk of his Cadillac, surrounded by a gang of his little homies.

They were discussing Lil' Bangers appearance at The Dawg House and how many hoes they speculated would be in attendance.

Mickey was hardly interested in any of it. Smoking a blunt, he looked out onto the street and the smallest of smirks appeared on his face once he seen the two familiar faces heading his way. It took a minute but his small gang finally noticed the men too.

"You must be from outta town nigga, because you damn sure heading the wrong way," a young man in a Chicago Bulls jersey moved to cut them off.

Ace looked amused at the boy as he continued walking. "It's all good little homie. I know where I'm heading," he said coolly.

The boy stepped in his path, while his friends quickly moved to back him up.

"Nah, my dude, it's about to be all bad," he warned, placing his underneath his shirt. "Who you know over here?"

Ace looked the boy directly in his eyes, and though he wore a scowl across his face Ace could see the coward lurking beneath the surface.

The fact that he was with his friends was giving him courage, and even then Ace could almost hear his heart beating out of his chest.

Beside him, Ace felt West tense up as he prepared to make his move but before the kid got the life snatched from his body, Mickey intervened.

"Y'all chill out," he called in a lazy drawl. "Show these niggas some respect. They're family, ain't that right, cousin?"

Ace brushed past the boy with the Chicago Bulls jersey. The sarcasm in Mickey's voice was hard to miss but he chose to ignore it for the time being.

"Last time I checked the DNA chart I was," he said easily. "Which is why I'm confused."

"About?" Mickey asked.

In response Ace pulled a zip-lock bag from his pocket and tossed it to him. Mickey caught it with one hand and glanced at it briefly before setting it on the car.

He chuckled softly as he looked up at Ace. "Damn, I know I got some fire, cuddy, but did you really have to rob my niggas for it? Your blood, I would have hooked you up if you needed it."

"Cute," Ace replied dryly. "But we got this from some niggas that was on my block, pitching it like someone had gave them a pass to. Now I wonder who would have gave them the green light to make money on my street," Ace asked, looking Mickey in the eyes.

Never one to back down, an angry sneer crossed Mickey's face as he slid off the car. "Nah nigga, you know what I wonder?" he asked, an edge in his voice now. "I wonder why my young boys came back about an hour ago talking about how a muthafucka that matches your description," he pointed at West, "Came by and robbed them on a block that Calvin Cole gave me authority over. That's what the fuck I wonder."

Never one to lose his composure Ace kept his game face on at this surprising bit of information.

"How's that nigga going to give you access to my shit?"

Mickey's sneer turned into a cocky smirk as he climbed back on top of his car.

"Hey, that's the price of fucking with a boss, instead of muthafuckas that got bubblegum dreams and licorice money. You got a problem with that go take it up with the big man himself, but in the meantime I appreciate it if you kept your hands off my employees. They didn't sign up to be in a hostile work environment."

A rare roar of anger exploded in Ace's chest as he stared into Mickey's arrogant face, and he found himself contemplating pulling his gun from its holster.

Giving a brief glance at West, he seen his friend giving a questioning look and he understood what he was asking without speaking; life or death. Ace gently shook his head before turning back to Mickey.

"And I thought we were family," he said matching the sarcasm from earlier.

Mickey flicked ashes from his blunt and hit it before replying. "Ace, it's only because we're related that I'ma let you walk out of here without having my young boys tear into your ass. But if you ever come back through here trying to check me on anything I'm doing, I might not be so generous. Now shake." Mickey pulled out his cell phone and began to type away on the buttons.

Ace stared at him for a few extra seconds, still contemplating whether or not he should let West finish him off, before deciding to let it be for the time.

"He said shake from around here nigga," the same dude from earlier with the Chicago Bulls jersey barked at them.

By this time, he had his gun dangling from his hand. Ace tapped West and began to head back to the street. West backed away from the group, making sure he looked each of them in the eye, but he locked eyes with the one in the jersey. Smirking like he knew something they didn't, West turned and followed his partner to the Buick. Ace was already in the passenger seat, a rush of emotions soaring through him at what he had just heard.

West climbed in behind the wheel. Reaching in the backseat, he tossed the Batman blanket he had back there to the floor, revealing the sawed of shotgun he had concealed underneath. Lifting it up, he cocked the slide, mumbling to himself.

"Aye Rambo, where you think you off to?" Ace said, grabbing his arm as he prepared to get out of the car.

"I'm 'bout to hit these niggas," West fumed. He was so angry his eyes had turned bloodshot red, as if he was now in touch with his inner demon. "Did you hear these faggots popping off? And you told me not to blast?"

"Yes, exactly like I'm telling you right now," Ace cautioned. "Just chill out. Mickey and them popped they shit, but I already have his ticket pulled. If you go out there right now the only thing that's gonna happen is me having to go explain to my nephew, why his father's laid in a box with a suit and tie on. We're on these muthafuckas turf.

They automatically got the drop on us. Just chill out for right now while I try and figure why this bitch ass nigga Cole think he has the authority to hand my turf off to this nigga." Ace nodded towards Grant Ridge.

"That's easy as fuck to see," West snapped. "This muthafuckas trying to exterminate us and replace us with his people. He's tryin' to get his people in order so he can put the smash on the streets. You said you didn't want to kill Mickey because it might start a war with The Family but by the way things are looking right now, we're going to have to go head up with them niggas anyway. They're trying to take all our shit."

As much as Ace hated to admit it he knew West was right. It seemed as if Calvin Cole had deemed them not adequate enough to make money in the streets and had instead told a whole different set that they could have his territory, without so much as giving Ace word about it. But if that's the way Cole wanted it Ace wasn't going down as quietly as the drug lord apparently thought.

"Fuck that, I'ma need to have a sit down with this nigga, Cole," Ace said, trying not to let his anger overflow. "He's trying to play us pussy, and I need to show him the error of his ways."

"You want to go see this nigga now?" West asked, anxious to aim his anger at someone and lash out.

Even though he wasn't attempting to get out of the car again, he still held a firm grip on his shotgun.

Ace shook his head. "Nah, in due time," he replied looking at his watch. "As of now we need to head over to the block and see what the little homies is doing. If these niggas want to take our street they're going to have to fight for that shit. We need to tell the soldiers from now on smash on any nigga that walks on the block not talking right."

****

The sun began to set, bringing about the usual suspects. Stepping out from the growing shadows, Seven pulled his hood over his head and looked around the dark street before heading to his destination. A few people were wondering around outside, and Seven examined each face he passed. His hands were shoved deep in his pocket and he had something ready, in case someone wanted to come around acting stupid.

At only seventeen years of age, Seven had a head start on being remembered in the streets long after he was dead and gone. He was a beast when it came to the hood and everyone knew it.

The streets were something he was born into and they had a hold on him. Nothing gave him more of a thrill than being on the block and putting in work, two things he did frequently.

This evening was no different. Watching a police cruiser go by, Seven crossed the street and cut through the Lamont apartments. Once behind the apartment complex he went through an alley and walked to the end of the street.

It was a quiet, residential street that would be hard to find if you weren't shown the exact location. There were no cars passing by, and the echo of people's voices were left back on the main street. It had been awhile since Seven had to come over this area and he was hoping he could just see who he needed to see. Reaching the house on the end of the block he tightened his grip on his gun's handle as he walked down the driveway.

Two young men were situated on the front porch. They both wore hoodies and were passing a blunt back and forth. They had been in the middle of a conversation but they stopped once Seven drew closer. The taller of the two stood up, grabbing a shotgun from off the porch table.

"What business you got around here homie?" he asked with hostility.

"Come to see Baron." Seven answered simply.

"About what?"

"I don't think that's your business dawg. You can let him know I'm here though."

The young dude glared Seven down and Seven glared right back. He looked like he was considering busting a move but Seven already knew he could air him out before the dude could get his finger on the trigger of the shotgun. His partner slowly stood to his feet, face twisted in a sneer.

"You might wanna chill with that shit around here nigga," the first dude stated, trying to lay his gorilla down.

Seven smirked, and slid his finger around the trigger so he could pull out blasting at any second. "I hear that shit, just let B know I'm here."

The first dude pulled his phone out and placed a call. He talked low in the phone for a few seconds before nodding and hanging up. "C'mon." He stepped off the porch and headed towards the back of the house. Seven followed behind, while the second dude brought up the rear.

They reached the garage which looked quiet on the outside but everyone knew how the inside operated. The first dude opened the side door and they got inside. Without turning the light on, he knelt down and tossed a large raggedy rug to the side, revealing a hidden door.

Giving it a tug the first dude held the door open while Seven stepped down the stairs and into a smoky tunnel hidden beneath the ground. Loud voices and music could be heard now, and the strong scent of drugs and money filled Seven's nose as he followed the two down the tunnel and into a large basement.

People were gathered around like they were at the club, music playing and partying in full effect.

Seven recognized a few people as he moved through the crowd. He pulled the strings of his hoodie, shielding his face even more. He was on solid terms with Baron, but that didn't speak the same for some of Barons affiliates. Keeping his senses on live alert, Seven turned his hard glare to the first dude as he tapped his arm.

"Baron said he'll meet you in here."

"Yep." Seven answered and the two dudes both left to go resume their post in front of the house.

Still looking around Seven leaned back against the wall and took in the scene. There was a lot of bumping and grinding going on, and he had no problem watching the females shaking their asses.

If he wasn't there on business, he might have made a move to push up on something, but he had other plans. He was watching the skirt on a fine young chick rise higher and higher as she twerked as if she were in a video, when he felt someone staring at him.

Looking up Seven instantly made contact with a group of grimy looking young cats across the room. They were all looking at him with distain but the leader of the group had a look of pure hatred as he and Seven made eye contact. Eyes narrowing, Seven stood up straighter as he continued watching the group.

At first Seven didn't recognize the dude but then the light hit his face and Seven realized he did know him.

Just a few weeks back he and Angel had been outside the club, smoking and waiting for the club to let out so that they could snatch up a few of the females straggling out when Chance had walked past their car.

Chance was a dude from around the way who didn't really have a name for himself but he did move a little weight for some heavier cats. Seeing that it was just him and his homey, Angel decided to see just how much work the young hustler was really worth.

Seven played lookout while Angel ran up behind Chance and his boy and robbed them both for everything down to their nose piercings. Seven remembered the cold look that Chance had given Seven while he handed Angel his jewelry, but Seven didn't pay it much attention, exactly like he wasn't now.

"You Seven right?" Chance spat as he finally made it across the room.

"Last time I checked." Seven said boldly.

He was outnumbered, in close quarters, but he was willing to wild out if need be. People nearby began to move aside as they sensed an altercation brewing. Chance was so angry he was almost shaking.

"Yeah, I thought so. You already know what it is." Chance took a fighting stance while his crew began to mutter encouragements for him to cause harm to Seven. "You and your nigga were real hard the other day. I'ma need my bread back before shit turn ugly in here, my nigga."

Seven let out a humorless laugh. "Nigga, you coulda kept your ass in your seat for this shit. If you run up on me, you better be doing more than talking." While he spoke Seven slipped his Glock from his jacket, and prepared to end the party early.

Chance snarled but before he or his crew could bust a move, a loud voice came booming over the music. "Fuck is going on in my spot?"

Everyone cleared the way as a large man stepped through the crowd, a group of goons following nearby. He was easily six feet tall, built with solid muscle and a powerful physique.

His head was shaven but his beard was thick and hung to his chest, while his eyes were hidden behind a pair of dark shades. Baron was a monster of a man and his size played a big part in his dominating demeanor. Everyone respected Baron and the ones who didn't were smart enough not to be vocal about it. He looked between Chance's crew and Seven.

"What's going on here?" he asked, his deep voice easily audible even over all the noise.

"Ain't shit Baron. Just checking this little nigga over some shit he and his man owe," Chance said, never taking his eyes off Seven's face.

"B, you know we go back a cool minute, and I would never disrespect your spot." People standing nearby screamed as Seven put his gun in full view and cocked the slide back. "But these niggas keep on with that gangsta shit I'ma let them hold something hot."

"All you niggas need to chill before I get involved and it won't be nothing nice," Baron warned. "Whatever y'all got to handle, handle it on your own times. While you in my spot, you're gonna let that shit ride out or get stomped out, feel me? I ain't feeling how y'all got my li'l nigga hemmed up in this corner. Go take a seat Chance."

Chance's jaw worked back and forth like he had something to say, but he knew better. Baron and his crew were brutal, and no one had ever got the best of them in a battle. He knew he wasn't ready.

"Yeah, I got you Baron. I'ma see you and your nigga soon though," he told Seven.

"You see how good that worked for you last time you seen us." Seven smirked and winked as Chance walked off. Baron gave Seven a look.

"I see you're still up to the same ol' shit, huh?" he asked, before his face split into a grin.

"Ain't that why you fuck with me?" Seven asked.

"You already know." They exchanged handshakes, and Seven nodded at the rest of the crew. Baron clapped his hands together. "So you got that for me?"

Seven reached in his jacket and pulled out an envelope. "It's all there."

"Oh trust me, I don't doubt it. You really tracked that nigga down huh?" Baron asked impressed. He looked inside the envelope and passed it to one of his boys.

Seven shrugged. "Wasn't too much to it. Just gotta have the right resources."

One of Barons employees had decided to try and go into business for himself, but before he quit he decided to walk off with all of Barons money he had made and a little bit of work. Taking a few of Barons disloyal associates with him the traitor went to San Jose and decided to lay low for a while.

Baron needed to get to him but he didn't want to send anyone from his crew because the traitor would recognize them immediately. That's where Seven came in.

"You didn't kill him did you?" Baron asked.

"Nah, I figured I'll leave that bit of gold for you. I just roughed him up a little bit."

By rough him up a little bit, he meant that the traitor now had thirteen stitches across his face, a mouth full of shattered teeth, and a broken arm.

"He's taking a vacation at O'Connor's Hospital. You can probably still catch him."

"Yeah, I intend to." Baron dug in his back pocket and pulled out a bank roll that had a rubber band holding it together. "I think this is yours. You gonna offend me by counting it?"

"Nah, I trust you. Besides, if it ain't right, I know where you be at." Seven half joked, accepting the money.

"That's one beef you don't want, li'l homie. You need a few more stripes first." Baron threw a playful punch that Seven deflected.

"I hear that shit."

"Nah, fa'real. When you gonna quit fucking around and ride with me and my people. I could use a real nigga like you on my team Sev. I still remember when you and Angel's little ass was out there hustling dime bags. You got potential, and you're wasting it if you're out here robbing niggas like Chance."

"I make enough to get by." Seven shrugged. "Besides, you know I don't fuck with following anybody. I run on my own rules. We would bump heads too much, and that's something we both don't need."

Baron laughed a booming laugh. "You right, my nigga, you right. Well the offers always there if you want it, and you know I'm here if you ever need it."

"I respect it." Seven nodded in appreciation. They gave each other dap.

"Now, I know you're gonna try to snatch up one of these bitches before you walk out of here. Shorty over there been eyeballing you since we've been talking."

Seven followed Barons gaze to a section in the opposite corner. A trio of females were sipping drinks and not even trying to hide the looks in their eyes as they watched the young men. One, a short caramel beauty with a beautiful face gave Seven a smile and he nodded at her.

"As tempting as it looks, I'ma bounce. Me and Angel got a few things to take care of before the night is over with."

"Always on the prowl, huh? I feel it. Good looking out again on making sure that got handled."

"You already know. Hit me when you need some business done."

"I got you on speed dial, my nigga. You gonna be good or do I gotta set some niggas straight?" Baron nodded towards Chance and his crew. They were seated on the couch with a few girls now, but Chance was still eyeing Seven with evil intentions.

Seven smirked at the mean mug. "Them boys don't wanna run the issue." And with that Seven turned and left.

8

Sammy sat in the backseat of the car, smoking a cigarette and toying with the gun he had in his lap. Wick and Randy were in the front seat having a discussion that Sammy wasn't interested in. His mind was focused on the same thing it had been all day.

Since the run in with Junnie the night before Sammy had been walking around with zero pride. Not only had Junnie stolen all of his work but, he had slapped him in front of his boys. Even though Wick and Randy hadn't said anything about the altercation Sammy felt like he had lost respect in their eyes and he couldn't rest until he got it back.

Sammy had insisted on rolling past the block that Junnie and his boys usually was seen around but they hadn't been out. Sammy's heart had been beating hard as the rolled through the street searching for Junnie's familiar face. In reality Sammy knew he was no match for Junnie but he had to prove himself.

"I'm telling you bro, we should just go to this party on the west side." Wick called back to Sammy. "We go to the party, drink on something, smoke good, and find a bad bitch for you to get under for the night. Trust me, it'll be good."

"Yeah, fuck Junnie and them niggas he roll with. When we do run into them we're gonna bang it out, but for now let's go kick it." Randy encouraged.

Thinking about it Sammy nodded. Going to get fucked up sounded a lot better than any confrontation with his enemies.

"Alright, we can for a minute. But I still want a line on that nigga Junnie. This shit ain't over."

"You might not have to wait long." Randy sat up in his seat. "Ain't that the car them niggas drove away in the other night?"

Wick and Sammy both sat up quickly to look at the car that was a little distance from them.

"Yeah it is. Look, it still got bullet holes in the side!" Wick pointed.

"Oh shit." Randy excitedly pulled his gun from his jeans. "What you want to do, Sam?"

This was the time to prove he was as solid as he had always claimed he was in the streets. Taking a deep breath Sammy nodded towards the car.

"Pull up beside these niggas."

****

Allah blew weed smoke up towards the sunroof as he slowed down at a red light. He was already high from smoking majority of the day but to him there was no such thing as being too high.

Beside him Harlem was in the passenger seat, arguing with someone on his phone.

After dropping Junnie off at his house the two had decided to keep going on with their journey to the party. Allah hadn't been to a hood function in a while and he was ready for some action. Before he walked inside the party he planned on finishing at least two more blunts.

"Stupid bitch." Harlem cursed as he ended his phone call.

Allah looked at him. "Why you always pissed off? You need to invest in more of this." he held the blunt out, which Harlem greedily snatched.

"Nah, these females be on some stupid shit. That's why I could never be in a relationship. I don't see how you and Junnie does it."

"It's called love, bruh. You have to be willing to settle down with a chick. These hoes don't last forever."

"Whatever you say, Romeo." Harlem shrugged him off.

"You want to know something my uncle taught me?"

"Not really."

"He taught me that anger is your second strongest emotion. If you can't control it it's probably because your weak minded."

"Ain't your uncle a dope fiend?"

"Yeah, but that doesn't mean what he said isn't true."

"If I were you I would have told him he could keep that advice." Harlem laughed. "What's the first?"

"First what?"

"You said anger is your second strongest emotion. Whats the first."

"Love." Allah revealed.

Harlem glanced at him. "Love?"

"Yep. Anger will make you kill someone, but love will make you give your life for them, which is the biggest sacrifice in the world."

Harlem continued staring at Allah before finally shaking his head in disgust. "Don't run up in this party talking this sappy ass shit. You ain't gonna get any pussy for the night."

"Whatever nigga." Allah laughed.

He was reaching for the blunt in Harlem's hand when there was suddenly a loud screech of car tires. Allah turned in time to see a car pull up beside them. When he seen the guns aimed in his direction Allah's heart dropped.

"Get down!" Allah yelled to Harlem right as the gunfire started. Their windows shattered as Sammy and his crew tried to take their heads off.

Even as they were surrounded by bullets Allah was still able to get his mind right enough to drive the car forward. Staying ducked down he steered the car without being able to see where he was going.

"Fuck that shit!" Harlem climbed half out of his window and aimed his gun over the roof of the car. He fired back at the three shooters, not concerned with getting shot himself.

"Get these niggas!" Wick yelled driving after Allah's car. The two vehicles sped side by side as its passengers exchanged gunfire.

"Cut these niggas off."

Randy directed, taking charge. Wick sped past Allah's car and crossed him off. Randy hopped out the car and prepared to finish Allah and Harlem off. He was surprised when Allah opened the drivers door and stuck his gun out. Randy's jaw dropped but it was too late. Allah squeezed the trigger.

"Randy!" Sammy yelled as he watched his friend get lifted off his feet from the bullets.

As soon as Randy hit the cement Allah closed his door and drove around Wick's Buick. With no barrier in his way Allah drove down the street and away from the crash site.

"Randy."

Sammy called out, not caring that his targets had got away. He was still in shock from seeing one of his best friends sprawled out on the concrete with a large hole in his chest. He made to get out the car.

"No. We gotta go." Wick yelled. Without wasting another second he directed the car in the opposite direction that Allah had driven.

"Wait, we have to go back!" Randy yelled angrily. "He can still be alive."

"Yo fuck that, that nigga is dead! If you want to stick around and get booked by the cops hop out the car, but my black ass is getting out of here."

Sammy looked out the rear window, back where Randy was surely dying. He said a prayer for his comrade as Wick led them away.

****

It had been awhile since Junnie had taken Essence out anywhere so it was long overdue. Their first stop was the Cheesecake Factory downtown that they had gone to only once before when they had first started dating.

After a fantastic meal they went to catch a late night movie that was pretty entertaining. Now they were at home in bed, and Junnie couldn't stop laughing.

Essence had the next two days off from work, so she decided she wanted to try something risky. She had never really been a weed smoker, but she wanted to join Junnie tonight, even against his warnings. The weed he had picked up from Charlie was more potent than he had expected and he knew Essence couldn't hang, but she protested so he let her hit the blunt.

Three puffs later she was staring at the television screen with a dazed looked on her face. She had been talking and laughing nonstop before smoking, now she seemed like she was moving in reverse.

"You good, baby?" Junnie asked, looking into Essence's bloodshot eyes.

"Yeah, I'm just watching… the show," Essence replied softly, staring straight ahead. Junnie chuckled, and she turned her attention to him. A slow, goofy smile spread across her face.

"What?" she asked innocently.

"You're faded, that's what. Didn't I tell you that you wouldn't be able to handle it?" Junnie shook his head. "Now look at you."

Essence stared at him for a second, then her smile grew even wider.

"You're so cute," she gushed, pinching his cheeks.

"Move with your weird ass," Junnie hit her in the head with the pillow. "See, this why I don't smoke with you. You're a rookie."

"Shut up." Essence scooted closer and laid her head on his chest. It was nights like these that she appreciated.

To her, having Junnie next to her was better than anything else in the world. Usually he was out at night making moves, even against her protests, and by the time he came back she would be sleep. But on the nights she was able to keep him home Essence was always content.

In the streets people viewed Junnie as a powerful player in the game, and either feared or respected him, but when he was at home with her he was Essence's big baby.

"Thank you for taking me out tonight," Essence said softly, rubbing Junnie's chest. "I'm always happy when we spend time together."

"You act like I be away at war or something." Junnie replied. "We spend plenty of time together."

Essence rolled her eyes. "Yeah, you playing video games while I'm snoring every night isn't exactly 'spending time' in my book. You spend more actual time with Allah and Harlem's rude ass then me."

"That's because I'm taking care of business with them. It's not like we're just hanging around, going on picnics and shit.

I'm trying to get this money so you and I can get up out of here one day. You don't want to work at Macy's forever, do you?"

"No, but I also don't want you out here risking your life for this rich ass lifestyle you seem to think I want."

Essence lifted her head and stared into Junnie's eyes. They were just as beautiful as the day she had first looked into them. They only showed love when she looked, but she often wondered what Junnie's enemies seen when they looked into them.

"I don't need an extravagant life for us to be happy together. We can be just as happy with you working a regular job, instead of out here looking over your shoulder every time we go out."

Junnie chuckled. "We both know you can't picture my black ass trying to flip any damn burgers. A Nine to five ain't my thing and I wouldn't even attempt it."

"Not even for me?" Essence asked seriously.

"You shouldn't want to change me Essie. This the nigga you fell in love with, so why change that?" Junnie held his arms open.

"No, who you are is what made me fall in love with you. Robbing people, shooting, and dealing drugs isn't who you are as a person. That's just the stupid shit you do."

"I'ma product of my environment." Junnie kissed Essence's forehead. "But your high right now and you're getting deep in your feelings. I'ma let you sleep it off while I go make a sandwich. I'm hungry as a muthafucka. You want something?"

"No." Essence replied, turning over in the bed.

Junnie laughed and smacked her on the butt. He slipped in Essence's Scooby Doo slippers before heading for the kitchen.

"Junnie?" Essence called out softly.

"Yeah?" He turned towards her.

"I love you, baby."

"I love you too ma. Now get some rest."

Junnie went to the kitchen to see what he could find to cure his hunger. Grocery shopping was more of Essence's thing but she knew what he liked. Junnie didn't like cooking, so he was pleased when he looked in the cabinet and found a box of Captain Crunch.

He had just grabbed a bowl when his phone rang. It caught him by surprise because he had forgotten that he had left it on the table when they had got back home.

"Yeah?" Junnie answered.

"Fam, what you up to?" Allah's voice came from the other end.

"At the house chilling. What's good?" Junnie questioned curiously. Allah sounded a lot more agitated then his usual chill demeanor. In the background, Junnie could hear Harlem cursing and yelling about something. "Y'all at the party?"

"We were on our way but hit a detour. You remember how we threw that surprise party for our friend the other night?"

"Yeah."

"Well he just tried to do the same for us."

"The fuck!" Junnie stopped fixing his cereal "You two good?"

"Yeah, don't trip. He brought some presents for us, but we gladly returned the favor."

"I'm on my way, bruh."

"Nah, chill it's all good. Tonight's your night with wifey. Me and Harlem just going to head to the house until all the excitement from the party dies down. I just called you to let you know."

"Aye, come get me first thing in the morning, hear me?"

"Solid." Allah ended the phone call.

Junnie shook his head as he tossed his phone to the side. Sammy was causing too much trouble that didn't need to be caused. Junnie had planned on him just taking his lost, and moving on, but it seemed that Sammy thought he had something to prove. Now Junnie had to kill him.

Junnie didn't mind killing, but he only tried to do it when necessary. It was only a matter of time before the police caught wind of somebody leaving dead bodies all over the city, and so far, he had remained off their radar, which was how he intended to keep it.

Junnie planned on going back to the room with Essence but once in the living room he opted to just sit in his favorite seat of the house. His armchair was positioned next to the window which gave him a direct view of the street below. Sitting down, Junnie ate his cereal and stared at the empty street below.

For as long as Junnie could remember, he had been in the streets. Even when he was a small child, his father would bring him along as he walked around the hood talking to all his friends. There was something luring about being in the streets that Junnie couldn't let go.

He hadn't expected a relationship when he first met Essence, but he ended up falling for her. She was everything to him, and now he couldn't imagine living life without her.

The fact that their relationship had started before he had planned to settle down complicated things. Essence wanted him to stop what he was doing but Junnie wasn't ready to leave the underground life yet.

He had established himself at everything he had been working on. Unlike a lot of people who played the game, Junnie knew it wouldn't last forever, but he still had work to do.

He needed to stack enough money for him and Essence to escape and live comfortably. Getting a regular job will never be an option for him so he needed to make sure he had enough cash to fall back on.

Essence wasn't the type of female that wanted the luxury life. She always made sure her appearance was kept up but she was completely fine with going to a discount store to get her purses and clothes as opposed to wanting Michael Kors or Prada.

Junnie had seen her come home with more than a few nice summer dresses that she had found at Target. It was one of the things that made Junnie love her more and more of a reason why he wanted to give her everything she could possibly want.

Finishing his cereal, Junnie put his bowl in the sink and grabbed his pack of cigarettes from the coffee table. He cursed silently when he realized they were empty. He went to the bedroom so he could grab his hoodie and walk to the store.

Upon walking into the bedroom Junnie found the TV still on but Essence was curled underneath the covers, fast asleep.

Junnie walked over and couldn't help but smile down at her. Her lips were slightly parted as she snored softly. A wisp of hair in her face fluttered with each breath she took.

Junnie gently brushed the hair away and planted a kiss on her forehead. At that moment, he realized there was nowhere else he rather be then with his lady.

Pulling the cover back he climbed in beside Essence and pulled her close. The day must have taken more of a toll on him than he thought because in a matter of minutes, Junnie was snoring too.

9

Calvin Cole got out of the car, squinting his eyes in the harsh sunlight. The heat was getting worse as the summer continued and there wasn't indication of it letting up.

Running his hand over his fresh haircut, Calvin walked up the gravel path of the warehouse. He had purchased the building for the needs of stashing any goods or as a secret bank, but it was being occupied for another use today.

It had been awhile since he'd come out this way, but his presence was needed. A group of rough looking young men stood posted outside the entrance, including Polo. The young leader walked over to greet Calvin as he got closer.

"He in there?" Calvin asked with a grim face. Polo nodded the confirmation.

"Wolf and the boys brought him through about thirty minutes ago. They been in the room with him ever since." Polo opened the door for Calvin and he stepped through.

The inside of the warehouse was dimly lit, but you could see that there were many more soldiers inside standing around.

Calvin led the way through the large room and down the hallway to a solid metal door. Giving a solid knock, they waited for a minute before the clanking of a lock could be heard and the door swung open.

There was a single light bulb inside the room, it swung back and forth causing the shadows to shift. Beneath the light there was a man slumped in a chair. There were a few goons situated around the room, all wore serious expressions on their faces.

Wolf stood shirtless with a link chain wrapped around his fist. The Wolf was a stocky cat with a hideous face and a lazy eye. His evil streak was just as scary as his facial features, and he had an incredibly high taste for blood.

Whenever someone needed to be killed Johnny usually went. Whenever someone needed to be made an example of, Wolf was summoned. He looked up as Calvin and Polo entered the room.

"Boss man." Wolf nodded at Calvin. "You said don't kill him, that's the only reason this bitch is still breathing," he said, motioning towards the man tied in a chair.

It would have been hard to describe what the man looked like unless you had seen his face before he had been tied to the chair. Currently, his face resembled a slab of bloody ground beef. One eye was swollen shut, while the other was busted, and had turned solid red. His nose was leaking blood down his swollen lips and seemed to be turned at a very painful angle.

When he opened his mouth to groan, you could see some teeth struggling to stay intact to the gum. Polo tried to stop from grimacing at the sight of the man, and did his best to keep a straight face.

Calvin however didn't bat an eye, patting Wolf on the arm to let him know it was okay, Calvin stepped close to the man. Giving his face a gentle slap he watched as the man stirred.

"Rise and shine, Doughboy," Calvin spoke softly. Doughboy stirred again and opened the eye that wasn't swollen shut. "How you feeling?" He didn't respond, but then again Calvin didn't expect him to. "Yeah, probably not as good as you have been for the past few days, right?"

"What is this about?" Doughboy croaked.

Calvin's eyebrows raised. "You really don't know what this is about?" Doughboy managed to give his head a little shake.

Calvin began to pace around his chair. "You mean in your wildest dreams you couldn't imagine why Calvin Cole might have you tied to a chair, and beaten three blows away from death?" Again silence. "See, I pride myself in being a compassionate leader, Dough. In my time on the streets there weren't exactly too many cats out here that were interested in giving niggas fair work.

It was dog-eat-dog. I told myself I wasn't going to be like that. So that's when I put together a team of young hustlers, and still gave a fair share to niggas not even a part of The Family. So can you imagine how I would feel if I find out that someone's been stealing from me this whole time? Someone I let eat off my fucking plate?"

"C'mon Cal— "

Whap!

Calvin slapped Doughboy so hard it sent a shock up his arm. Doughboy slumped in the chair but the restraints kept him in a sitting position. Calvin bent down so he and Doughboy were eye to eye.

"Don't ever speak my name again, you cock sucking faggot," he spit venomously. "I paid your pockets so that you could take care of your little girlfriend and your bastard son and you repay me by stealing my fucking money and work? If I could kill you two times I would."

"Cal—I mean, wait please. I'm sorry." Doughboy croaked, hearing the seriousness in Calvin's voice. "I got greedy and I'm sorry! Please don't kill me over this shit! Please!"

Calvin looked at him, disgust written all over his face. "You already proved you're a rat. At least don't spend your last few seconds in life as a bitch." Standing up straight Calvin looked down to make sure no blood had got on his shoes. "But I'm not a complete monster," he told Doughboy.

He turned to Wolf, who was looking as if he couldn't wait to finish Doughboy off. "Give him a quick death," he ordered, before heading towards the door.

Polo quickly followed, not wanting to be in the room with the beaten Doughboy any longer. They shut the door behind them, leaving Doughboy's fate to Wolf.

As they were walking down the hallway Johnny almost bumped into them.

"My bad, am I late to the show?" he asked, looking over Calvin's shoulder. At that precise moment they heard the roar of a chainsaw coming to life and the final screams of a man dying.

"Yep," Calvin nodded before continuing outside the warehouse. "Where you coming from?" he asked Johnny.

"Headquarters. I was finishing up a little business when Smitty came through and said Ace wants a meeting with you."

"Who?" his thoughts still on Doughboy.

"Ace Boon. He and his boy West were running Foster Avenue, but you told the young boy Mickey he could move work over there."

"Yeah, I remember Ace. The nigga never hit me back up about going into business together, and Foster is way too profitable for me not to have a piece of it, so since he didn't want to play ball he got benched. Fuck he want now?"

"Probably wants to see what the deal is. You did muscle him off of his block, but from what I know Ace isn't really a threat," Polo spoke up.

"Anybody's a threat if you give them a reason to be," Calvin replied, stopping outside of his driver's door.

"Well, he wants to meet with you later on today. You down for it, or do you want me to just eliminate the problem altogether?" Johnnie asked.

Calvin thought on it for a second. "Nah, we're going to let him breathe for the time being. Once we meet with him if he doesn't like the way things are going we'll just exile his ass. He won't ever eat on my streets again. Besides there's a loose end I need you to tie up."

"What's the word?" Johnny gave his full attention.

"Doughboy might have been a thieving muthafucka but Queenies the one who put the battery in his back. I don't want her living to see the sun set, feel me?"

Queenie was Doughboy's girlfriend and had served as a runner in The Family for a while.

"So you want me to get rid of her?" Johnny clarified, gently surprised. Calvin usually had a strict code against hurting women or children, but then again Queenie had violated.

"Like a case of the mumps," Calvin responded seriously. "We seem to have a case of thieves running among us. Make sure you guys are still keeping an eye on this nigga Jonah. If he really was stealing I'm sure he was a part of this shit with Doughboy. If you have to miss the meeting with this nigga Ace, then so be it. I'll have Polo come with me."

"What time are you meeting this guy?" Polo questioned suddenly.

"Why, you got somewhere to be?" Johnny asked curiously.

"Well yeah, Lil Bangers supposed to be coming out to the Dawg House tonight," he informed.

"Really? I didn't hear anything about it," Johnny frowned.

"I did. His manager hit me up earlier this week and let me know," Calvin said.

"Yep, all the skeezers are going to be flocking out tonight so you know I have to go out hold it down for the team." Polo popped his collar, and thumbed the tip of his nose.

"You might want to be careful going around to all of these functions, Po," Calvin cautioned. "You're a made-man now and the last thing we need is some clown running up on you just to try and make a name for himself."

"You don't think I tell the hard headed nigga the same thing all the time?" Johnny said, jerking his thumb at Polo.

Polo just smirked at his mentors. "C'mon big homies, these fools know who I am out here. I'm untouchable, that's why I'm still around to brag about my record."

Johnny just shook his head. "Speaking of niggas who think they're untouchable, the young boy we had making a few moves for us got pushed off last night."

"Who?"

"Jericho and some of his crew."

"Damn, is it going to hurt us any?"

"Not that I can think of. He wasn't signed on with us, just ran a few errands here and there."

"Fuck him then," Calvin shrugged. "At this point if they're not directly tied in with us I can care less about their well-being. I have a few runs to make then I'll meet up with y'all later on," he told them, getting inside of his Charger.

"You don't need one of us to roll with you?" Polo asked leaning in the window. Calvin looked at the young boy and smirked.

"I was a soldier before I was a don," he told him, putting the car in gear. The car Sent gravel flying in the air as he pulled out of the driveway and down the road.

****

Sammy sat in the Chinese restaurant waiting impatiently for Wick to get his food. It was hotter than it had been for the past couple weeks, so there was more activity on the street than usual.

Sammy looked around suspiciously at every person that walked past him. He knew that either Junnie or the police were going to walk up on him at any second and that's why he had his hand wrapped tightly around the handle of the .22 he had in his pocket. He didn't plan to go with either one.

Randy's death from the night before was affecting him hard. He had grown up with Randy since they were youngsters and to know that he was dead because of Sammy would always weight on his heart. Even worst Junnie would be coming for him any day now.

Junnie and his crew were known for being wild when it came to beefs and Sammy knew he wasn't ready to tangle with the deadly trio, but his pride had backed him into a corner and now he was going to have to either kill or be killed.

Wick came back over to the table with his food. He was stuffing his mouth with rice and orange chicken as if he didn't have a care in the world.

"I like that you can stuff your face in the middle of a crisis," Randy said, shaking his head. He stood up so they could leave.

"I have to be well fed and energized for what's about to go down," Wick replied seriously as they exited the restaurant.

"And what you planning on doing?" Sammy asked.

"We're about to kill this nigga, Junnie." Wick responded as if it should be obvious. "Him and his homies. They killed Randy and that shit ain't about to be forgotten. I'm banging on all them muthafuckas."

"Junnie wasn't there," Sammy pointed out.

"Maybe not, but he's still responsible for that shit. He started all of this the other night when they ran up. His crew, his orders. He's dying tonight, and that's on my momma."

They crossed the parking lot as Wick continued to eat and explain how he was going to torture Junnie and his squad. Sammy was only half listening. Truthfully, he wasn't in a rush to see Junnie or any of them. Randy was dead and gone. This beef was the real deal.

Sammy was thinking whether or not Junnie would end the feud if he admitted defeat. Sammy was by no means a sucker, but he didn't want to die over something stupid either.

They were almost to Sammy's car when a beat up Toyota revved towards them. Sammy barely had time to register what was happening when the passenger window rolled down and a man wearing a black bandana wrapped around the lower half of his face leaned out the car.

Sammy didn't need to see the man's full face to know who it was. Junnie's pale gray eyes were narrowed in anger as he aimed his gun out the window.

"What's up now, nigga!" Junnie barked before squeezing the trigger.

Sammy was so surprised he didn't know that he was hit, but he sure felt the next two shots.

Wicks food dropped out his hands as he tried to reach for his own weapon. Harlem grinned as he leaned out the back window and joined Junnie in shooting. Wick was hit a couple times but when a bullet knocked off half his face it was obvious he was done.

Sammy lay on the ground coughing up blood as he tried to grab at the large holes in his chest. The last thing he seen before he died was Junnie's harsh glare, and the next second the car was driving off.

****

Rango stepped out of his apartment building, shielding his eyes from the harsh sunlight.

It was blazing and the day was just getting started. Smirking smugly, Rango brushed imaginary debris from his fresh t-shirt and stepped down the stairs. Someone across the street called out to him and he nodded in response as he pulled his car keys from his pocket.

Rango was a young hustler whose dreams were bigger than his bank account. You wouldn't be able to tell from all the jewelry he sported and the 2015 Cadillac he had just bought but he had spent every dollar he had to his name just to get those things.

He believed in keeping up a solid image and he did better than most. Young boys wanted to be like him and women wanted to be with him. If they knew he only had a couple hundred left until he came up on a job again.

Reaching his car, Rango's jaw dropped slightly when he noticed a girl walking past with more ass than any of his favorite porn stars. Instantly, he arranged the Rolex on his wrist and adjusted his chain before speaking.

"Now, you know damn well them feet too pretty to be walking on this concrete, ma," he called out.

The girl looked up and seen the D-boy eyeballing her hungrily. Noticing the sun shining off of the jewels he was rocking and the car he was standing next to, a smile crossed the girl's face as she prepared to go give him a minute and see what she could get out of him.

She paused once she noticed two young men walking up behind Rango. Seeing the look in their eyes, the smile left her face and she turned and walked the opposite way.

"Aye, where you going, angel?" Rango called out confused.

"I don't think Angels like the sight of devils," Seven retorted.

Rango jumped in surprise and turned around. Two young boys he didn't hear were standing behind him with less than friendly faces.

They looked slightly familiar, maybe from around the block but Rango didn't know them personally. He looked between the both of them.

"Why you niggas sneaking up on a muthafucka?" Rango asked angrily.

His surprise was now replaced with anger as he looked at the teenagers. The one with the dreads was looking like he wanted to bust a move but the Smith & Wesson Rango had in his jeans would make the little dude change his mind.

"Our profession calls for us to be a little sneaky." Seven smirked. "We don't know each other but we have a mutual friend. You're Holly's boy, ain't you?"

"I ain't nobody's, "boy", li'l nigga," Rango snapped. "Check that shit. Who the fuck is you?"

Seven ignored the comments. "The other day your boy Holly and some rag-toe niggas ran up on my li'l homie and stuck him for some bread. I'ma need that back in full."

Rango's face twisted up.

"Nigga, if you just ran up in my face with this dumb ass shit you clearly got me confused with the wrong nigga. If Holly stuck your dude for some bread, the li'l dumb muthafucka probably had it coming. If you need some change go run up on Holly and try to get him for it, but I doubt you'll get far. Fuck outta here." Rango opened his car door but Seven slammed it shut.

Rango didn't even pause to think about it. He swung, but Seven was quicker. Ducking the blow, Seven came up with a vicious right hook that rocked Rango's cranium.

As his body slumped to the side Seven hit him with a left, that sent him leaning in the opposite direction. Seven came with the precision of a boxer as he landed three more punches to Rango's exposed face before the older man could hit the ground.

"You niggas always want to show out huh?" Seven spat, reaching down and slapping Rango. "Now word on the street is you run a little crew of bitch ass niggas, and with that being said, I don't approach soldiers. I approach leaders, no matter how pathetic they are."

Seven began searching Rango's pockets for any valuables. A frown crossed his face when he came up with a few twenties and a cellphone.

"Nigga, I thought you were out here slinging shit. How you making major moves with eighty dollars in your raggedy ass jeans?" Seven shook his head before throwing the bills in Rango's face. "Take this shit and this old ass Blackberry homie. I'll hold on to these though." Seven ripped the chains from his neck, and slipped the watch from his wrist.

"You might as well let this bitch keep that shit," Angel drawled from the sidelines. "You know it ain't real."

"Probably not, but somebody will still cop it." Seven looked at Rango. "I'ma come holla at you again in a week. That should be enough time to get your weight up. Tell your boy Holly I'm head hunting his bitch ass too. You touch mine, and I'ma touch everybody from your momma to your mailman, dawg. Remember that."

Blood pouring from his nose and busted lip, Rango raised his head from the ground in time to see Seven and Angel jog away from the scene and hit a nearby corner. Still trying to clear his mind, Rango unsteadily stood to his feet and leaned on his car for support.

He had no idea what had just taken place but he planned to get to the bottom of it. Looking around to make sure no one saw what took place, Rango clenched his fist as he burned the young boys faces into his memory.

Looking at the corner where they had disappeared, he nodded slowly as he bit down on his lip. He had plans for the day but they just got canceled.

10

After leaving Allah and Harlem to dispose of the car, Junnie decided he wanted to stay out of the streets for the day. Sammy was a piece of shit that Junnie was sure no one would miss too much but that didn't mean the police wouldn't be looking into the murder that took place in broad day light. With that being said, Junnie decided that a day off from the hood would be an obvious choice.

Catching a cab to the house, Junnie hurried and took a quick shower and changed before making his way to the mall. It had been awhile since he had stopped by Essence's job to see her and he figured he could surprise her by taking her to lunch.

It was a nice Saturday so it made sense that the mall was crowded. Junnie walked through the sea of people, trying not to bump anyone. It was rare that Junnie came to the mall unless it was to see Essence or he was really in need of some new clothes. Back in their younger days he & Allah would come just to chill and crack at the females, who were there for the same reasons.

It was wild back in the day when their main goals were to get as many girls as they could and then hit up every store and steal as much as possible. Since he had gotten older, the mall had lost a lot of its appeal.

Junnie made it to Macys and walked through the large store to the area Essence was usually at. Women came to this section to check out the high priced make up.

Essence was one of the make-up artists, and was exceptionally good at her craft. One day, Junnie had arrived early and waited patiently while Essence worked on an older lady's eye shadow. He smiled with pride as he watched the look of concentration on her face while she worked.

Walking through the aisles, Junnie searched for Essence and a slight frown crossed his face as he spotted her. She was behind one of the perfume counters but she wasn't alone. Some kid with cornrows was in the middle of a conversation with her, and from the way he was smirking while he leaned across the counter, it was obvious he was in the middle of spitting some game.

He was wearing slacks and a button up so Junnie assumed he was a coworker but the part that was bothering Junnie was the full tooth smile Essence was giving the dude as she responded to whatever he was saying. Junnie made his way over, bumping into people as he went.

Essence happened to see him as he got closer and her eyes opened with surprise. Her smile grew even wider as she walked around the counter to meet him.

"Baby, what you doing here?" She asked rushing into his arms. Junnie hugged her back.

"Clearly interrupting something." Junnie answered her, but kept his eyes on the kid with the cornrows. "Who is this nigga?"

"Oh, this is my coworker, Caleb. He was just telling me about some old lady that was cussing out our manager. It was funny as hell."

"Is that right?" Junnie replied dryly, still staring the dude down.

Caleb shifted uncomfortably under Junnie's hard glare. "What's up with you, bruh? You must be Junnie." He stepped forward with his hand out.

"Yeah, I am." Junnie looked at the hand in front of him but didn't touch it.

Caleb nodded like everything was cool. "Yeah, Essence talks about you all the time. I'll leave you guys to it though. See you later Essence." Caleb walked off without waiting for a response.

Junnie finally looked at Essence and when he did he found her giving him a very disappointed glare.

"What?" he asked innocently.

"What was that about?"

"You tell me. I walk up to find this square ass nigga showing you all thirty-two of his damn teeth, and you giggling like he's the funniest thing since Eddie Murphy."

Essence shook her head. "He's a coworker Junnie. He was just telling me about something that happened."

"Yeah, from the way he was cheesing he was trying to tell you something alright, but it ain't what you think."

"So I can't talk to any dude now? Just females for the rest of my life, huh?"

"Damn straight."

"What about Jesus? I talk to him every night before I go to bed and when I wake up in the morning." The corners of Essences mouth twitched as she tried not to smile.

"Don't play, because I'll go up there and run the issue with him too."

Essence laughed as she hugged on Junnie. "Stop playing." She held his face in her hands and looked at him. "I'm not worried about any of these niggas at this job or anywhere else. You're my man and I respect you too much to even think about showing another dude more attention than I should be. But I have to interact with the opposite sex sometime, baby. You have to trust me."

"I trust you just fine," Junnie told her honestly. "It's these goofy ass dudes I don't trust."

"Well then trust me to set them straight if they ever get out of line." Essence gave Junnie a soft kiss. "Now I know you didn't just come up here to be mean to me, right?"

"I figured you were going to lunch soon and that you would probably be hungry."

"You were right in both instances. I'm supposed to be on break now and I'm starving. What did you have in mind?"

Junnie shrugged. "You know I'm pretty much down for whatever."

Essence rolled her eyes. "Very helpful. I have to go let Jennifer know I'm about to leave. Think about what you want to eat and please don't start any trouble before I get back."

Junnie gave her a look. "If I see ol' boy cheesing again I'ma knock his teeth out."

Essence shook her head before walking off.

Junnie sat in one of the empty salon type chairs and waited for his lady to come back.

Macys had a good selection of women employees but Junnie made it a habit not to look whenever he came in. He was no saint when it came to checking out an ass or two if a female with prospect walked past but he wouldn't be caught doing it at Essence's job.

Junnie could only imagine the shit he'd hear if her coworkers bragged about how he was checking them out when he'd visit her.

Junnie pulled his phone out to check out the score from the Raider's game that took place earlier that day. Thinking about the game drew his mind back to Sammy and how his life had to end over a simple bet.

He wasn't exactly broken up over Sammy's death. He had tried to give the man a chance by taking all his drugs and money and not his life, but Sammy had something to prove. Now he was in the morgue with bullet holes throughout his body.

In all honesty, he'd be lying if he said killing didn't affect him. He remembered every life that he had taken and even though his conscious mind pushed it far away, his subconscious wouldn't give up so easily.

Many nights Junnie had nightmares about the lives he had ended and the families he had torn apart. It wasn't as if he planned to rob and kill for the rest of his life but for now it's what he needed to do for his dream life with Essence.

Essence returned with her purse on her shoulder and her apron in her hand. She was smiling real hard about something.

"What's so funny?" Junnie asked suspiciously.

"I told Jennifer you were here and she said she wanted to come say hi," Essence giggled as the look on Junnie's face turned to slight disgust.

Jennifer was Essence's manager. She was an older fat Hispanic woman, with a face her momma probably didn't love and a stomach that made her always look hungry.

Junnie had met her once before when he had come to pick Essence up, and the lady fell in love with him instantly. He had only spoken about two sentences to her to be polite but she swore he had feelings for her as well.

Essence thought the whole thing was funny, but it wasn't so humorous to Junnie.

"Hell nah, let's get up out of here." Junnie stood up and made hurried steps for the exit. Essence couldn't stop laughing as she chased after Junnie.

"Wait, you have to say bye to your boo!" she called loudly. Junnie took off in a slow jog and Essence almost fell on the floor laughing as she rushed to catch up with him.

****

Rabbit sat on his couch in shock. He had just got a call from one his homies from the block with bad news. Rabbit's older cousin, Sammy, had just been killed an hour ago and he couldn't believe it.

Rabbit was a young cat who was trying to make his way up in the street ranks. He and his crew had been putting in work for months but that had only been because of the help of Sammy.

Sammy had been the one throwing his little cousin and his boys a bone to get them started in the game and Rabbit had never been more appreciative. When his father died, Sammy had stepped up as a mentor for Rabbit and had been fulfilling the duty perfectly. Now some hater had taken him away.

"Bruh, this shit is crazy." Chucky mumbled from the kitchen.

He had been in the middle of making a ham sandwich when they had received the call. He was Rabbit's best friend and comrade. "These niggas really took the big homie."

"Yeah," Rabbit replied sadly. He hadn't shed any tears, and he probably wouldn't. Sammy had been a soldier so he knew the risks they all played, but that didn't mean Rabbit wasn't hurt.

"They know who did it?"

"Speculation right now, but word is that he had a beef with a nigga named Junnie."

"I know that nigga." Hassan spoke up. He was the third member of the group, and the chilliest among them. He was running a lighter back and forth beneath the blunt he had just rolled. "They say that niggas a beast."

"If he did touch my cousin, he ain't shit but a dead man now." Rabbit vowed darkly.

"We about to go ride out on this nigga?" Chucky asked, anxious to let his gun bust. Sammy had been like an older brother to him as well, so he would be more than willing to kill for him if necessary.

"Nah, not yet. We're going to wait patiently to see what the next move is."

Honestly, Rabbit was hesitant in approaching Junnie. He had heard horror stories about the older goon, and he was truthfully scared to approach him. Rabbit wasn't a punk but he knew when he would be putting himself in danger in trying to check Junnie and his team.

"You say the word, and I'm going to murk this nigga." Hassan swore, sparking the blunt. "Real talk."

"Nah, we'll wait for now. But this nigga will pay." Rabbit accepted the blunt from Hassan and took a deep pull as he watched the sun setting over the horizon.

11

By the time Junnie stepped out of his apartment the next day, the hood was already buzzing with daily activities. Essence had already left for work by the time he woke up and he found that it was well into the afternoon again.

Getting dressed, he decided to skip breakfast and placed a call to Allah to come pick him up. He still hadn't got around to getting his hair braided so he just pulled it back into a busy ponytail that hung past his shoulders.

Now, sitting on the concrete steps, Junnie wished for nothing more than a cigarette. He watched as the kids rode their bicycles in the street, while the younger ones ran past with water guns, spraying relentlessly at anything moving. Junnie and Essence had lived in the same apartment since they first decided to move in together two years ago, so they knew everyone on the block.

Junnie nodded as Mr. Kony waved at him from across the street. He was a good natured man who loved to tell Junnie stories about life in the sixties. Just from the way he spoke, you could tell Mr. Kony had been a part time pimp and a full time gangster back in the day.

Junnie was just considering going across the street and asking him for a cigarette, when he heard footsteps coming down the stairs from behind. Turning around, he looked up into the grinning face of Horace.

"What's up with it, cuz?" Horace grinned as he stomped down the steps.

Charcoal black, with a shaved head, and a mouth full of yellowing teeth Horace was a stocky killer who hailed from Long Beach, California. Besides that, he was Junnie's upstairs neighbor.

When Horace had first moved in, Junnie figured it would only be a matter of time before the two came to blows, but one night while they were both outside smoking cigarettes, a conversation started and a mutual respect was formed.

"What I tell you about that 'cuz' shit?" Junnie cautioned, standing up and giving him a handshake.

"My bad, homie. I forget y'all ain't about that banging shit this side of the state," he said, pulling out his cigarettes and tapping one out.

"Oh we bang, but we bang money." Junnie told him. "Let me get a cigarette until tonight."

Horace gave him a look and tapped an extra cigarette out. "And I want my cigarette by tonight, nigga."

"Fuck you," Junnie pulled out his lighter and sparked it. It was refreshing when the nicotine entered his lungs. "What you doing up so early?"

"Up?" Horace snickered "I ain't been to bed yet. You must not have been here last night or you wouldn't have been either."

"What you mean?"

Horace lit his cigarette and nodded up the street. Junnie followed his gaze to the corner where he had missed the yellow tape that had been put up the night before.

"Oh shit, who got killed?"

"Some crack head bitch that was in the wrong place at the wrong time." Horace shook his head. "You know that nigga,

Gerry, had the Mexicans on his ass for that shit him and his man pulled last week, right?"

"Yeah, I heard something about it," Junnie replied, thinking about the robbery story he had heard about the two men.

"Yep, well the vatos came through last night, guns blazing on that nigga. He was blasting back though and the crack head got hit in the process. One-Time was through here thick, questioning muthafuckas and shit. You know a nigga got warrants so I peeped the show from my window."

"Damn. What happened to Gerry?" Junnie asked, knowing how the gun-slinging drug dealer got down.

Horace shrugged. "He survived, but he got hit I think. When he was running, he was limping like he got plugged, so I don't know. If he is okay, you already know he's tearing San Leandro apart, looking for the niggas. Shits getting real out here." Horace flicked his ashes, exhaling smoke through his nostrils. "What you doing sitting out on the steps like you homeless and shit?"

"I'm waiting for my nigga to come through real quick. There's a few moves I need to make uptown. Honestly I'm trying to stay ducked off from all this heat. This shits for the birds."

"Shit, who you tellin' but Jack and Helen." Horace looked up the street. "These your people right here?" he asked, nodding towards a car that was slowly creeping in their direction.

Junnie looked up and nodded when he seen the familiar dark green Monte Carlo.

"Yeah that's him."

"Oh okay. You can't be too careful." Horace said, staring at the car. That's when Junnie noticed that he had slid his Ruger from his pants and was holding it down at his side.

"You better quit smoking that shit before you come outside, my nigga. You be paranoid." Junnie laughed as he stood up and headed towards the car, which was bumping music so loudly, the tinted windows were rattling.

"You young niggas call it paranoia; us O.G.'s call it staying alive." Horace capped. "Get at me later, fam, and we'll burn one."

"Bet," Junnie called back, before hopping in the passenger seat. "What's good with the God?" he asked, slamming his door shut.

"Everything, long as I'm living." Allah nodded outside the window. "Who's your man with the ratchet?" he asked, placing his gun on his lap as he watched Horace, who was still outside smoking his cigarette and watching the car.

"That's my nigga Horace. Don't trip off him, He just didn't know whether you were friend or foe when you pulled up. But fuck all that. Let's go get what we need."

Junnie was wild but was nowhere near dumb. Whenever he pulled off a hit, he made sure he tossed out whatever gun he used. He had heard more than a few horror stories about dudes that had been caught with guns that had multiple bodies connected to it, and ended up serving life sentences. Junnie didn't plan on making that mistake anytime soon.

Whenever any of them needed new firearms there was one person they always referred to. Maliki was a young cat from the south who was known for the nice artillery kept in his house. Junnie had been doing business with him for a while and had always been satisfied.

"Damn, I kinda liked that gun too," Junnie said, thinking on the nice chrome Beretta he had just got a month ago.

"See, that's why I always keep me an extra one right here." Allah tapped the compartment that usually stored an airbag in it. "So you really want to go see what this nigga Ace is talking about?"

"Yes sir, we can use some work right now. We haven't made any real money since we went to San Jose and hit Finger Freddy."

"Yeah, that was a helluva night," Allah recalled, thinking on the night the three of them barely escaped with their lives as they robbed a drug lord that was only a few notches below Calvin Cole himself. "I'm still eating good off that hit though."

"Me too, but it's not going to last forever." Junnie sighed as he looked out the window. "I've been thinking about getting out of here, Lah."

"What, out of the game or out of this town?"

"Both," Junnie replied seriously. "Just think about it, this shit isn't long term. Ain't no retirement plan in this shit, Lah. The way we're aiming with this, there's only going to be two options on getting out; a box or a cell, and I'm not planning on either."

Allah nodded solemnly, his eyes focused on the road. "I know exactly where you coming from. I think about the same thing too, most the time. I mean, you have a family. You and Essence going to settle down and have a whole bunch of nappy headed, gun toting ass kids running around.

I don't have any of that planned for the near future, so I always figured I could play the game for a little longer, but luck only goes so far. When we were shorties, we figured we would have a good run."

"And we have. Think about it; we've had more money in our pockets at sixteen then doctors have at thirty-four. We've fucked some of the baddest bitches Cali has to offer. Remember you pulled that Persian bitch when we went to the All-Star game in LA?"

"Natasha," Allah smiled.

"Yeah, I knew she was a freak when we saw her. But my point is, we've wild out bro and we haven't even hit twenty-one yet. I'm ready to take a crack at this normal life that doesn't involve looking over my shoulder every time I run to the store. That's why we need to make this money," Junnie concluded, sitting back in his seat.

It had been awhile since they made the drive to Hayward but it had always been worth it.

Allah exited the freeway and turned off the main road. They drove through the backstreets, looking at the familiar surroundings. It took no time to reach the run down house that was half hidden behind a jungle of trees. The two men got out of the car and walked up the gravel path. A pit bull stalked around the front lawn freely, sniffing in random spots of the grass until he noticed the visitors. His light blue eyes locked onto Allah's, who's hand cautiously reached towards his gun.

"You told Maliki we were coming?" he asked wearily, never taking his eyes off the dog.

"Yeah, he told me."

A voice called out. Maliki came from behind a tangle of trees, a bottle of rum in one hand and a machete in the other. He was a skinny man, with a long neck and big teeth which made him resemble a horse.

Maliki was from the bayous of Louisiana. Though his accent wasn't strong as it used to be, it would resurface sometimes.

He held the machete on his shoulder like a baseball bat as he took a swig of his drink.

"And you need not worry about ol' Nunu here. She might look like a killer but she hasn't bit a nigga since the slave days," he laughed looking at the Allah's face.

"Yeah, comforting," Allah mumbled, getting a good look at Nunu's teeth as she yawned.

"How's it going with June the Goon?" Maliki asked, giving him a firm handshake. "Hear you been putting in a lot of work up your way. Word is you been kicking up dust lately."

"Is that what they're saying?"

"Yes they are, but I'm doubting that this serves as news to you, seeing how you're the one kicking the dust."

"You can't believe everything you hear." Junnie revealed.

Maliki smiled, showing off his gold tooth. He rubbed his chin where his scruffy beard decided to grow wildly.

"Ahhh yes, I've never been one to feed too much into the gossip that makes it down my way, but just the fact that you're standing in my yard right now makes me wonder how much of it is true."

Giving Junnie a knowing wink, he motioned for the two men to follow him. They stepped onto the porch and through the back door into the house.

Once inside, Maliki led them through the kitchen to a door leading into the basement. As soon as he opened the door, Nunu slipped through and ran down the stairs. Leading the way, Maliki flipped the light switch and stomped down the stairs into the dark abyss.

"I was wondering when I would see you again," Maliki said as they reached the bottom.

Junnie and Allah looked around the basement like kids in a candy shop. There were firearms of all shapes and sizes inside. Assault rifles rested against the walls as if they were umbrellas that someone had simply put to the side for the time being.

Shotguns were strewn around almost as if it were dirty laundry. Junnie picked up an AK and examined it. Through his criminal career he had never got to hold one, and now that he was he felt like he was in an action movie.

"Goddamn Maliki, what war you arming up for?" Allah asked, examining something that strongly resembled a rocket launcher tucked in the corner.

Maliki stood in the center of the room with his arms crossed over his chest.

"The battle y'all fight in the streets is one of that with each other," he drawled, looking around at his weapon gallery. "The battle I prepare myself for is against a much more sensible enemy."

"Being?" Junnie asked.

Maliki looked at him. "This government grows more and more corrupt as time passes by, but no one seems to notice because they are much more concerned with killing each other over stupid shit such as drugs and chump change. When they decide to finally stop fucking with us and start rounding niggas up, y'all are going to be caught with your pants down, but me." he patted the revolver he had tucked in the front of his pants "I'm going to be right here waiting for the final song to play."

Junnie stared at him before letting out a laugh. "You might want to lay off the booze, Farrakhan. Before you get busy with that, let me grab a couple of these pistols over here and that bulldog you have next to your feet."

"Laugh if you want to Junnie." Maliki bent down to grab the shotgun. "But I'm guessing your biggest enemy is Calvin Cole?"

"Actually I have no beef with Calvin Cole as long as he stays on my good side." Junnie dug in his pocket and pulled out the roll of money. He tossed it to Maliki who caught it with one hand. "Good looking out on the merchandise."

"Good looking out on the money." Maliki held it up before stuffing it in his shirt pocket. "I want to take you to my native town one day. It's a lot different from the California lifestyle but I have a feeling you would still feel in your comfort zone there."

"Whenever they have Marti Gras, let me know and we'll get the plane tickets." Shoving the guns in the duffel bag he had brought Junnie gave Maliki a handshake. "I don't mean to buy and dip on you but we have a meeting to get back to across town."

"Then get to your meeting, my brother, now that you're properly equipped for the job. You sure you don't want anything a little heavier though?" Maliki swept his hand towards the machine gun placed on the wooden table. Junnie looked at it and shook his head.

"When I get ready to take over a small country I'll come back for it," he promised before walking up the stairs and out the house.

****

Bobbi impatiently sucked her teeth as she checked her phone for the hundredth time in the past ten minutes. She shoved the phone in her purse and crossed her arms as she laughed to herself, but there was no humor in it.

Xavier was late meeting her as usual and didn't seem too concerned with answering her phone calls. This exact situation had happened countless times before and here she was yet again setting herself up for failure. Even after checking and double checking to make sure he was going to be on time Xavier still decided to leave her looking stupid.

She had been waiting outside the restaurant for almost an hour, with her temper slowly rising with each minute. Every guy with eyes and a mouth, tried to holler at her while she waited impatiently but as usual she didn't even spare a glance in their direction.

Finally deciding she had enough Bobbi walked away from the restaurant, the fury burning in her chest, more than likely expressed on her face. She had cancelled all her plans for the day so that she could spend it with Xavier but she should've known what would happen.

Tavae and Yalani had made plans to go to a picnic but Bobbi didn't feel like calling them and hearing Tavae's, 'I told you so', speech.

Letting out a slew of curses only she could hear, Bobbi pulled out her phone. She called Xavier again but instead of ringing it went straight to voicemail this time. Letting out a few louder curses Bobbi began to type Xavier a paragraph of a text message. She was so focused on her message she bumped into someone.

"Damn shorty, open your eyes."

Bobbi's head snapped up to find Seven's grinning face staring back at her. His eyes were red and low and he reeked of marijuana.

"If you bumped into me than that means you weren't looking where you were going either right?" Bobbi snapped, playfully pushing him. "If you made me drop my phone I would've whooped your ass."

"Yeah I bet," Seven teased, receiving another push.

"What are you doing out here? I thought you never left the block," Bobbi questioned suspiciously.

"I come to enjoy the scenery from time to time." Seven said casually, taking a look around the street.

When he turned around his shirt shifted and Bobbi seen the butt of the gun he had hidden. She shook her head.

"You always on some hot shit, ain't you?" she asked disapprovingly.

"Nah, I'm always on some staying alive shit," Seven corrected. He pulled a cigarette from behind his ear and sparked it. "What you doing over here, since you wanna interrogate my ass."

"I came to see Xavier but our plans got cancelled."

"Who?" Seven feigned ignorance.

Bobbi gave him a look. "You know exactly who, don't play."

Seven shrugged and grinned, taking a hit from the cigarette. "Whatever li'l homie. You heading back to the east?"

"Yeah, I guess. I don't have any other plans so I might as well." Bobbi could still feel the anger below the surface and was trying not to let it show.

Seven must have picked up on it anyway. He simply looked at her as he exhaled smoke. Grinning slightly, he nodded his head to the side.

"Come on. I'll give you a ride," he told her, turning and starting to walk.

"Oh you got a car?"

"Nah, I got a horse and carriage. Bring yo' ass on." He retorted.

"Don't get fresh, boy," Bobbi told him, slipping her phone in her purse again.

She decided to put her text on hold as she followed after Seven who was moving across the street at a steady pace.

They reached a secluded parking lot behind a corner store and Seven led them to a gray Dodge.

"This yours?"

"Yes ma'am," Seven unlocked the doors and they climbed inside. It smelled like vanilla freshener and marijuana. "Her names Priscilla and she usually gets jealous when I invite other women over."

"Well I've been your best friend long before you had this shit, so I'm Queen B around here," Bobbi joked.

Seven's eyebrows raised in surprise, as he started the car and pulled out of the parking lot.

"Best friends huh? Don't best friends usually stay in contact with each other?"

"Don't even start that shit because your name surely doesn't pop up on my phone either."

"I didn't want ol' boy beefing if I called. You know how these niggas be in their feelings."

"His name's Xavier."

"Whatever."

"He don't be beefing like that. Shit, he doesn't have the right to." Bobbi huffed, feeling her anger still flaring.

Images of Xavier being laid up with another female kept rushing through her head and it was making her more furious than she wanted to be. If she had any hint of his location she would be over there acting a fool and she already knew it. She had done so before.

Seven snickered. Bobbi gave him the evil eye. "The hells so funny?" she demanded.

Seven raised his hands in surrender. "Aye, don't take your anger out on me because that goofy nigga left you standing out here."

"Who said he left me doing anything?"

Seven gave her a look. "C'mon B. You're across town, by yourself, talking about you're meeting the clown but the plans were cancelled and some other shit. Oh and let's not forget that stank ass face you've had since you bumped into me."

Bobbi's eyes narrowed. "First of all, you bumped me. Second, don't act like you know anything because you don't. Just worry about all your little hoes you got on you."

"I don't have any hoes to concern myself with."

Bobbi sat up in her seat. "Oh is that right? Because Chantel was surely on the block the other day talking about the little rendezvous y'all had a few weeks back."

Seven laughed. "Word? I knew that bitch talked too much."

"Out of all the hoes out here, you're gonna fuck with her? That bitch is nasty."

Seven glanced at her. "Trust me, I know," he replied.

"I have no hope in the male species," Bobbi sat back in her seat, shaking her head.

"I'm reduced to these big mouth tramps because there ain't no solid females out here. They either tricks or taken already."

Bobbi gave him a look. "So out of all the females you know ain't none of them worth anything?"

Seven's face turned slightly serious. "There was always one I thought was worth it, but she'd rather waste her time on simple niggas."

Bobbi gave Seven a curious look but he kept his eyes on the road as he sped through an intersection. A small smile fluttered across her face for a second so she turned her head so she wouldn't be seen.

Digging in her purse, she pulled out her phone to see if she had any messages but she let out a small growl when she seen she didn't.

"I swear I'ma kill this nigga," she said softly, looking out at the clouds.

"You're stressed. Open that glove department for me."

Bobbi leaned forward and popped it open. Her eyes grew when she seen all the weed that was stuffed inside. There was one large shopping bag sized zip-lock that was busting at the seams, along with a dozen miniature baggies and a large pistol placed right in the center of it.

Bobbi looked up at Seven who didn't seem at all worried about the contents that were being shown.

"Who the hell did you just rob?" Bobbi asked.

"You been asking a lot of questions in the past ten minutes. Just take this swisher and roll one up for us. Unless your skills are rusty?" Seven grinned as he held out the cigar. Bobbi snorted and snatched the swisher.

"Let me show you something, youngsta."

Seven turned up the radio as Bobbi began to split the swisher. He drove on the freeway and they cruised back to their side of town.

A lot of people described Seven as being some type of monster or goon with no respect but Bobbi knew better. If you were on his good side, then Seven was one of the coolest people on the planet.

He was a laid back guy with a witty sense of humor and Bobbi found herself laughing to tears for most of the car ride. For a brief moment, she actually forgot her anger at Xavier who still hadn't called her. They smoked the blunt, filling the car with smoke and discussing the hottest songs that played on the radio.

After they got off the freeway, Seven drove to the In'N'Out burger drive-thru. Both high and feeling good, the laughs only got worse as they went through the drive-thru and gave young cashier a hard time.

When they left, the young pimple faced white boy probably hated them. By the time Seven pulled onto her block, Bobbi had completely calmed down. She wasn't sure if it was from the weed or Seven's company.

Bobbi looked for any signs of life inside her house as they pulled up in front. The living room light was on, letting her know Charity was home.

"That burger was bomb as fuck," Seven said, cutting off the engine.

"You ain't lying. I was starving all day. I still got the munchies though thanks to you."

Seven grabbed a cigarette and lit it. "That haze wasn't no joke huh?"

"It was a'ight." Bobbi downplayed it, but the dazed look on her face told it all. "Thanks for the ride. I wasn't really feeling having to catch the bus back."

"If you quit wasting your time with this buster then you would never have to worry about it."

Bobbi looked at Seven. His voice had shifted to serious again but his face remained its usual blank expression.

"Oh, and let me guess, you could take care of me right?"

Seven shrugged. "Maybe I could but, the fact is you're too scared to find out."

"No, the only thing I'm scared of is getting shot or kidnapped and held hostage over some of your shit. You think I don't hear about your name ringing out here Sev?"

To Bobbi, Seven would always be a close friend but others didn't feel the same. There were a lot of people who hated the young goon and he had made a lot of enemies in his young life.

Seven made a face. "Ain't nobody worried about these square ass niggas out here. You know how I move, B. I wouldn't let anything happen to you."

"Yeah, I do know how you move. That's why I'ma go inside this house and leave you to your antics." Bobbi leaned over and gave Seven a hug. He smelled like marijuana and cologne, and Bobbi found herself holding on a little longer than usual.

"You be safe out here, big head. Text me later to let me know you made it home, okay." She opened the door and grabbed her purse from the seat.

"Yeah, yeah get the hell out my car. Got it smelling like watermelons and shit." Seven started the car, cigarette bobbing from between his lips. "You be good ma and think about my offer."

"Boy, bye." Bobbi shut the door and stepped back on the curb.

Seven gave her a wink and pulled off, tires screeching and music bumping. Bobbi continued watching the car's taillights until they went a couple blocks and turned off the street. A small smile formed on her face, Bobbi turned and went inside the house.

Opening the front door, she was shocked to see everyone waiting for her. Charity was sitting in the recliner, with a glass in her hand.

Tavae and Yalani were on the couch, both laughing as if they had just heard the funniest joke ever told. A bottle of Grey Goose was on the coffee table and it wouldn't take too much guess work on why it was empty.

"There she go!" Charity announced as if they had just been discussing her. Charity raised her glass in a salute. "There's my mini-me."

"Please Momma, you know I'm the big homie." Bobbi dropped her purse and slipped her shoes off. "I see everyone was awaiting the star of the hour to get back."

"Don't gas yourself up. We thought you wouldn't be back until later tonight." Tavae told her. "Weren't you supposed to be going to the movies or something? We just talked like an hour ago."

"Ahhh if she's here that means one thing; the nigga stood her up." Yalani laughed and the other two joined in.

"Ha ha that's funny but umm which one of you heifers have a man? None?"

"I rather be single than have a nigga like Xavier." Yalani claimed.

"I rather date a dog than have a nigga like Xavier," Tavae put her two cents in.

"Ain't that the same thing?" Charity pointed out. Bobbi shook her head while they had another round of laughter.

"Comedians huh? Damn, couldn't even save me a drop?" she grabbed the empty bottle and held it up.

"You know your ass ain't grown, no matter how much you try to fake the funk," Charity told her.

"First of all; 'fake the funk'? Eww, you're old Momma. Second, I'm older than both these hoes, and I know you didn't kill this bottle solo."

"Quit hating," Tavae told her.

"If you want some so bad go get some." Charity suggested.

"As good as that sounds, I'ma pass." Bobbi went into the kitchen and flipped the light on. She was on her second wave of munchies and she needed something to eat.

Opening the cabinet, it didn't take her long to decide on her box of Cocoa Puffs. She was just opening the refrigerator for milk when her cell phone vibrated.

Looking at the screen, she couldn't believe what she seen. Her stomach began to bubble from the anger that had settled down. At first she wasn't going answer it but decided to unleash her fury.

"I know it didn't take you that long to grow some balls," Bobbi answered, her attitude apparent out the gate.

Xavier laughed. "What are you talking about?" he drawled, playing dumb. Just from his voice Bobbi could tell he was high off of whatever his drug of choice was today.

"Oh, so leaving me standing outside waiting for hours in the cold is funny to you?" Bobbi snapped, slamming the gallon of milk on the counter.

"It wasn't no damn 'hours' so chill out. Something came up and I had to make a run with Chris to go handle some shit. Where you at though, I'll come get you."

"Nah don't trip about where I'm at nigga. Somebody gave me a ride and made sure I was okay, while you were out holding hands with Chris." Bobbi told him.

Xavier ignored the last part. "Who the fuck was you with?" he asked suspiciously.

"You wasn't worried about it an hour ago so don't scratch your head over it now."

"A'ight you talking real fly over this phone but you're close to catching an ass whooping. Don't go out here showing your ass Bobbi, because I'll hurt you and fuck your little boyfriend up."

Bobbi smacked her lips. "Nigga you don't put fear in anyone but those pussy ass niggas you run with. I'm tired of you doing whatever the fuck you want and then sit up here and come at me like I'm the one in the wrong. We've made plans for today a week ago, now all of a sudden something came up huh? You're a punk ass nigga Xavier and I'm tired of this shit. There's lines of dudes waiting to give me their resumes for your position and I think I'ma start taking applications."

"Bitch keep talking that shit and I'ma run up on—"

Bobbi hung up the phone and tossed it on the counter. Feeling better that she had succeeded in pissing Xavier off, Bobbi finished preparing her cereal and went into the living room with her women.

12

Queenie let out one last moan as she rolled over in the bed, gasping for air. Gerald climbed off of her and laid to the side, grinning as if he had just accomplished a great feat.

The two had woken up and had started with some early morning 'exercises'. Queenie swept a loose strand of hair from her face as she watched Gerald hum to himself proudly.

"Fuck you grinning for?" she asked, still working to catch her breath.

"Same reason why your pussies still smoking. I put in work."

Gerald laughed, swinging his hips in a circular motion. Queenie hit him with a pillow and grabbed her watch from the nightstand. Jumping up she cursed when she realized what time it was.

"I'm going to be late," she said, searching for her bra.

Gerald sat up in bed and watched Queenie as she rushed around the room searching for her items.

"So what, I'm late to work all the time." Gerald shrugged as if it were no big deal. Queenie let out a wild laugh.

"Baby, I'm not talking about clocking in at Wal-Mart five minutes tardy. I'm talking about a whole bunch of people depending on me and me not being there. They're going to fucking kill me," Queenie mumbled, searching for her panties.

"Damn girl, who the fucks your boss, Freddy Krueger?"

"I wish," Queenie replied, tossing the blanket to the side.

Queenie had first been introduced to Calvin Cole by her then boyfriend Doughboy. Doughboy was just a youngster so the big boys didn't give him too many heavy jobs to take care of, but over time he began to build his resume.

When he began to eat good, he asked permission to put Queenie on. Her pass was granted and pretty soon she was making more money simply by delivering drugs here or there, then she had in a whole week's pay at Safeway.

Things were going well until Queenie noticed a flaw in Calvin's design. Then things were going perfect. Queenie told Doughboy how he could actually skim the drug he sold, and she could take a little off of what she delivered and pretty soon after collecting some here and a little there the two had enough to actually eat off of.

They were living so good Queenie decided she didn't need Doughboy anymore and he was fine with that since he was doing his own thing. They remained friends and thieving partners, while Queenie decided to start seeing Gerald.

They had to keep it a secret, however. It would have been frowned upon if anyone found out she had left Doughboy for his cousin.

"You want to help me look, or keep staring at my ass?" Queenie asked irritated.

She picked up her leggings and pulled them on. Gerald continued to stare and stroke his manhood.

"I prefer to just keep staring," he answered honestly. "But aye, how about you come show me how good you are at that head again before you get out of here?"

Queenie frowned in disgust. "Nah, my lips are chapped," she said before heading in the living room to find her shoes.

She looked around the sofa where she and Gerald had stumbled in drunk the night before. She spotted one of the gold heels, and was still searching for the second when a familiar voice spoke softly.

"There's no need to rush, Queenie. We don't need you to come in today."

Queenie jumped in surprise and let out a yelp. Johnny was sitting at the kitchen table, watching her calmly from the sidelines.

His face was calm but there was something taunting lurking behind his eyes as he stared at her. It took a few moments for Queenie to see the gun in his hand.

"What the fuck, Johnny. You scared the shit out of me," she snapped, trying not to show her fear. "What are you doing here, how did you know I was here?"

Johnny didn't answer the questions. Glancing at his watch, he stood up and walked over to the window, his pistol dangling at his side. Queenie watched as he peeked out the blinds before closing the curtains.

When he was done looking outside, he turned and looked at her. "I don't want to prolong this, Queenie," he started, walking slowly in her direction. "We know about you and Doughboy's side hustle."

"I don't know what you're talking about Johnny," Queenie lied, backing away.

"They never do." Johnny grabbed one of the couch pillows. "Sadly, Doughboy gave you up shortly before his life ended. This hurts because I actually liked you, Queenie. But like most, you let greed run you and in the case, destroy you." he said raising his gun, he saw from the corner of his eye someone coming out the bedroom.

"Queenie who you talkin'—"

Instinctively Johnny lifted the pillow and covered the gun's barrel before squeezing the trigger twice. The muffled shots tore through Gerald's chest sending him crashing into the wall before sliding to the carpet.

He was dead before he got an answer from Queenie. She screamed and made a break for the front door but Johnny was across the room in a few strides. He grabbed Queenie by the back of the neck and threw her on the couch.

"Please don't do this," she pleaded, thinking of how she was gasping her last few breaths of life. "What can I do? What can I do to fix this?"

Johnny sadly shook his. "We're past that stage ma," he told her. "But I promise, it'll be a lot less painful than Doughboy's farewell. That I guarantee."

Without another word he raised the pillow and fired two shots into Queenie's head. Her body slumped to the side as she came to rest on the cushions.

Leaning down Johnny closed her eyelids gently. Moving quickly, he gathered his four shell casings from the floor and left the apartment as stealthily as he had come.

****

Ace stood outside his Jeep Cherokee, with his arms crossed and waiting impatiently for the man of the hour. West stood beside him, smoking a blunt and staring into space.

They had been sitting in the parking lot for the past thirty minutes and Calvin Cole had been late for twenty of them. Ace was beginning to feel more and more disrespected but he kept his anger in check.

Anger was for the weak minded and he had long developed the skill of confining his true emotions. He had no idea what he expected to come from this meeting but he wanted there to be a resolution. If not, he was going to have to resort to plan B which he hadn't formed yet.

"What the fucks taking this nigga so long?" West snapped, coming out of his quiet time.

No sooner had the words left his mouth a black-on-black, Range Rover pulled into the parking lot, and parked a few yards away from Ace's jeep.

Ace stood up straight as he watched Calvin Cole's tall frame ease from out the passenger seat, followed by three of his men. They walked towards Ace, and Ace walked to meet them.

"Calvin Cole," Ace smiled in greeting. "We finally meet."

"Ace, right?" Calvin shook his hand, his face remaining blank.

Ace's smile faltered from the dry reception but he made sure not to let it show.

"The one and only. I hope I'm not taking up any valuable time..."

"Trust me, if you were, I wouldn't be here." Calvin pulled his cell phone out and read the text he had just received from Johnny. Nodding grimly, he looked up at Ace. "I don't mean to sound rushed, fam, but I do have somewhere to be after this. My man Johnny told me you had a problem with something?"

West glared at Calvin but wisely didn't speak. One of Calvin's men noticed his facial expression and slowly inched his hand towards his gun. Ace looked taken aback by Calvin's attitude but just continued to grin.

"Well, it's more of a misunderstanding than it is a problem," he said, crossing his hands behind his back.

"Someone who used to work for me now works for you. Mickey from Grant Ridge. Trust me, I don't care about that at all. Keep him. But someone seems to still be confused because even though he doesn't work for me anymore, he's still making money on my block."

Calvin stared at Ace, waiting for him to continue but he didn't.

"That's it?" he asked, not bothering to hide his irritation. "Where's the problem, because right now the only misunderstanding I see is you thinking I give a fuck about this information."

Ace's smile finally vanished as he stared at Calvin to see if he was serious. He was.

"The problem is you're giving my shit away like you got ownership to it. I was working that street before you were in the position you're in now, don. So I'd appreciate it if you kept you're monkeys out my space."

Now it was Calvin's turn to grin. "You got brass balls, Ace, I'll give you that," he chuckled, rubbing his beard. He seemed to be thinking about something. "I did tell Mickey he could have the block. Believe it or not, there's a lot of money to be made over on that side."

"Yeah, I know," Ace said with pride.

"And you're right, my approach was out of pocket. We should have talked business. Listen, how about I buy you out?" he asked reaching in his pocket and pulled out the thickest wad of cash Ace had ever seen.

"It's not for…" Ace started but Calvin held his hand up.

"Nah, I'm not hearing it," he objected. "Not too many of these pussies out here have the heart to come check me when

I'm wrong. So let me give you a little something to show you how much I think it's worth."

Peeling off a crisp one-hundred-dollar bill Calvin flicked the bill at Ace and it fluttered in front of his face before falling to the ground. Ace looked at the bill, then up at Calvin whose fake smile had been replaced with a scowl.

"Let me tell you something, homie. I don't know what rock you been living under, but Calvin Cole runs this shit and I have a problem with a nobody coming to try and check me on some shit that I already own. I reached out to you working with me and you never responded so you missed your chance to eat at my table.

As for Mickey, that little nigga runs that street until I get tired of him doing so. If you feel some sort of way about that let it be known now."

As if on cue Calvin's men reached under their shirts, or behind their backs, producing their guns almost synchronized. Ace kept his eyes locked on Calvin's, his face set in stone.

"You're making a big mistake," Ace warned, Calvin stepped closer so that they were almost nose to nose.

"Like I said, bust a move." Calvin challenged.

West shifted as if he considered taking him up on his offer and Calvin snickered. "If you draw nigga you'll be dead before you could put your ashy ass knuckle on the trigger."

West dropped his hands back at his sides as he exchanged sneers with Calvin's goons, who had the drop on him.

"I came to work it out and this is the reception I get, huh?" Ace asked, still staring into Calvin's eyes. "I see why you and Mickey work together. You're both crazy."

"I've been called worse," Calvin turned to leave. "See you in the unemployment line, Ace Bone."

Calvin and his entourage climbed inside the truck, laughing at Ace's expense as they left. Ace continued to stare at the truck long after it had pulled down the street and around the corner.

He had been backed into a corner first with Mickey disrespecting him, now Calvin Cole. A fire began to burn in Ace's chest as his face contorted into anger. It had been a long time since the beast in his chest had called for blood but now that it had been awaken it was up and starving.

13

Once they were back on their side of town, Allah wanted to stop at the store to get a swisher. They were only a few miles from Ace's meeting place and still had thirty minutes to kill.

Allah pulled up to the corner store and hopped out. Junnie got out the car and decided to wait outside. Sparking a cigarette, he leaned against the hood of the car, his eyes sweeping the street.

They had tried calling Harlem a few more times but it was going straight to the voicemail. Junnie was beginning to worry if something had happened to him.

Harlem was a thorough soldier, but even he could have got caught slipping. Junnie was just thinking of cancelling the meeting and going to search for his comrade when he heard it. To the average person the footsteps would have gone unnoticed but Junnie picked up on the soft patter of someone trying to sneak up on him. Spinning around in a fighting stance he looked in surprise and anger when he seen who it was.

"Give me all your money, muthafucka!" Harlem growled in a deep voice, his gun trained on Junnie. He burst out laughing when he seen the look on his friend's face.

"You getting slow on that response time, fam," he said, waving his gun in plain view as if the people walking past them didn't matter.

Junnie snatched the gun from his hand angrily, the smile left Harlem's face.

"Where the fuck you been nigga? We've been calling your goofy ass all day."

Harlem raised his hands in surrender. "Damn mom, calm down. My phone's been dead nigga. Fuck you tripping for?"

"Because you know we have shit to do, but you rather lay-up with these hoodrats than handle your business."

Harlem made a face, just as Allah walked out of the store with a swisher. "You act like we were going somewhere important. Ace ain't shit, fuck him. Y'all don't even need me there. If he starts acting crazy, slap him. And second, who said I was with a bitch? Today is Sunday. I could have been at church."

Junnie and Allah both looked at each other, shook their heads then got inside the car. Harlem laughed as he climbed in the backseat.

"You niggas too serious all the damn time," he chuckled.

They would be a few minutes late but Junnie could care less. He didn't move to the beat of anyone's drum but his own. Hitting the blunt and trying to ignore Harlem tell a story about where he had been, Junnie's mind drifted to what his life would have turned out like if he had only decided to stay on the right path. Odds are he wouldn't be sitting in the car on his way to a possible job opportunity that would more than likely involve killing someone.

Driving down International Avenue, Chino's soon came into view in the distance. Allah pulled the car into the parking lot, hitting the corner hard enough for the front bumper to scrap the cement.

The people occupying the sidewalk looked at the vehicle as it sped around cars and didn't bother to slow down at the sign of pedestrians. Finding a spot near the entrance, Allah pulled in, cutting off the engine. Now that the car was quiet, he looked back at Junnie.

"That shit was just as good as it was the first time," he said, passing the blunt to Junnie. "I'ma need to fuck with him on the regular."

"Yeah, he told me to let you know he's always got some available."

Putting the blunt clip in the ashtray, Junnie looked towards the restaurant's entrance. Chino's was a small building, with tinted windows to keep passer-byes from seeing the customers while they ate.

There were three thugs standing outside the entrance, laughing at an unheard joke amongst themselves. Unlike the Mexicans, that were at Charlie's house, Junnie actually knew about these henchmen.

Ace might not have been that vicious but he was surrounded by bloodthirsty goons who would let their guns bust for the slightest offense. Taking in their movements for a minute, Junnie quickly scanned around the area to see exactly how many they might be dealing with.

"Yo, so what's the plan when we get in this muthafucka?" Harlem asked.

He also was staring the young men down and from the frown on his face, it was obvious he was already considering starting some trouble.

"Because I'ma let you know right now, if these niggas start acting stupid the only talking I'm doing is with my burner, fam. I ain't fucking with these pussies."

"The plan is we go in and see what this nigga Ace is talking about. If it's legit, we're gonna rock with it. If it's some bullshit we ain't gonna rock with it. Pretty simple."

"Or if I feel like it I might just rock him," Harlem muttered, opening his car door.

The trio exited the vehicle and made their way to the restaurant's entrance. The thugs outside stopped talking and glared at the group but had no words to speak.

Just as Junnie placed his hand on the door handle, it flew open and a man stepped out. He stopped in surprise and looked at Junnie and his entourage before a smile crossed his face.

"Oh shit, what's good June?" Deray greeted, tucking a brown paper bag under his arm as he gave Junnie dap. "Ace said you was supposed to be coming, but I didn't think you would really show."

Junnie shrugged. "I figured I could come see what your boys jawing about."

Junnie and Deray knew each other from being locked up together, they still ran into each other occasionally at different functions, but they never kicked it intentionally.

Deray nodded. "Yeah, he up in there waiting. I'm just making a run really quick but I'll probably be back before y'all done talking business."

"Fasho. Do your thing fam."

Junnie entered the restaurant, with Harlem and Allah flanking close behind. Chino's was a nicely decorated establishment, with the lights dimmed and candles lit at every table.

Even though it was smack in the middle of the hood, not too many people ever went inside. Junnie had only been once before, and that had also been to conduct business with a shady cat named Frick.

Leading the way through the tables Junnie turned the corner, towards the back of the restaurant and found the welcoming committee.

There was a collection of round tables set up relatively close to one another, with most of the seats being occupied by rough looking young men who seemed out of place in the nice restaurant with their hoodies and caps on.

Sitting in the center of it all was Ace. He had been talking with one of his people but he looked up and grinned when he seen Junnie approaching.

"Well... well... June the goon in the flesh, huh?" Ace called out, standing to his feet. He held his hand out. "I almost thought you lost your way getting here."

"C'mon Ace Boogey, you should know I was born in these streets. If I'm late, it wasn't because I didn't know how to get here." Junnie gave him a firm handshake. "How's it kickin'?"

"Shit, its kicking."

Ace motioned towards the chairs and Junnie and Allah had a seat. Harlem remained standing, with his arms crossed over his chest. Ace gave him a look.

"What's good, New York?" he asked.

His voice was friendly but there was a look of dislike in his eyes. Ace and Junnie had never directly had a problem, but Harlem was responsible for quite a few altercations with Ace's people.

The feeling must've been mutual because Harlem merely nodded in response. West, who was standing at Ace's side clenched his jaw as he stared at Harlem as well, but he too didn't say anything.

"And how's the God doing?" Ace asked Allah, once he was done exchanging glares with Harlem.

"Maintaining in this world of demons," Allah responded smoothly.

"Aren't we all." Ace grinned. He looked down at the plate in front of him, then back to his guest. "I know y'all want something to eat? Oscar put his foot in this gumbo, no lie."

"Sounds promising, but if it's all good with you I'd prefer to just get down to business," Junnie said politely. "We got other shit to take care of once we shoot out of here."

Ace nodded, wiping his mouth with a napkin. "Fair enough," he said easily. Rubbing his hands together, Ace took his time to chew his food before he continued talking. "I think we both know why you're here. I just need a little work put in, nothing heavy."

Junnie nodded. "Who's the mark?" he asked, sitting up in his seat.

"I know you familiar with a nigga named Mickey right?"

Junnie had to think on it for a second before the name rang a bell. Mickey was a dealer who was just as much of a killer as he was a hustler. Junnie had never met him, but the kid was infamous for his violent streak.

"Yeah, I heard of homie," Junnie confirmed. "Dude from the west right?"

"Same one." Ace rubbed his beard. "Let's just say me and fam have come to a disagreement that can't get resolved unless one of us is maggot food, feel me?"

"That is the easiest solution to most beefs," Junnie agreed.

"Exactly," Ace smiled broadly, glad that Junnie was going along with it. "But as I'm sure you know Mickey ain't one of these toy soldiers out here. This nigga lays his murder game down."

"I heard."

"Yeah and I figured what's better than putting a monster against a beast?" Ace nodded at Junnie.

Junnie simply stared back, letting the thoughts swirl through his head before sorting them out completely.

"That sounds good, but from the look of it you have a whole crew sitting around you right now," he said, waving his hand at the many men surrounding them. "Why don't you just have one of them put the hurt on this nigga?"

"Naturally I would, but me and Mickey use to do a little business together. He knows there's no love between us so if he sees one of my people in his area he's gonna know what time it is. I need unfamiliar faces to get the drop on his bitch ass."

"Yeah, I dig what you're saying." Junnie thought a second more. "Check it, I'ma sit on it for a minute, get at my people about it and see what the deal is, A'ight? I'll get at you tomorrow and see what happens."

The smile on Aces face faltered for a split second, but remained in place.

"I see why you might wanna sit on it, but I kinda need this done ASAP. I have some prior arrangements that can't be made until this nigga is out of the way, so they're kinda at a standstill."

"And I respect that Ace, but when I do business I like to see exactly what's going on before I just jump out the window, know what I mean? You're not asking me to help you change a flat tire, homie. This shit requires research and tact."

Ace smile turned into a confused grin. He stared at Junnie, before pushing his plate away and leaning forward on the table.

"Now, maybe I had this wrong, but I thought you and your people put in work for bread?"

"Nah you got it right, but for me to bang out I have to completely believe in the cause," Junnie replied, folding his hands in his lap.

Some of Ace's crew muttered at Junnie's statement but Ace didn't stir. Lightly tapping his fingers on the tabletop he continued to look amused.

"Well, this isn't what I expected," Ace said finally. "I was expecting to pay you so you could go take care of what I'm fucking paying you for, like a soldier usually does." He chuckled but there was no humor to it.

Junnie's facial expression didn't change but if you looked closely you could see the darkness spreading behind his eyes.

"Oh, don't be mistaken, my nigga. I have no problem banging on a nigga that I feel deserves it," he said, never shifting his gaze from Ace's, "but I ain't nobody's soldier, homie."

West snickered and went back to clenching his jaw as he watched the exchange. Harlem's attention snapped in his direction.

"Something funny, B?" Harlem asked roughly. West looked him up and down.

"You should know. Y'all the fuckin' joke," West told him without hesitation. "How y'all killers but scared to put in work? Niggas pump you up but so far I'm not impressed."

"Oh, keep giggling and I can turn you into a believer, son," Harlem uncrossed his arms, and made to move forward but Allah held him back.

As soon as Harlem had moved Ace's crew stood from their chairs. From their movements they made it clear they were ready to get the scene popping if given the chance.

Harlem wouldn't be deterred. He looked at the group while Allah continued to hold him off. Things had taken a turn quicker than anyone could have expected.

"How you niggas wanna do it?" he asked, waiting for the first person to make a stupid move.

"Y'all be easy," Ace said waving his hand at his squad. "I'm sure my niggas didn't mean to get shit heated. Right fellas?" he questioned Junnie.

From his tone it was clear he was trying him. Ace felt that he had the advantage because he was surrounded by his people, but what he didn't know was that Junnie was prepared to wild out at any second and if he gave the word Allah would gun Ace down first.

"Whatever you want to call it," Junnie gave a shrug. "But shit is going to the left, so before I have to make it right me and mine are just gonna split. Thanks for the offer, but I'ma pass."

Scooting his chair back, Junnie stood to his feet. Ace leaned back in his and smirked.

"So I'ma offer you some bread and you just gonna spit in my face huh?" he asked like it was all cool.

"If that's how you wanna spin."

Ace nodded. "Nah that's what it is. It's straight though, you too good for my money it's all gravy baby, but you should know I'ma boss, my nigga. Everything I want I get, and if I don't it usually ends bad for the nigga that prevented it. You hearing me?"

The threat was so loud and clear you would have to be Hellen Keller to miss it.

Junnie raised an eyebrow. "Yeah, I know how you like to give yourself that title, but I think you're forgetting something about me." He turned to face Ace. "I remember when you were a nobody out here, my nigga. When you were just plain ass Richard Jefferies and nobody would hand you the short on a Newport, let alone hand you some drugs to pump, so I'm not really feeling your tone.

But I can see why you would pick someone to do your work for you. From what I heard about Mickey, he might be too much for all the killers in here."

Junnie laughed as he motioned for his people to follow him out of the restaurant. West looked at Ace in disbelief.

"You're gonna just let this nigga walk up out of here?" he barked, already digging in his jeans to grab his burner.

Ace gently shook his head, a trace of the grin still on his face.

"Nah, we straight. I'ma see you again real soon, right J?" he called out.

Junnie turned around, continuing to walk. "You know where to find me if you ever want to finish this meeting," he winked. A few seconds later the trio was out the door.

"Want me to go after them?" West asked Ace, his eyes on the door that the trio exited.

"Nah, it's all good." Ace pulled his plate back to him and continued his meal.

"That didn't go as planned, but it's okay. One monkey does not stop my show or flow, but some shit is going to need to be rearranged."

"Shit let's rearrange these niggas right now."

"Oh don't worry I'ma have something special cooked up for this fool, Junnie," Ace grinned wickedly. "Don't even worry about that yet, we have bigger issues than that little nigga. Since he's too spooked to put the lean on this muthafucka I'ma need you to go pay this buster Mickey a visit. He's my uncle's only son make sure you leave enough of the nigga left to bury."

West turned to him and nodded his understanding. His face was set and determined.

"Don't worry, fam. This nigga won't live to see another sunrise. That I'll make sure of that."

****

Bobbi walked out of the library, holding onto her papers she had just printed. The summer was just starting and she had started looking up colleges early so it wouldn't be a hassle later.

Most of her friends were talking about going to universities but Bobbi didn't want to go that route. With her GPA it would be easy for any school to accept her, but the payment methods were a different story.

A partial scholarship would have been nice, but Bobbi wasn't going to fool herself into believing that would be close to enough to pay for everything. Besides, community colleges weren't as bad as the rep they had been given. Feeling good about the prospects she was holding, Bobbi was on her way to the bus stop when she heard someone call her name. Looking up, her good mood instantly turned sour.

Xavier came jogging over to her, cocky grin plastered on his face as usual. He walked up to her and tried to plant a kiss on her lips, but Bobbi backed away.

"Damn, like that huh?" he laughed.

Bobbi once thought he had the sexiest laugh in the world. Now it made the breakfast sandwich in her stomach turnover.

"What the hell are you doing here, Xavier? I know damn well you ain't up here using the library," Bobbi said in disgust.

"Course not. That nigga Skeeter told me he seen you come in here so I whipped it over. You about to hop on the bus?"

"That's exactly what I'm about to do." Bobbi looked at him real foul and turned to leave but he grabbed her arm gently.

"C'mon B, why you acting like this? Because I missed a fucking movie date? You haven't answered my calls or tried to hit me up. I miss you." Xavier said sincerely, pulling her close.

Once Bobbi's head fell on his chest she found herself succumbing to his touch and she almost gave him a hug back, but she fought it off.

"Nah, I'm sick of your shit Xavier," she told him, pushing away. "You really believe you can do whatever you want, when you want and expect me to be okay with it. I don't have time for the games. I have a life to live, and I'm not going to live it constantly stressing over a nigga who can't do me right. So if you really think this is over one single date, then you're letting me know how hopeless you really are."

"I know I've been fucking up lately, but that's gonna change, baby. Look, I was thizzin' the other day that's the only reason I was tripping like that. You know I don't be going hard any other time. But I'm done with that baby, I swear. No more drugs, no more bitches, none of that shit. I'm not trying to lose you." Xavier was staring into her eyes seriously, and his voice was filled with emotion.

To the uninformed, it might have seemed sincere but Bobbi already knew how he operated.

"Xavier go ahead with that shit because we both know you're full of shit. It's the same thing every week, and I'm tired of it. Just go ahead and fuck with these hoes, we both know that's what you want. Now you're absolutely free to." Bobbi turned to leave and Xavier grabbed her arm again, this time more forceful.

The sincerity was gone from his face and replaced with a look of pure evil.

"So what's really good? You out here trying to fuck with these niggas huh?" he asked angrily, shaking her arm. "That's why you trying to fucking leave me."

"Xavier," Bobbi started calmly. "let go off my fucking arm."

"Nah, call your nigga to make me let go of your arm, bitch," Xavier snapped, giving her an extra tug. "Who you fucking with Bobbi? Let me holla at the nigga."

"You sound fucking crazy. That's exactly why I'm done with you. I'm not going through your bullshit anymore. Now let go of my fucking arm Xavier!" Bobbi yelled angrily.

"Try to leave me and see what happens. I'll fucking kill you out here," Xavier said angrily, spit flying from his mouth.

"Oh, tough guy," Bobbi said sarcastically.

Xavier bit down on his lip and balled his fist up but before he could make a stupid move a police cruiser pulled up beside them.

"Is everything alright over here?" the officer asked, looking between the two suspiciously. Xavier hurriedly let Bobbi's arm loose and took a step back.

"Yeah, we all good, blood," Xavier said with attitude.

"I'm not your fucking blood," the officer told him. He looked at Bobbi. "You okay ma'am?"

Bobbi shot Xavier a dark look before nodding. "Yeah, I'm good. Just heading to the bus stop."

The officer nodded. "I don't think she needs a chaperone," he told Xavier with dislike. Xavier smirked and raised his hands before slowly backing away.

"It's good. Aye, we can finish this talk later, B."

"Don't hold your breath," Bobbi told him before continuing on her way.

14

There was a loud noise as Harlem slammed his fist into the car door.

"Fuck, why y'all stop me from getting at son?" he asked angrily.

They were in the car and on their way back to their own territory. Junnie was in the front, seat reclined, smoking a Newport while Allah drove nodding his head to the music, seemingly chill about everything. Harlem was in the back fuming over the scene that had just happened.

"I was 'bout to floor this nigga but you two always want to be on some diplomatic shit." Harlem barked, looking up at the two of them. "That nigga was in there yapping out the side of his fucking neck, b."

"That wasn't diplomatic, that was some smart shit," Junnie told him smoothly. "If you would have made the wrong move we wouldn't be shit but three corpse getting tossed in a gutter somewhere. They had us outnumbered and outgunned in closed quarters. You really think we would have made it out that bitch in good terms?"

"Hell yeah!" Harlem said seriously. "I don't give a fuck if they had rocket launchers, them niggas ain't have no heart. I would've hit six of them before they even thought about busting back."

Allah chuckled. "You a fool, my nigga. You ever heard of having tact?"

Harlem looked at him as if he had spoken Russian. "Nah nigga, I don't know anything about that shit. I know about Techs, Millis, and this here Ruger." he held up his gun.

"Put that shit away before you get us knocked," Allah cautioned, looking ahead at a police cruiser, which had just turned the corner.

He turned his attention to Junnie, who was watching the scenery pass with a blank expression on his face.

"So what you think about that shit?" Allah asked, referring to the meeting with Ace.

"I don't think shit about it," Junnie replied. "Ace already knows I don't fuck with him like that, so for him to make it seem like he's doing us a favor by tossing a job this way he got me fucked up. I know this niggas type. Even if we put the work in for him he would look at it like a fucking hand out and you know that's a no-no."

Allah nodded, already understanding.

"I can dig it, but if these muthafuckas come around on some shady shit, you already know what time it is; rock-a-bye baby."

Junnie waved his hand. "Ace is the least of my worries. I got bigger plans for our team and I've been thinking about it for a while now."

"Well don't keep an asshole in suspense. Lay it on me." Allah turned the music down so that he could hear. Junnie sat up in his seat.

"Check it, we've been putting our shit on the streets for the last few years. Everything from robbing heavies, pitching drugs, wiping these pussies off the face of the earth, and yet, bitch ass nigga like Ace, and that fool Mickey are on higher ranks than ours. Why is that?"

"Because Calvin throws them a bone," Harlem said. "Without him looking out for them they ain't shit."

"Exactly. Calvin Cole is the answer to these niggas eating good. See, these fools running around wouldn't be shit without Calvin, but we're eating good without ever having dealt with him. How well off do you think we would be if we decided to do business with the duke?"

The thought had been in Junnie's head for the past few weeks but this was his first time running past the other two.

Harlem leaned forward to the front seat. He was giving Junnie a strange look.

"Hold up, you talking about being down with the Family?"

"Why not?" Junnie challenged.

"Because most of those niggas are fucking wannabe niggas. They're more into living the Hollywood shit but turn to pussies when it's time to get into some G shit." Harlem shook his head in disgust. "I don't fuck with them niggas."

"Luckily we wouldn't be doing business with them. We'll be doing it with Calvin Cole."

"You really considering it?" Allah asked. He always knew it would be a good opportunity to work with Calvin Cole, but he never figured Junnie would go for it.

Junnie nodded seriously. "We're making good money with the moves we make but them niggas are making retirement money and I want some of it. It's just a thought so far, but it's not something I would turn down if the opportunity arose.

"I feel you on that." Allah pulled to a slow stop at a red light. He looked down at his phone and read the screen. "Well that meeting was a big ass waste of time honestly, but we might be able to make up for it tonight. The Dawg House is about to be crackin'"

"Oh yeah, I heard some shit about that," Harlem said, rolling down the window to spit.

"What's going down?" Junnie asked.

"Lil Banger is in town. He's supposed to be performing tonight."

"You know the whole towns about to be there. Remember last time that nigga was out here?" Harlem asked. Everyone did.

Lil Banger was one of the hottest main stream rappers, he had just dropped his first album "Tales from a Trap God", which had sold a million copies in its first week.

You couldn't turn it to BET, or turn on the radio without seeing his video or hearing one of his songs. But before he had turned into a rap megastar Lil Banger had been your average troublemaker, selling drugs on the corner or fighting in an alleyway.

Everyone from the hood remembered him from those days, and his rise to fame had given hope to the young boys in the hood. Lil Banger had come and performed for his Wild West tour a month before. As expected the show was a huge turnout, with people coming from all over the Bay Area to see the rapper.

Everything was going good until a joker threw a water bottle on stage. Lil Banger shut the music off and waited until the culprit was identified. When he was, Lil Banger hopped off the stage and proceeded to beating the boy to a bloody pulp while his entourage jumped on anybody that looked like they wanted to help the boy.

"I heard it took the janitors a week to clean all the blood up," Allah said.

"So you guys trying to go see him perform?" Junnie asked, raising his eyebrow. Harlem turned and gave him a stupid look.

"Is you crazy? Fuck that busted ass nigga. I'm going for the bitches!" he shouted at the top of his lungs, pounding on the roof of the car.

"The bitches!" Allah shouted equally as loud, beating on the horn. Junnie just looked at them and shook his head.

"Well while y'all celebrate your quests for pussy drop me off at the crib. If we're going out I need to get dressed and shit." Junnie told them, looking at his current attire.

The T-shirt and jeans he had on would hardly suffice to get past the bouncers.

"Yeah Lah, drop this nigga off. He's dressed like a construction worker and shit." Harlem laughed, leaning forward to get a good look at Junnie. "You ain't pulling no bitches like that."

"Wasn't planning to anyway. I'm going to go see my lady right now."

****

Junnie walked in the house and found Essence in the bedroom bustling around. She looked up as he walked in and a bright smile formed on her face.

"Hey baby," she greeted, walking over and giving him a kiss. "I wasn't expecting you back so soon."

"I see." Junnie looked around the room.

Clothes were strewn everywhere and there were so many heels and boots on the floor it looked like a shoe department.

"Looking for something?" he asked, watching Essence dig through the shoeboxes she had stacked inside the closet.

"Yeah, I am actually. I'm looking for some boots that match my outfit for tonight."

"Tonight?"

"Yeah." Essence stopped searching to look at him. "You don't remember when I told you, me and Nubia were going out tonight?"

"It must have slipped my mind." Junnie sat on the edge of the bed and slipped out of his Jordans.

"Where you going?"

Essence gave him a look. "Are you serious? I'm going the same place everyone in this state is going. The Dawg House to see Lil Banger."

"I don't know about that, Essence," Junnie said with uncertainty. "It's going to be wild out there and you remember what happened last time this fool came to a show. Niggas were getting gunned down like this was Iraq."

"I know, but I want to go Junnie." Essence argued. "Nubia's already on her way over here to pick me up. Its possible things are going to get crazy, especially thinking about how many stupid niggas are going to be there gang banging and shit, but something could happen to me just walking down the street any normal day. I ain't never scared," she said, putting on a gangster sneer.

Junnie laughed. "Alright killer, do your thing. Just know that I'm going to be there keeping an eye on you."

"Really? Is it for my protection or are you just trying to get an eye full of all this?" Essence turned around and did a quick twerk. Junnie watched as her ass bounced wildly in her pajama shorts.

"C'mon, we know who that ass already belongs to." Junnie stood to his feet and walked over to her. Palming her behind, he pulled her close. "How about you get naked before you get dressed, and we go fuck these sheets up?"

Junnie kissed her on the neck, and let his tongue flicker over her skin. Essence moaned softly as the touch sent a sensation straight throughout her body. She allowed Junnie a few more kisses before gently pushing him away.

"You know I could never argue with that, but it's very near that time of month again." she said, gently patting his cheek. She laughed at the expression on his face. "I'm sorry baby."

"It's good, I'll live." Junnie playfully pushed her away. "But one good thing about that is I don't have to worry about anybody sliding up in you tonight, Bloody Mary."

"You wouldn't have to worry about that anyway, dumbass." Essence picked up a pillow and threw it at his head.

"Take a joke." Junnie walked past the dresser mirror and froze. "Hold up, before you leave can you take care of this?" he asked, tugging at his busy ponytail. Essence walked over it and examined it.

"Yeah, I guess I can hook you up, playa. Its gonna run you about fifty bucks."

15

Seven hit the blunt and tilted his head back towards the ceiling. Blowing the smoke in the air he nodded his head to the hard beat banging out of the speakers.

Across the living room, Angel sat on the edge of the sofa, focused on the television screen as he flicked the sticks on his Xbox controller. The afternoon was early, so they had been in the house for the majority of the day. Once the sun went down and the street lights came on they planned to make some moves.

"These bitch ass niggas, man" Angel mumbled, as he received the losing end of Call of Duty. "This AK ain't shit. I hit this muthafucka ten times and he still throwing grenades."

"That's because that's a fucking video game. Ain't nobody surviving a hit from this shit." Seven lifted the assault rifle they had leaning against the wall. It was one of the largest weapons he had ever held, but he had no plans of using it in real combat.

"Fuck you need this big muthafucka for?" Seven asked examining it.

"For the exact reason you just said. Nobody's gonna survive a hit from that bitch. Its gonna wipe out a niggas squad and every witness on the block."

Seven shook his head and set the gun down. "To each his own, I guess. I get by just fine with my nine." He pulled his gun from his jeans and aimed at an imaginary enemy. "Split a niggas melon with ease."

Angel snickered. "That old ass gun, bruh. You're gonna need an oil change on it soon. You been banging that same shit since we first started making moves."

"I'm used to it. It's gotten me out of a lot of situations." Seven looked at his gun. It had been the first gun he had and it had become sort of a good luck charm to him.

"Yeah, it's going to get you in to a lot of situations too, if the boys find you with it. That shit got more bodies on it than a cheap motel mattress. Didn't you knock Ving with that on our first run?"

"Nah, I hit that nigga with the blade to his stomach like eight, nine times."

"Ah you right, I remember that."

There was a light knock on the front door. Angel put the game on pause and stood quickly. Holding up his sagging pants with one hand, and holding a pistol with the other he crossed the room and peeked out the peephole. Turning the lock, he opened the door.

"Where you been at, li'l nigga?"

"My bad, I had to make a run for my aunty." Wiz stepped inside the house. He was small, even for his fourteen years of age, but he had the soul of an older person. His small dreads hung in his face, covering his eyes, and his baby face was void of any hint of facial hair.

Seven had found Wiz in the streets a couple years back and was drawn to the youngster. He reminded Seven of a younger version of himself.

"Yeah yeah, did you bring it?" Angel asked, shaking his dreads out his face.

Wiz grinned, digging in his pocket. "You ready for this ass whooping, nigga?" he asked, holding up the Xbox controller he had brought.

"You young bucks these days. Fresh in the game thinking you know it all."

Seven shook his head and went into the kitchen. He had never really been into the video game thing, but if he was going to play he stuck with old school Nintendo. Opening the refrigerator his stomach let out a growl as he looked inside and only found a jug of milk and a carton of eggs.

"Aye, before you niggas get started on that bullshit, lets run to the store. There ain't shit to eat in this muthafucka."

"Aye, don't be in here dissing my shit nigga." Angel warned. "Shawna's ass is supposed to be going grocery shopping when she gets off."

"When is that?"

Angel looked at his phone. "Three hours."

Seven instantly grabbed his hoodie and pulled it on. "I ain't waiting for that, my nigga. We need a Swisher too, if you wanna roll up this sticky."

"You got me there." Angel tucked his gun in his jeans, before pulling a t-shirt on. "Get your jacket and let's go. I want you to be well fed before I dish out this beating," he told Wiz.

"I don't need my jacket, it's like eighty degrees out here, cuddy. And you ain't never beat me in your life, what you mean?"

With the two of them arguing Seven followed them out the front door.

****

The streetlights were on, meaning that the criminals were out and about. Mickey was posted outside of the corner store, crouched over a dice game shaking his fist furiously.

He had just hit the homies for a rack and was quickly working on his second. The front of the mini-mart was almost like its own party. A few females had stopped by and spotted the ballers, called up a few more of their girlfriends and pretty soon, someone had turned the bass all the way up on their car's speakers and bottles were being passed around. It was a warm summer night and everyone was feeling good.

"Twenty, he don't make it," a spectator called out as Mickey shook the dice.

"Fifty, he's good on it," someone else bet.

"You're smarter than you look," Mickey told the man. "Because I'm sure about to knock down the back door and help myself to a sandwich. Count 'em."

Throwing the dice against the side of the store everyone held their breath as the dice landed showing a six and a one. The majority of the crowd let out groans and more, while Mickey just showed off his gold teeth.

"Pay up, muthafuckas, just pay up," he motioned for everybody to toss their money on the ground. One by one the crowd began tossing an assortment of bills, and some fool even tossed some coins in the pile.

"That's what the fuck I'm talking about. Pay homage to the king of this dice shit. I'm tired of hitting you fools with seven so I'm about to show you what my bottom bitch eleven is looking like," Mickey claimed as he started shaking the dice again.

"Can't nobody stop this nigga?" a hater asked from the sideline.

"Hell nah, my homie got it on lock right now," Lonnie spoke up.

He was leaning against a car, with his arms wrapped around a thick Puerto Rican broad, with curly hair. Lonnie was only fifteen, but constantly tried running with the big boys. He reminded Mickey of himself when he was that age, so he decided to take the young boy in.

"Yeah, or he got some loaded dice," someone else mumbled.

A few cats snickered. Mickey looked up at the joker and his face turned serious.

"You got something to say, nigga?" Mickey asked, a hint of threat in his voice.

"I already said it nigga," the cat said matching Mickey tone.

"Nah, you mumbled it like a bitch. Speak up if you got something to say."

Putting the dice game on hold Mickey stood up. The cat he was talking to was a few inches taller and had at least a hundred pounds on him, but Mickey wasn't one that was easily swayed.

"Nigga, I said you're out here cheating niggas. What's good?"

The man stood up to his full height and walked over to meet Mickey. Before he could reach him someone stepped through the crowd and delivered a vicious blow to the side of the man's face.

Without so much as a grunt the big man leaned to the side and fell to the ground, out cold. Mickey's enforcer, Murder, glared down at the unconscious man he had laid out.

"Bitch ass nigga," he barked.

The crowd let out "ooooohs" and laughed at the knocked out man who was sleeping like a baby. Murder rubbed his knuckles and stepped back into the sea of spectators.

"Anybody else got something to say?" Mickey asked the crowd, nobody responded. "Good, now back to the show."

Taking his place back over the money Mickey began shaking his dice again. Grinning cockily, he rolled the dice again. Six and five. The crowd let out shouts of protests but Mickey welcomed them with open arms.

"Damn, he's cleaning up out here," one of the females watching commented.

"That's my nigga," Lonnie said like a proud papa.

"You know what, I'm done breaking you muthafuckas for tonight. Go re-up on that rent money then come holla at me."

Scooping up all his money Mickey stood to his feet and began to sort through it all. The crowd broke away from the circle and began to discuss what they were getting ready to get into for the night. Mickey stood next to his people and began to count his money.

"We eating good tonight?" Lonnie asked, while he palmed the Puerto Rican girl's ass.

"No better than usual. I only hit busters for some short change," Mickey said counting.

"I don't get these niggas. Every week they come out here just to lose their money, then come back for more and more,"

Murder shook his head. He was a large man, with a gruff beard and long cornrows.

"Aye, as long as I'm hitting them I wouldn't care if they were using their kid's college funds to play me. As long as I'm getting cashed out," Mickey said, folding the bills and stuffing them in his pocket.

"Yo, who's that creeping?" someone asked.

As everyone looked up there was a loud screeching as a car burned in their direction. The back window rolled down and West stuck his body out.

Biting down on his lip he aimed the rifle and began squeezing the trigger. Windows shattered and people screamed as the bullets tore into the side of the building.

Two men who had been standing by the curb didn't have time to cry out as the bullets ripped their bodies apart. Everyone began scattering and ducking for cover but it did little to help.

His street instincts kicking in, Mickey pulled out his burner and started busting back at the car as he jumped behind a parked Ford.

Not long ago he had snuck into the McDonald's bathroom to snort a quick line, so his adrenaline was pumping full throttle and he felt like he was in a war movie. Standing up he began firing at the car while everyone tried to stay out of the path of the bullets.

Murder stood beside him and started letting off with his revolver. Setting his sights on them, West took aim and began letting loose. Mickey and Murder put up a good fight but they were no match for the powerful automatic.

Mickey let out a grunt as a bullet ripped through his side, knocking him back. Murder tried to come to his defense and ended up catching multiple hits to the body, sprawling him on the sidewalk.

Seeing that he was the target of the enemies' anger, Mickey decided that a good run would be better than being dead. Turning around he took off in a full sprint into a nearby alley.

"Hold on, wait!" Lonnie called after him.

Leaving the screaming girl behind, he ducked down and tried to run after his best friend but two bullets to the back sent him flying forward onto the cement.

"Stop the car!" West barked at his driver.

Without waiting for the youngster he hopped out the Dodge and went to chase Mickey. Lonnie was still moaning and crawling when West ran past and without breaking stride he fired another shot to the back of Lonnie's dome knocking his brains out of his forehead and onto the sidewalk.

Mickey had a good head start and was almost a block away as he ran through traffic without slowing down.

A rusty Cadillac smashed on its breaks to avoid hitting him. Mickey jumped onto the roof of the car and kept it moving without slowing down.

West was catching up but still wasn't close enough to fire a shot off. Mickey hit the corner so hard he lost his footing and almost crashed to the asphalt.

Catching his balance, he continued running, but the numbness that was spreading through his right side began to slow him down. Mickey's breathing became ragged as he held onto his wound, blood seeping through his fingers. The world was spinning and before he knew it Mickey had fallen onto the sidewalk and had smashed his head on the ground. There was nothing he could do as blood drenched the entire side of his body. Staring up into the dark sky his heart skipped a beat when West's wide face appeared above him.

"What's good, nigga?" he grinned.

Without bothering for an answer West raised his boot and smashed it down on Mickey's face repeatedly.

Mickey's face was cracked and covered with blood.

"Yeah, you ain't poppin' that shit now, are you bitch ass nigga?" Another kick to the face. "Where's that tough guy shit now, faggot ass nigga?"

Mickey tried to speak but the only blood came out. Smiling at the mess he had created, West reached in his pocket and pulled out his blade.

"I'ma enjoy this shit," he laughed, leaning down over Mickey.

He began to slash Mickey across the face, spilling blood onto the ground and causing Mickey to cry out in pain. Without mercy West continued to slice and dice Mickey's face until pieces of flesh was hanging from his skull.

Once Mickey was done squirming West reached down and slit his throat open. Satisfied with his work West picked up his AK-47 and ran back to the awaiting car.

16

Rango sat behind the wheel of the car, high and getting impatient. His .40 sat in his lap, fully loaded and ready to put in work.

He had been driving around for hours and was starting to get pissed at the lack of results. Beside him, Philly was rolling another blunt mumbling to himself. He had been riding with Rango most of the day and his impatience was growing more rapidly than his partner.

After the run in with Seven, Rango had asked around about the young boys and had acquired some information. It was no secret that he ran in the Westside of the city but where exactly he could be found was a different matter.

Rango had been ready to load up his whole squad to make sure he did Seven and Angel dirty but he didn't want to have to explain why he was so intent on taking out a couple of teenagers.

Instead he settled for Philly, who would kill without question, and Holly who was following them in his car with another one of the loyal soldiers named Lynx. It was Holly's fault that Rango was in this situation in the first place.

"Man, if we don't find these muthafuckas soon you're gonna need to drop me off back on the block," Philly said in his gravelly voice. He began to lick the blunt to seal it. "I got shit to do, and we out here looking for some run-of-the-mill ass niggas. You could have got the li'l homies to do this shit."

"Chill the fuck out, dawg. You get paid to put in work right? So do what you get paid for." Rango snapped, searching out the window as they drove through the streets. "These niggas are out here somewhere and I'ma get them while they are."

"You can't handle two teeny boppers nigga?" Philly asked in disbelief. "You already let them black your shit," he nodded towards Rango's black eye.

Rango glared at him. "Nigga, didn't I say chill out? These niggas snuck me on some bitch shit, but I got something that's gonna make them realize who I am."

"Yeah, I hope you let that thing bark just as much as them lips."

Rango ignored Philly. He was used to his best friend's shit talking but he wasn't in the mood today. Rango's cell phone vibrated in his pocket. "What?" he answered roughly, keeping his eyes on the street.

"Man, I don't see these niggas out here and I'm burning up my gas," Holly's voice came through the speaker. "Let's do this shit another day."

"Nigga you out your fucking mind?" Rango barked into the phone. "I'm in this shit because of your dumb ass! I should have you out here all week until you find these li'l niggas."

"Come on, fam," Holly replied, but he knew Rango was right.

He had seen the little boy Wiz, walking by himself late night while Holly was out searching for a quick hit. He needed to come up on a few hundreds to help support his coke habit and he was scoring his fix in a couple of hours.

So when he saw the young boy with a gold chain and diamonds shining off his wrist, Holly had thought he found himself the perfect mark.

"Well shit, can we stop at this store up here? I need a swisher and some chips or something."

Rango was about to go off on Holly for even suggesting wasting time when something caught his eye. Sitting up in his seat Rango stared at three young men walking to the corner store up ahead.

The one in the front was none other than Seven himself. It didn't take long to recognize Angel by his dreads, but Rango didn't know the third boy.

"Yo, I see these niggas!" Rango exclaimed excitedly. His heart started pounding at the sight of his targets.

"Where?" Philly looked up from his blunt rolling. "Those little dudes right there in front of the store?"

"Yep." Rango slowed the car down as he tried to figure out what he wanted to do. "Holly, pull over to the side up here. We're gonna hit these niggas fast. I'ma pull up on them dumping, then I want you to hit them with the next round, got me?" he spoke into the phone.

"Yeah, I hear you." Holly spoke up, but half-heartedly.

He wasn't sure if he wanted to run up on the young boys but if they were going to go through with it he was going to make sure they did it right.

Rango ended the call and tossed the phone aside. Cocking the slide back on his gun he sat up and stared at Seven, who wasn't even aware of what was about to happen.

Rango could feel his hand shaking with anger and adrenaline as he prepared to make his move. He had never actually killed anyone but he was more than ready to pop his cherry.

"You ready nigga?" Philly asked, his Desert Eagle in one hand and his other hand on the door handle. "We been looking for these dudes all day, you better be ready."

Rango took a deep breath. "Let's do it," he said, opening the car door. Both crouching down low, the two men slowly crept towards the corner store.

****

Seven, deep in his own thoughts, walked with his hands shoved in his pockets. Angel and Wiz followed close behind, still arguing about who was going to get the worst end of the ass whooping when they got back to the house.

Seven had blocked them out a while ago. His mind was on a different matter. When they got outside the store, his cell phone rang. He looked down in surprise at the number.

"I know this ain't who I think it is," he answered coolly.

"Nope, this ain't Chantel," Bobbi laughed. "You got in my head the other day about how I don't ever hit you up so I figured I finally dust the cob webs off your number."

"About time." Seven turned to his two comrades. "I'll be in there in a minute. Grab me some Cheetos and a soda," he told Wiz, handing him a ten-dollar bill.

"Oh, you gonna post up when the bitches call, huh?" Angel snickered.

"Nigga, kill that shit," Seven called back before returning to his phone call.

Angel just waved his hand, dismissing Seven's comment while Wiz followed him in the store, laughing.

"So what you up to?" he spoke in the phone.

"Just getting ready for the night. Me and Tavae are going to see Lil' Banger perform. Are you going?"

"I forgot that shit was tonight. I'm probably not gonna go though. The niggas kinda corny to me."

"Hell no, you're tripping. His song 'Gun Sauce' is the shit."

"Yeah, you could call it that." Seven leaned against the side of the corner store, looking around the street while he talked.

"Shut up," Bobbi giggled. "Listen, I was thinking—"

Bobbi's voice trailed off as Seven looked up the street and noticed a black Cadillac parked almost a block away.

There was something familiar about it but he couldn't place it. He didn't have too long to think about it as two men exited the car and started creeping in his direction. There was a determination on their faces that Seven was used to. He wasn't sure if they were coming for him but, when he seen the gleam of metal in one of their hands he knew he wasn't going to wait around and find out.

"Aye sorry to interrupt, but I'ma have to call you back B. Something just came up," he spoke into his phone keeping his eyes on the men who were doing a terrible job of trying to stay hidden.

"Oh okay, want me to…"

Seven hung up the phone before Bobbi could finish speaking. Placing his hand beneath his shirt he waited patiently for the men to get closer.

The darker one he had never seen before but once the lowering sunlight hit Rango's face, he knew what the deal was.

"What's up, pa'tna?" Philly called out as he raised his revolver and fired.

Seven jumped to the side and slid across the gravel, skinning his arm up, but it was better than the bullet to the head he would have surely received.

Ducking behind a car, Seven waited as Rango and Philly shot up everything in sight but didn't get close to hitting Seven. Easing around the side of the car, Seven popped up and sent some shots back in response.

Rango hurriedly dropped to the ground, and Philly ducked behind the side of the building. Glass shattered as bullets hit the car that was providing Rango cover.

While they were down, Seven seen the boy Holly running towards them from the distance, shotgun out and ready. Seeing that the scales were tipped against him, Seven decided to end it quickly.

Looking underneath the car, he seen Rango crouching down and fired. He wasn't sure where he hit exactly but he was satisfied when he heard Rango cry out in pain.

Seeing Rango holding his arm and withering in agony gave Philly all the fuel he needed. Feeling like an action hero, he leaned from the side of the building and began to squeeze.

He couldn't hear the screams of the pedestrians over the roar of the gun, but he seen everyone scattering for safety. He was so involved with trying to get Seven, he never heard Angel creeping out of the store.

"Aye homie."

Philly turned and the last thing he seen was Angel's evil grin before the young boy put his life to an end with a bullet through his skull.

Philly's head snapped back and he collapsed to the ground in a heap. A roar suddenly shook the whole street and if it wasn't for Holly's bad aim, the shotgun blast would have surely cut Angel into half.

Holly cocked the shotgun and let off another lick that caused Angel to back up out of sight. Reaching down, Holly grabbed the injured Rango and lifted him to his feet.

He considered trying to save Philly but one look at his brains on the cement told Holly not to waste his time.

Rango wrapped his arm around Holly's shoulder and allowed him to guide him back towards the car. His eyes landed on the youngster who had been with Seven when they arrived at the store.

Raising his gun, Rango prepared to send the boy to the afterlife. Wiz froze as he looked down the barrel of Rango's gun and there was nothing he could do. Before Rango could fire, Seven returned to action and sent a hail of bullets his way.

Holly gave one last shot with the shotgun to provide cover while they made tracks back to Rango's Cadillac.

Seven and Angel both made it to the sidewalk at the same time and began running towards the car, guns blazing.

The Cadillac started and burned rubber as it pulled away from its parking spot, swerving to avoid parked cars. The two teenager's bullets hit the car and shattered the windows but they couldn't tell if they hit anyone. The car faded off in the distance as it sped away.

"Let's get it," Seven demanded tapping Angels chest. "Aye, come on!" he yelled at Wiz, who was only a few steps behind them.

Without needing to go into a plan, the three began to run as fast as they could before anyone could remember their faces.

****

"What the fuck happened?" Lynx asked as he whipped the car through traffic. He looked in the rearview at Rango's sweaty, panicked face. "Is he dying?"

"Shut the fuck up and drive this muthafucka, Lynx," Holly demanded, before turning back to Rango's wound.

Lifting up his shirt, Holly examined it. There didn't appear to be a hole but there was a nasty jagged gash, as if he had been sliced. "I don't think it went through. It just grazed you."

"Nigga this shit still hurts like a bitch," Rango grimaced, as he held his hands over the gash. "Damn, did we even hit any of them niggas?"

"I don't know, I don't even know." Holly looked out of the back window to make sure they weren't being followed. "They shot Philly though. I think that nigga was dead."

Rango felt a pang in his heart. He had just been snapping at him a mere twenty minutes ago, now Philly was in the afterlife. What was even worse was that Seven and Angel had seen their faces.

They knew that Rango just made attempt on their lives and what he knew from their reputations, they weren't going to let that ride out.

"They killed Philly?" Lynx asked in shock. "What are we going to do?"

"Just start by getting us the fuck away from here," Rango told him, watching the blood seep from between his fingers. "Then get me to Walgreens so I can get some aspirin, Icy Hot, alcohol, or something. This shit hurt."

"I got you, I got you!" Lynx said, speeding through the traffic.

17

"What the fuck was that shit?" Angel demanded once they got inside the apartment.

Seven double checked the hallway before shutting the front door behind them and bolting the door shut. Angel had crossed the room and peeked out the blinds before closing them and drawing them shut.

He turned to his comrades. "I know that wasn't Holly's punk ass trying to earn some stripes?"

"Yeah that was him." Seven sat down on the couch, tired from the run. That's when he noticed blood dripping down his fingers. "The fuck?"

"Oh shit, you good Sev?" A worried look crossed Wiz's face as he walked over to his mentor. Hearing his concern Angel frowned as he walked over to Seven and noticed the hole in the sleeve of his shirt.

"Damn, you got hit." Angel observed.

"You think?' Seven eased the hoodie off and Angel and Wiz crowded around to examine the wound.

Blood covered his entire bicep and dripped down his arm and his forearm was skinned up badly where he had slid on the pavement. His arm was looking bad overall.

"We gotta take you to the hospital." Wiz said, looking at the amount of blood that covered Seven's arm.

Seven smiled at his young protégé. "Going to the hospital with a gunshot wound right after there was just a big shootout is just as good as going in the precinct and copping to a murder."

"That's just a scratch, we'll clean it up." Angel went back to the window and took another peek. "Where the fuck did they even come from?"

"They rolled up as soon as we got to the store. They got out the whip with the guns out already, so I knew they weren't there for any convo."

"That shits hot as hell." Angel mumbled, looking for any sign of red and blue lights.

"Wiz, grab me that bottle off the table," Seven instructed. "Angel grab me some peroxide, a Band-Aid or something. This ain't no paper cut, my nigga."

"I got you," Angel walked away from the blinds, gun still clenched in his hand. He went in the back to find something to clean Seven up with.

Wiz walked back over to Seven with the bottle of Jack Daniels that had been sitting there from the night before. Seven nodded in appreciation as he popped the top off and took a deep swig. The burning sensation was a calming relief from the pain that was radiating up his arm.

"Let me see your belt," he told Wiz who readily obeyed.

"Angel blew that niggas head damn near off," Wiz said, remembering seeing Philly's head snap back and his brains pouring out the back of his cranium. "That niggas brains popped out."

"Yeah, I can't say I feel too sorry for the nigga." Seven took Wiz's belt and wrapped it around his bicep, right beneath the bullet wound.

"I would have felt sorry for you though if that nigga Rango had let his ratty spit. Why didn't you draw your gun?"

"I left it here in my jacket." Wiz said, feeling disappointed with himself.

If Seven hadn't provided him with cover then he would be laid out back at the corner store with his body riddled with bullets.

"We were only running to the store so I didn't think I would need it."

"As you can see, that dumb ass logic almost had you up at the pearly gates," Seven said seriously.

His arm felt like it was on fire but it was important that he teach Wiz this.

"In the line of work we're in there are no days off. You being off guard could get your life span cut short and there's no coming back from that. You hear me?"

"Yeah, I hear you Sev." Wiz said quietly.

Angel came back in the living room with a bottle of peroxide, a towel, and a squirt bottle full of water.

"Trying to stop that blood flow huh?" Angel said, noticing the belt around Sevens arm.

"Hell yeah, this shits starting to hurt."

"Don't trip, bruh, I got you." Angel propped Seven's arm up as if he were preparing for surgery.

They both had sustained similar injuries in the past so they knew enough to clean them and patch them pretty decent, but it would still need professional attention.

"So you know what this means right? With these niggas coming for our lives."

"Yep. It means its killa season in Cali," Seven said, taking another drink from the bottle just as Angel poured the peroxide over the hole causing it to bubble and hiss.

18

The outside of the Dawg House was more crowded than it had ever been. Crowds of people stood outside the entrance and in the parking lot anticipating the arrival of Lil' Banger.

Females strutted the streets in their best attire, which surprisingly didn't consist of too much. Dudes called out and tried to gain the attention of the women who were coming through in all shapes and sizes, showing off enough skin to leave little to the imagination.

The club event had also called out every dope boy and hustler the town had to offer. They showed off their jewels and chains, while the rest slow cruised through the streets, blasting Lil' Banger's music from their trunks. The police knew what time it was. They worked crowd control on each end of the block, setting up perimeters.

"This must be what heavens like," Harlem commented, watching a group of women walk by.

He had dressed to impress, he wore a baby blue Polo, dark Enyce jeans, and crisp white Nikes.

The platinum chain he wore caught the eye of one of the women and she looked back to give him a seductive smile as her friends led her across the street.

"Yeah, don't be surprised if I don't ride back with you losers," he told them, running a hand over his fresh fade.

"Ride back? We planned on leaving your ugly ass here anyway." Allah said, adjusting the cuff of his sleeve.

He was decked out in a tight gray thermal and black jeans. His gray and black Blazers still had the tag on it, letting everyone know they were fresh from the box.

"I'ma have too much pussy in the whip to be trying to let you squeeze in," he said, rolling his up sleeves so his tattoos could be visible.

"Are you serious?" Harlem looked at him and laughed. "The only pussies that's gonna be in the car is you two muthafuckas and I rode here with you just fine."

"A busted lip sure would crack your style tonight," Allah threatened. He tapped his partner on the arm. "You see anything you like?"

Junnie hadn't been listening to the exchange between Allah and Harlem. He smoked his cigarette and observed the number of people who had all chose to spend their Friday night all in the same location.

Junnie decided he didn't want to get too dressed up for the event and kept it settle. He decided on his red and black lumberjack flannel, black Dickies, and original black Chuck Taylors.

Essence had done a quick but efficient job braiding his hair. His cornrows hung to his shoulders, but he still decided to pull a wool cap on his head.

"There's a few sheep walking around," he replied, taking a deep pull from his Newport. "I'm sure y'all going to clean up tonight."

"Oh yeah, I forgot wifey is going to be here. Sucks for you." Harlem said, not sounding remotely sympathetic.

He peeped a thick white girl walking past from the corner of his eye.

"Aye what's good, Snow White. Make sure you save a dance for a nigga," he called.

The white girl looked him up and down "If I see you inside," she flirted.

"See that shit?" Harlem asked his comrades once she left. "I'm going wild when we get in this muthafucka, no exaggeration."

"While we're on the topic, how are we going to go about getting in?" Allah proposed.

"You're right, this line is long as fuck," Harlem said, looking towards the end of the line, which stretched around the corner.

"Nah, I'm talking about me getting past the bouncers. I still have my burner on me."

"I left mine in the car."

Allah looked at him in surprise. "You're walking in here naked?"

"Never that. I got a few tricks up my sleeve."

Harlem moved his tongue around and smiled, showing off the razor he had concealed in his mouth.

"I swear you east coast niggas stay with razors."

"Don't trip, I don't think we're going to have to worry about getting in," Junnie assured them, seeing who was at the door.

There was a group of bouncers patting everyone down, and checking female's purses. Junnie spotted a familiar face amongst the large men.

"Let's go."

Leading the way across the street, Junnie and his crew headed for the front of the line as opposed to the end, which had disappeared down the block.

One of the bouncers was roughly patting a dude down, while the second stood back with his arms crossed over his massive chest.

He looked over as Junnie approached. At first he looked ready to bark at them for skipping the line but when he seen who it was his facial expression changed.

"What it do, Junnie?" Tone greeted, giving the smaller man dap.

"What's up with it Tone. I haven't seen you around the block for a minute."

Tone swept is hand towards the building. "Yeah, I know. I been working steady now. Trying to get shit right, you know?"

"Trust me, I know how it is." he nodded his head.

Only a short time ago, Tone had been on his way to becoming a heavyweight in the town's underworld. He was a beast who would give it to anyone when necessary, but once his little brother was tortured and killed over revenge. The life seemed to have lost its appeal to him and he disappeared from the radar. He and Junnie had lived on the same street for a while but a few months ago Tone had up and moved.

"You came out to see Lil Banger too huh?" Tone grinned.

"More for sights than that nigga." Junnie told him. "This lines crazy though, I was thinking..."

"You already know you don't even have to ask."

Unhooking the velvet rope, he motioned for Junnie and his crew to step through. One of the other bouncers gave them a hard stare as they stepped past.

"Tone I don't think…"

"What don't you think?" Tone asked, a hint of threat in his voice.

He stared the dude down, daring him to finish his sentence.

"Nothing," the dude mumbled, going to check the ID of the people coming up.

"Aye, good looking out Tone. I respect it." Junnie gave him a handshake before walking inside the club, with Allah and Harlem following.

Tone grinned as he looked down at the hundred-dollar bill that was left in his hand.

****

"Damn, baby boy, you see this shit?"

Lil Banger slowly lifted his head, dreads swinging and looked through the tinted windows of the Maybach. The back was filled with smoke from the blunts that were in circulation but he could still make out the hundreds of people filling the streets on both sides.

His right hand man Alley was staring out the window in amazement at all the people who had shown for the turnout.

"This shit happens in every city and you still shocked by it?" Lil Banger asked, more focused on the blunt in his hand.

"Hell yeah!" Alley answered. "These muthafuckas wouldn't look twice at us a year ago, now their putting on their Sunday's best just to come see us. That shits crazy, cuddy."

"I'm pretty sure they're coming to see Banger. Not his buff." Lil Banger's bodyguard, Lucius spoke from the front seat.

"Yo, shut your big ham hock eating ass up, nigga. We know ain't nobody coming to see you. When's the last time you got pussy, the mid-eighties?" Alley cracked and everyone in the car laughed.

Alley had insisted on bringing some females with them so that it would give them a good look when they first entered the club, but from the way the females outside the club were looking, it was more than possible that the ones currently in the car would need to find a ride home afterwards.

"Alright, B, it's show time," Mannie, Lil Banger's uncle and manager, said excitedly.

He was a throwback goon who had decided to get into the business the moment "Drop it Hot records" had offered his nephew a contract.

"We're going to go in here, chill out for a little bit to check the scene, then we'll see when the owner wants you on stage," he said, craning his neck to get a good look at the people standing in line.

"Yeah, that's what's up." Lil Banger responded.

He had been smoking for a couple hours straight now and it didn't help that he had combined that with the lean that Alley had fixed him as soon as they had got in the car.

"Y'all act like this is my first time doing this shit," he drawled, making sure his shades were covering his droopy eyes.

"Nah, I'm acting like you need to stay on your toes, nephew," Mannie told him seriously. "I reached out to Calvin Cole before we came out here and he assured that he would make sure that these niggas kept peace while we're here, but he doesn't have control on all these hating ass niggas. I want you to stay with either me or Lucius at all times, hear me?"

"Man, you didn't have to reach out to any fucking body," Lil Banger said angrily. "Niggas know what's up with me out here. Don't forget, I was a shooter before I was a rapper. And muthafuckas better stop getting it twisted."

"Save that killer shit for the fans, nigga, and do what I said," Mannie barked.

The car came to a stop directly in front of the club's entrance.

"Put that fucking cup down and get yourself together. We're getting paid fifty G's just to basically show up to this bitch, so get right. Alley, take that fucking blunt from him. I want you and these bitches to get out first, then me, then Banger last for the dramatic effect."

"Bitches?" One of the girls cried angrily. "I ain't no bitch!"

"You are as long as your black ass is sitting in this fucking car," Mannie snapped, he had more on his mind than the attitude of a random groupie. "B, you ready?"

"Whatever man, open the door." Lil Banger snapped angrily.

"I'll check you on that attitude later." Mannie tapped the window. "Let's go, Lou."

The crowd outside the club had started going wild as soon as the Maybach parked. The crowd waited in anticipation for the star of the main event to exit the vehicle.

They were so excited they started cheering when Lucius stepped from the passenger side. His leather jacket hugged his massive frame as he went straight to the back and opened the doors.

Alley hopped out, welcoming the shouts and cheers as if he were the one they had been waiting to see. Next, came the three women they had picked up earlier that day at the mall.

They weren't as beautiful as the usual girls they ran into in the industry, but they were the sexiest chicks in the hood. Mannie stepped out, mug intact as usual as he scanned the crowd. He stepped to the side and waited for his nephew to come.

As soon as one of Lil Bangers shoes came out and landed on the sidewalk the crowd went wild. Cell phones came out and females professed their love for the young star as he stood to his full height, dreads swinging.

His face was hidden by his dreadlocks but you could make out a mouth full of platinum teeth as he sneered in greeting. He nodded at a few people here and there but for the most part he ignored them.

"It's going to be a good night!" Alley yelled over the shouts of the clubbers as the bouncers unhooked the ropes and let the rapper and his entourage through.

19

The inside of the club was almost packed to capacity but that didn't stop everyone from hitting the dance floor and doing their thing. For the people who weren't as confident with their dance moves they stood around watching the women who were twerking as if they were getting paid to.

The Dawg House was usually packed on any given Friday but it had never been this wild, this early. Junnie and his crew made their way to the bar and were lucky enough to find some open stools.

Junnie ordered a shot of Yak, while Allah got a glass of brandy. Harlem was too preoccupied looking around at every woman that came within eyesight.

"That's how I know this is some bullshit," he said, turning to his team. "I ain't never seen half these bitches in my life. Like her, where the fuck does she be at?"

He nodded at a thick Latino girl, whose skirt was so high you could just see the cuff of her ass cheeks. She was on the arm of some dude who looked like he couldn't believe his luck at getting her.

"You know these females came from all over just to see homie perform," Junnie said, downing his shot.

He slammed the glass down, then waved to get the bartenders attention.

"Essence told me her home girl was driving down from Sacramento just to come tonight."

"Dudes nice on the mic, but he ain't Pac or nothing," Allah said, taking a sip of his drink.

At that moment there was a loud roar of cheers towards the front. People all began to move towards the door to see what was going on.

Lil Banger walked through the crowd, followed by his people who were surrounding him closely. To have so many females throwing themselves at him, Lil Banger didn't seem to care too much.

He simply waved his hand once before heading to the VIP section that club had set up for him.

As soon as he was settled a large man with a leather jacket stood outside the booth and crossed his arms over his chest. A few people surrounded the area but nobody was stupid enough to try and get past the bodyguard.

"Look at that shit." Harlem shook his head in disgust. "The niggas are on that groupie shit just as hard as the bitches."

"They always are," Junnie said, uninterested in the arrival of the rapper.

The bartender brought him another shot and he swigged it down just as quick as he had the first one. Looking around the club his eyes fell on two women who were clear across the room.

Dudes who were next to them were trying to talk or compliment them but the women ignored them. They sat down at a table, oblivious to Junnie's stare.

He slid off the stool and tapped Allah on the arm. "There's the ass I'm taking home tonight," he said, nodding towards the table.

Allah turned and looked. He let out a laugh. "You're hella corny nigga." his laughter stopped abruptly as he got a better look. "Hold up, is that Nubia?" he asked, referring to the dark skinned female.

"Yep, let's go."

Junnie began to walk through the thick crowd of people. Allah killed the rest of his drink before standing up and following after him.

"Awe, you niggas are some busters. Just gonna leave me behind, huh?" Harlem called after them.

"Watch our seats." Allah called over his shoulder.

He couldn't hear Harlem's reply over the music but he was willing to bet it wasn't pleasant. Junnie led them through the crowd, nodding at people he knew and ignoring the ones he didn't. There were so many people Essence didn't notice him until he was directly in front of her.

"What's up ma, where your nigga."

Essence looked up and a smile stretched across her face. She had always been naturally beautiful so when she actually went out of her way to fix herself up she was on a level of something that didn't even have a name yet.

She had straightened her usual curly hair, so it now hung past her shoulders. Besides eye liner and lipstick there was no makeup on her face and it was still flawless.

The strapless Dereon dress she wore stopped mid-thigh, and she had settled on her blue pumps which gave her an extra three inches.

When she stood to give Junnie a hug, the men around the table sneaked looks at her ass which was stretching through the fabric of the dress. Junnie glared at them and they hurriedly looked anywhere but Essence.

"You just got here?" he pulled away from Essence and looked at her.

"Yeah, we got here as soon as Lil Banger was pulling up. People were losing their minds. You would have thought Jesus himself was coming out the Maybach. That line is ridiculous. It's circling around Lamont Avenue. Luckily, Nubia knew one of the bouncers."

"Same way we got in. What's up Nubia?" he asked turning to Essence best friend.

"Same shit, different day," Nubia responded, adjusting her top.

Nubia was a beautiful, dark Nigerian, who had the body of a porn star and the temper of Ike Turner.

She was wearing a black blouse, that was cut in a v neck, giving you a clear view of her large breast, and leggings that showed off her curves.

Nubia had no problem attracting men but once they actually made a move on her and realized that they were talking to a witch with a heart made of ice it usually scared them off.

"What's good with you Nubia?" Allah greeted from the sidelines.

She looked up noticing him for the first time, and a blank look crossed her face.

"Mmm."

"Don't be like that, Nubia," Essence scolded her friend.

Nubia looked back at Allah and gave him a phony smile.

"Hello Allah," she said with false cheerfulness. Then her scowl was back on.

"You know that attitude ain't shit but a turn on for me, shorty." Allah told her grinning.

As cold as she was, Allah had actually been able to reach her where no other man had ever been able to and for a few months he and Nubia had actually been messing around.

"Fuck outta here," Nubia mumbled with attitude, but the smile she was trying to conceal gave her away.

"You guys been here long?" Essence asked, wiping a smudge from Junnie's cheek.

"Nah, we just got here too. Just been checking shit out. We aren't trying to cramp y'all style. I was just coming to tell you I got my eye on you," Junnie warned.

"You told me that earlier," Essence teased. "You sure that's the only reason you came over here?"

"And I came to tell you that ass is mine as soon as I walk through that front door tonight," he told her quietly.

"Now that's what I wanted to hear," Essence told him.

She gave him a deep kiss, letting all the surrounding men know who she already belonged to.

"I'ma have my eyes on your ass too. There's too many hoes in here tonight and I won't have any problem knocking a bitch on her ass."

"I'll be sure to let them know." Junnie winked and patted her on the ass before walking off.

****

Lil Banger sat on the plush sofa, with his feet raised on the table they had set up in the booth. More of his entourage had arrived to the club late and Alley had allowed a herd of women past the ropes, so now the VIP was packed with people bumping and grinding to the music. Mannie was walking around the club shaking hands and setting up meetings with important people who had showed up to the event.

Lil Banger accepted one of the many blunts that was circling the booth in rotation. A pretty redbone was sitting right next to him, so close she might as well had been in his lap.

He looked her up and down from behind his shades and was debating whether or not he should mess with her when a man suddenly walked into the booth.

"What's up everybody, how's everything going?" he asked clapping his hands.

He was a handsome man, with a wide smile and a mouth full of white teeth. The suit he wore fit perfectly, and the crisp creases let you know exactly how new it was.

Lil Banger looked at him, not sure who he thought he was just walking past security, until Manny walked up.

"Yo B, this is Marcus the owner. He's just coming through to make sure everything straight."

"Yeah, it's all good, fam," Lil Banger drawled, putting his hand on the redbones thigh.

She giggled and scooted closer, letting his hand travel around to her plush ass.

"That's good, I had my people set the VIP up as nice as possible for you," Marcus told him.

He looked at the table and noticed the half empty bottles of Dom Perignon.

"I'll have someone bring some more drinks over when I pass by the bar. You going to have everything you need for your performance?" Marcus checked his watch. "It's still pretty early so I'm thinking we should wait about another hour for everyone to get here, before you go up and burn the stage down."

"Yeah, that sounds straight," Lil Banger said, more focused on the girl beside him, then whatever Marcus was talking about. "When we got here, Manny let me know you was paying us a good amount for this show. Fifty grand, I think."

"Yes sir," Marcus grinned widely. "We'll have the check ready for you as soon as you're done with everything. That's the best way to end a night in my opinion."

Lil Banger turned his head in Marcus direction. His shades were still on so you couldn't tell exactly where he was looking.

"Ending the night with a hundred g's is the best way to end a night. In my opinion."

Marcus continued to smile, but now he looked confused. He looked from Mannie, back to Lil Banger.

"I don't understand."

"Instead of fifty grand, I'll take a hundred," Lil Banger announced. "You can either re-write the check, or I'ma sit right here and chill."

Now the smile had left Marcus face. He turned to Mannie.

"Is this dude playing?" he asked, jerking his thumb at Lil Banger. "Mannie, I don't know what the fuck you two are playing at but we have a contract. There's no negotiating. If your boy backs out of this then you all need to get the fuck out of my spot, and the next time you'll see me is in court."

"Hold on, Marcus, the boys had a little bit to drink and he ain't thinking straight," Mannie said apologetically. "Give me a minute to talk to him."

"Yeah, you do that," Marcus snapped.

He gave Lil Banger a dark look before walking out of the booth. Mannie turned his angry gaze to Lil Banger who didn't look fazed about anything.

"What the fuck do you think you're doing?" he barked, kicking a stool out of the way as he walked over to his nephew. "You been smoking that shit again?"

"Check it, look at all these people in this muthafucka." Lil Banger waved his hand around the club. "Do you really think this shit would be popping like this if it wasn't for me?"

"Hell no!" Alley called, burying his face in a female's neck, and causing her to giggle.

"Exactly. That niggas getting paid off of me, fifty grand doesn't make me feel appreciated. Either he can up the pay or we can get the fuck out of here. Don't trip, Mann. He'll cash out."

"You dumb ass little nigga. Do you know what a contract is? It's a binding legal document, and if we don't abide by it we won't be worrying about him paying us any money. We'll be coming out our pockets to pay his ass." Mannie shook his head at Lil Bangers logic. "Listen, I'ma go smoke a cigarette and get some air. By the time I come back I expect you to be ready to go on stage."

Lil Banger watched as Mannie walked off mumbling to himself. Not paying him any attention, he moved off the redbone chick and reached for the blunt he was being handed. Alley pushed away from his chick and sat next to his friend.

"You really ain't about to perform?"

Lil Banger shrugged. "Probably, but this nigga better raise my pay check a little higher."

Hitting the blunt he looked around the club. He was about to tell Alley something but stopped when his eyes landed on a light skinned chick sitting at a nearby table.

She was laughing at something her friend was saying, and sipping on a colorful drink. Lil Banger watched her for a minute. He had so many of the baddest females throw themselves at him that he had grown use to it, but this chick was a different type of sexy. She had yet to even look in his direction and she was only a few tables away, which drew him to her even more.

"Yo, check that bitch out right there," he said, interrupting whatever Alley was saying.

"Where?" Alley asked, looking through the crowd.

"Light bright right there at the table."

Alleys eye's landed on the chick. "Yeah, she's bad, I noticed her earlier. You don't want her though. She seems like one of those stuck up bitches. She's been turning niggas away since she's been there."

"That's because none of these square ass niggas are me." Lil Banger said, staring at her hungrily. "Go get that bitch and bring her over here," he demanded, tapping Alleys arm.

"Man, c'mon fam. We got bitches right here," Alley pointed out, motioning to the women that currently occupied the booth.

"Fuck these hoes," Lil Banger said, not caring if the females were offended or not. "Go get that female and bring her over here."

Alley let out an impatient groan before getting up and leaving the booth.

****

Junnie made it back to the bar to find that their stools had been taken and Harlem was nowhere to be found. Allah went to the restroom, and Junnie knew as packed as it was, it would be a minute before they met again. Rapping his knuckles on the counter, Junnie signaled for another drink. As he waited he looked up just in time to see a familiar face walking in his direction.

"My nigga Jun, what it do, dawg?" Polo greeted, grinning from ear to ear.

He had a blunt in one hand and a drink in another. His entourage consisted of a gang of hard faced young men and a few chicks that looked like they belonged in a rap video.

"What's good homie?" Junnie greeted, genuinely happy to see his old friend.

He and Polo went back to days before either one of them even considered running the streets. They had been solid before Junnie had met Harlem, or even Allah.

They would have probably remained as close, until Polo decided to get down with a different crew. Once Polo became a part of Calvin Cole's inner circle, he and Junnie fell out of touch, but there were no ill feelings towards each other.

"Shit, you know me. Still out here trying to get this money," Polo said, his crooked grin still intact.

"You shouldn't have any problem there. I figured having the boss of the city as a big homie would have its perks," Junnie said.

Polo laughed. "Yeah, it's a nice setup, but best believe I work hard for all of it."

"Oh, trust me, I'm not doubting your G, my nigga. We've rolled out together on more than a few trips," Junnie reminded him of the times they had caused havoc on some of the locals.

"You ain't lying," Polo chuckled, shaking his head, "but from what I've been hearing you're still out here rocking niggas to sleep."

"I'll get at a nigga every once in a while if he deserves it," Junnie replied modestly.

"I know you would, that's why I'm saying, when you gonna get down with the Family?"

Back when Polo had first found out that he would be a simple soldier for the family, he had tried to get Junnie to go with him, but Junnie had other plans.

"I've been thinking about making some changes in some areas. I don't know if that's the one I need though."

"C'mon bro, my dude Calvin is the biggest don to run this shit in the past century. We could use somebody like you, Jun."

"Yeah, well you know 'me' is a team now. I don't go anywhere without my brothers."

"Shit, bring them too. I've heard stories about your boy Allah, and Harlem's a bonafide lunatic. We'll take them too."

One of Polo's men walked up and whispered something to him which Polo nodded to in response.

"Aye, I gotta run bro, but you still got my number?"

"No doubt," Junnie replied, giving Polo dap and pulling him in for a half hug.

"A'ight, get in touch with me when you want to start making big moves out here. I'ma holler at my people about it."

"I hear you," Junnie replied.

He watched as Polo and his people disappeared into the crowd. Back by himself, Junnie took to surveying the club.

He had spotted a few people he had beefs with in the past, but so far they hadn't given him a second glance. Still, he made sure to keep a close eye on them.

Accepting his drink, he paid the bartender and told him to keep the change. Before he could raise it to his lips, someone tapped his shoulder. Junnie turned around and was surprised to see who it was.

"I'm guessing you lost my card," Asia smiled at him.

She was looking stunning in a purple dress that looked more like a shirt that she had just pulled past her waist.

It hugged her body like a second skin, showing off every curve she had, and Junnie would be lying if he said it didn't make him feel some type of way.

"Nah, I just been busy. Nothing personal," Junnie told her.

He finished his drink and set the glass down. He had collected a nice buzz from the cognac, and it was feeding him thoughts as he found himself looking at Asia's nipples poking through the dress. Shaking his head Junnie hurried and looked away before she noticed.

"I wasn't expecting to see you here."

"Of course I'll be here. Me and Banger have worked together on a few projects. You didn't see his last video? It's been number one on the countdown list for the past two weeks."

"I honestly haven't followed the rap scene for a while, ma. It all sounds the same to me."

"Yeah, it kinda does." Asia agreed. She licked her glossy lips as she looked him up and down. "You want to dance?" she offered.

"Nah, I don't think I should," Junnie answered, even though the bulge in his pants was saying different.

Asia looked at him suspiciously, then a look of realization crossed her face. "You must be here with your girl," she said slyly.

"Nah, I'm here with my niggas, but she is here too." Junnie clarified.

Asia nodded slowly, walking towards him until she was close enough to smell the peppermint on her breath.

"Junnie, quit playing with me," she said, pulling at his flannel. "You know what I want. Ain't no female you've been with put it on you like I used to. Just let me get the dick tonight and I'll be out of this state tomorrow. You won't have to see me anymore."

Junnie was quiet as he stared in Asia's eyes. His sensible mind was telling him to walk away but the liquor was clouding his better judgment and soon he found himself considering what it would be like to be inside Asia's sweet walls just one more time.

Asia was smiling mischievously, thinking she had finally got him. Junnie was getting ready to tell her to beat it before they both got their asses whoop when something caught his eye.

Looking towards Essence's table there seemed to be some sort of commotion happening. When he seen who was in the middle of it Junnie's face hardened, and he was immediately sober.

Leaving Asia standing in confusion, Junnie pushed people out of the way as he rushed across the room.

20

Essence and Nubia were having a good time sipping on their drinks, watching everyone in the club. Nubia was a professional when it came to pointing out something wrong with someone that passed by.

She clowned on dudes from their jewelry to their mismatched outfits and their outdated sneaker game. The females didn't stand a chance. She had just begun a roasting session on a female that looked as if she were in her mid-fifties, when a young looking man walked up to their table.

He was nice looking, but he had the swag of a cocky dude as he stood next to them smiling.

"At ease ladies," Alley greeted smoothly. "How y'all doing tonight?"

"Fine," Nubia answered for the both of them. She stared him up and down as if she didn't understand why he was there. Alley gave her a look but turned his attention to Essence.

"My man would like a word with you," he told her, pointing towards the booth.

There were so many people in the section she didn't know who he was talking about.

"And who would that be?" she asked, looking but not seeing anyone that was paying them any attention.

"The black ass one with the dreads." Alley pointed again.

The crowd shifted and they could see Lil Banger sitting on the couch, staring in their direction. He raised his hand in a small salute.

"Oh hell no," Nubia said frowning. "Tell him we're good."

"I know you are because he wasn't asking for you," Alley snapped, not liking her attitude. "He's asking for your girl."

"Tell him that's okay," Essence said politely, as Nubia's nostrils flared open. "And for future reference, if he wants to talk to a woman that's a real lady, he should come do the talking himself, not sending for her like she's one of these groupies."

"I hear you shorty," he snickered, turning and walking back to the booth.

Essence laughed once he was gone and Nubia shook her head.

"These rap niggas are a trip," she said, going back to her drink.

"Did he really think I would go over there?" Essence asked amused.

"He's probably use to it." Nubia looked up. "And he's hard at hearing from the looks of it." Nubia nodded towards the booth and Essence turned in time to see Lil Banger and Alley coming back over.

"What's good with you ma?" Lil Banger drawled out, grinning lazily. "My nigga told me you denied my invitation."

"Yeah, I did. No offense, but I'm pretty sure my husband wouldn't approve." Essence told him, still being polite.

"Husband, huh?" Lil Banger snickered. Licking his lips, he stroked his chin hair. "Well how about you roll out with me and my people tonight and I'll have you home before your nigga even misses you."

"Nah, I'm alright. I'm actually leaving here with my man but, thank you though. I appreciate it." Essence raised her glass. "Have a good performance."

"Told you this bitch was stuck up," Alley laughed from the side.

"Bitch?" Essence repeated, all sweetness gone from her voice now.

"Don't mind him, he's retarded." Lil Banger said. He reached out and grabbed Essence's hand. "Listen, just come over..."

"Fucks wrong with your ears nigga?" Nubia said, finally having enough. "You didn't just hear her say she's in here with her man? Why don't you quit being a thirsty ass nigga and go fuck on them groupie bitches you already have at the table?"

Lil Banger's face slowly turned to anger as he glared at Nubia. "You know who the fuck I am, shorty? Do you really think I give a fuck about her nigga?"

"Probably not, but you should."

Everyone turned around to find Junnie standing there with a scowl on his face. He watched Lil Banger the whole time he approached.

"We got a problem over here?" he asked calmly.

"No baby, we're good. He was just leaving." Essence stood up and walked over to Junnie.

She felt disrespected by the way Lil Banger and his friend had come at her, but she knew if she told Junnie, the situation would escalate into something else.

"No the fuck I wasn't," Lil Banger said loudly, not worried about Junnie's arrival. "I wasn't done asking you to come roll out with me tonight."

"She's good, homie, but thanks for the offer," Junnie said evenly, fighting to keep his anger in check.

Lil Banger grinned smugly as he stared Junnie in his eyes.

"You must be the nigga, coming over here like you big and bad," he said, while Alley laughed in the background. "You came just in time, dawg. Your girl was about to get snatched up by a real nigga."

"You sure you got enough bodyguards with you to be talking that shit, homie?" Junnie asked, gently moving Essence out of the way.

People standing nearby eagerly began to run and tell anyone they could about the altercation that was taking place.

Essence grabbed Junnie's arm. "Baby, it's really not that serious," she pleaded. "Let's just go."

Lil Banger sneered. "Yeah, you better take your bitches advice, my nigga."

Junnie took a step towards him, and Alley hurriedly stepped forward, raising his sweater.

"You better think twice about that, nigga," he cautioned, showing the butt of his gun.

Junnie stopped in his tracks. He looked at the gun and slowly nodded. "You're right, homie," he agreed.

Lil Banger opened his mouth to add a smart remark, but before he could get it out Junnie's hand had reached across the table and slapped his glasses off.

Before he had time to realize what had happened, Junnie threw a punch that swept him off his feet and sent him crashing through the table behind him.

Alley made to move but an arm wrapped around his neck from behind and began to squeeze the life out of him. Alley struggled for air, as Allah began to apply pressure.

"I know you wasn't thinking about popping off at my brother, right?" he growled in Alley's ear, dragging him across the floor.

Alley tried to reach for his gun, but couldn't reach it as he was lifted from the floor. Junnie was standing over Lil Banger, stomping on every inch of his body he could.

"Who the fuck you trying to play nigga?" he barked, kicking him in the head. "You know what it is."

"Junnie, stop!"

Junnie spun around ready to swing on whoever was grabbing his arm, but he froze when he realized it was Essence.

Looking over her shoulder, he saw the bouncers forcing their way through the crowd to reach them.

"Lah, let's get it!" he yelled to his partner, who now had Alley pleading for help.

Allah gave one last squeeze before tossing Alley to the side, head first into the wall. By this time, Lil Bangers crew had realized something was wrong, and were running towards them from the VIP section.

Junnie looked back and forth between the entourage, and the bouncers, both coming from different directions. They were trapped. Allah noticed too, which prompted him to pull his gun from his jeans and aim it in the air. He pulled the trigger sending the club into pandemonium.

Junnie forced his way through the herd of people rushing for the exit. In the commotion he had managed to slip the securities sight, but he also lost Allah. Deciding to find him and Harlem later, Junnie pushed people out of the way, dragging Essence close behind. Seeing the red emergency exit towards the back Junnie fought for freedom, going the opposite direction of everyone else.

Pushing open the door he ran down the empty hallway, while Essence stumbled along in her high heels. She was asking a billion questions per minute but Junnie didn't have time to answer them.

Without slowing down, he kicked open the exit door at the end of the hallway and they stumbled into the cool night air. They were outside the back of the club, but could hear the screams and shouts coming from the front entrance.

Essence was breathing hard, while Junnie checked their surroundings. More gunshots went off and women screamed loudly as car tires could be heard burning rubber through the streets.

Junnie wished he had brought his gun as he heard people arguing and fighting on the other side of the building. He was prepared to go all out if he ran into any of Lil Bangers crew, but the scale would be tipped extremely if they were running up with guns, and all he had was his fist.

"I have to go back for Nubia!" Essence said suddenly.

She had been so preoccupied with Junnie beating on Lil Banger, and the threat of him getting jumped, that she momentarily forgot about her best friend.

Before Junnie could reply someone came crashing out of the side door, looking around wildly. His face turned angry as he spotted Junnie. He was one of the dudes who had been sitting in the VIP with Lil Banger.

"What's up, nigga," he said, stepping completely outside the door.

He opened his mouth to say something, but before he could get the chance Harlem suddenly appeared right behind him and punched him in the back of the head, sending him flying forward and crashing to the concrete for a nap.

"Bitch ass nigga," Harlem mumbled, spitting on the unconscious man. He looked up at Junnie. "I saw you guys heading for the exit, and seen this faggot chasing you. Niggas always trying to be a hero. What the fuck just happened in there?" he asked, pointing towards the exit door.

"Nothing, just a little disagreement," Junnie said. "You see Allah?"

"Yeah, and you fools call me the wild one." Harlem laughed. "That nigga was in there throwing tables at muthafuckas and shit like it wasn't nothing. The bouncers came through pepper spraying everything moving, and I saw him duck off with your girl," he told Essence.

"Thank God," Essence breathed a sigh of relief, knowing that her friend would be in good hands.

"We got to get out of here," Junnie said, glad that he had at least decided to drive his own car to the club.

"What about Lah and his shorty?" Harlem asked.

At times he and Allah seemed as if they hated each other but at the end of the day, that was his brother.

"Nubia drove her car here. They'll be fine,' Essence told him.

"Shit, let's shake then."

21

Over the next few days, the news of Lil Banger getting slapped was the topic of almost every discussion worldwide. The cell phone footage of the event had found its way to every media outlet possible from the evening news to Worldstar Hip-hop.

Since he had first arrived on the scene, Lil Banger had put out an image as being the baddest dude to ever touch a mic, so it was needless to say that his record sells were going to see a decline. To top it off, Junnie now had this situation with Seven being shot to deal with. With his little brother's track record, it was no surprise that someone wanted him dead.

Seven had crossed a lot of people in his few years running the streets, so it was going to prove difficult to find the shooters, but Junnie planned to get to the bottom of it.

"Yo, it was funny at first but now I'm tired of hearing about it," Harlem announced.

He was sitting at the table, focused on his cell phone. MTV was on the television screen showing the video of Lil Banger getting stomped into the club's floor by Junnie. You couldn't see Junnie's face in the video but for anyone who knew him it was easy to tell who it was.

"You're tired?" Junnie shook his head.

He was lounging on the couch with his arms crossed across his chest as he watched MTV go over the same story it had been for days. Beside him, Allah was smoking a blunt and watching the television with red hooded eyes.

"I never wanted this shit out there like that in the first place."

Since the altercation, Junnie had been at the house laying low. Word was the police were looking for him for the fiasco at the club. If they were indeed looking for him, it would be a hard task for them to accomplish. Junnie was a phantom when it came to being on the police radar.

"Nigga, what the fuck did you expect to happen when you smack one of the biggest rappers in a crowded ass club?" Harlem scoffed. "Don't trip though, they don't even know it was you."

"Maybe not the police, but everyone else in the hood do," Allah pointed out.

"Who gives a fuck about them? If anything they look at June as a hero. He exposed that bitch ass nigga, it needed to be done." he shrugged.

"I guess," Junnie said, checking the clock hanging on the wall.

Essence would be on her way from work in a couple of hours and he didn't want to be there when she arrived.

Since the club she had been nagging him more about staying out of the streets. She was scared that someone was going to retaliate from all the publicity that the situation was gaining.

Junnie cherished the fact that she was worried about him, but the streets were his home and he grew tired of telling her that. He had been through too many battles to let hurt pride from a low rate rapper scare him off.

"Yo June, you my man fifty grand, but I'm not trying to sit in this hot ass house all day," Harlem complained, turning off his phone and setting it on the table. "Let's get back out here and show our faces. I was talking to my guy Premo and he said it's going down on Sixty-First tonight. They 'bout to be going dummy at the sideshow."

Allah gave him a stupid look. "Dawg, after what just happened you want to take this nigga to a crowded ass public gathering? You don't realize that this nigga Banger still has family out here right?"

"Hell yeah I realize that but what you don't seem to realize is I don't give a fuck," Harlem said harshly. "Fuck him and his fam, they ain't built solid. What the fuck you trying to do tonight, go on a movie date or some shit? I'm trying to go out here and get shit crackin'. Besides, we can get a drop on whoever tried to get at li'l bro."

"Nah, I'm trying to avoid taking my brother somewhere where he could get shot," Allah spat back.

As the two continued arguing, Junnie stood and stretched. He walked over to the window and peeked out the blinds. The sky had turned a dark orange as the sun began to set over the horizon.

Junnie wasn't scared to go into the streets, but that didn't mean he was dumb enough to put himself in a dangerous situations either.

Still he couldn't deny that he was curious to see the hoods response to seeing him. For the past few nights he had been receiving texts from everyone asking if he had really stomped out Banger.

It was just like Harlem had said. People actually admired him for beating up the rap games bully. Even though Junnie had went at Banger for legitimate reasons, he couldn't help but see what fame had come with it.

"Yo, it's all good."

He turned to his bickering friends who had somehow got on the topic of Harlem owing Allah some money.

"Let's go out to the show for a minute just to see how it's looking. I could use some fresh air."

Harlem's gold grin stretched widely across his face. "My nigga, my nigga," he said patting Junnie on the back. "About time you listen to me and not this pooh butt muthafucka." he jerked his thumb in Allah's direction.

"You niggas ain't got no sense," Allah mumbled, hitting the blunt again.

Junnie went and plopped down next to him. "You know I'ma always take your advice over Harlem's dumbass."

"What?" Harlem cried out.

"But I've been cooped up in this house longer than my endurance can take, cuddy. I'm trying to get out here and vibe. Besides, if something goes down I got the silent assassin watching my back, right?"

Allah laughed. "I got you all day, no questions asked."

"Alright then." Junnie stood to his feet. "Let's get ready to get out here then.

****

The heat had been coming down in the streets the past few days, with five murders within the week. Seven and Angel knew they had to get at Rango and his crew but they also weren't dumb.

With the police stopping every black man walking the streets they decided to let things cool down for a couple days before they made their next move.

Seven decided it best to stay in the house, and only left for store runs. They had had a shootout in broad daylight and he knew that the cops might be on their trail so he was playing it cool. This gave him time for his arm to heal, but more importantly it gave him time to catch up with Bobbi.

They've talked on the phone frequently, more than any time since they've become friends. Seven had always had a thing for Bobbi, but never acted on it until recently.

He found himself distracted thinking of her, which he wasn't sure if it was a good or bad thing.

A few days after the shootout Seven was chilling in the house with Angel and one of the homies from the hood named Crow. They were crowded in the living room, smoking like it was going out of style, and going over a way to get at Rango and his clan of misfits.

Seven listened to Angel's latest idea, while he rubbed his arm. They had cleaned the injury the best they could but afterwards they went to an older cat known simply as "The Surgeon" in the hood.

He was an ex-military soldier who could patch you up just as well as a professional doctor. He stitched Seven up and bandaged the arm pretty neatly. It was still in pain but the constant weed smoking gave Seven moments of peace.

"I'm telling you bruh, we need to get a move on these niggas," Angel grumbled, tapping ash of the end of the blunt.

He had been ready to move on Rango and Holly the same day they had zoomed off in their car, but Seven had to be the voice of reason.

"We will, but we're not gonna risk getting booked over it," Seven explained again. He hit the blunt, tilting back in his chair. "Rango's going to get pushed back, and Holly's going to get done dirty, best believe. Just be patient my nigga."

"If y'all need help just let me know. I never liked that nigga Rango anyway." Crow declared.

Crow was a tall lanky kid, with large droopy eyes, and wild dreadlocks that stuck in every direction.

Seven and Angel smoked weed frequently, but Crow was a notorious pothead. He smoked blunts like cigarettes and probably hadn't been completely sober since he was eleven. He was known more for being laid back than he was for beefs or drama.

"Stick to rolling the blunts, zig zag man," Angel told him, tossing him a zip-lock bag full of weed. "As for this 'being patient' shit, it's getting real old. We gonna be in this house for weeks if we wait for the punk ass police to quit using their Tasers on niggas."

Seven shook his head as his phone vibrated. Checking the text message, a smile formed on Seven's face as he typed a reply. When he looked up he found Angel watching him suspiciously.

"Fuck you looking at?" Seven asked.

"You been acting different lately," Angel observed, rubbing his chin. "I think you holding out on yo' boy. There's only one reason you over there grinning at your phone like that, my nigga."

He and Crow exchanged knowing looks and smiled at the same time. "Pussy" they said together.

"And if he's grinning like that it's probably some new pussy," Crow theorized wisely.

"Either that or she just got some bomb punanny," Angel cracked, before they both started laughing.

"You niggas wild," Seven stood to his feet. "You busters need to go get you some ass and stop scratching your heads over if I am or not. On that note, I'm about to get up outta here. Hold down the fort for a little bit."

"Just tell me, do I know her?" Angel asked curiously.

"It ain't even that serious to find out if you do, or you don't."

Angel chuckled, hitting the blunt. "If you need some rubbers I got a few in the room back there," he called as Seven shut the door.

****

Bobbi had been busy the past few days, taking care of business. She had been working steadily and had taken a day off to get enrolled in community college.

Tavae would usually come visit at night and they, along with Charity would sit up talking and laughing. When she wasn't with them she was usually talking to Seven.

He had been like the sunshine gleaming through a dark cloud with getting past Xavier. She wasn't sure when they decided to start getting serious but it seemed like they were.

Xavier had been blowing her up non-stop the first couple days, but not to any success. Bobbi ignored every call and text that came her way. With Seven around it was easy to.

Sitting on her couch Bobbi watched Love and Hip Hop, while she patiently waited. Charity had decided to go spend the night out with Charles, and Tavae had went on a date with a guy she had met a few days prior. With everyone with their men Bobbi wanted to have some male attention as well.

That's why she tried to contain her smile when she heard the knock on the door. Going to answer it, she opened the door and smiled. Seven was standing there, a small grin on his face.

"About time," Bobbi said, giving him a hug.

"I couldn't rush over. Had to let it marinate." He told her. Stepping inside the house, Seven peeked back out the door before Bobbi closed it. "Where's Moms at?"

"She went out for the night with her boyfriend. I don't think she's coming back until the morning." Bobbi led the way to the couch and they sat down.

"Yeah Ms. Charity's wild. I went to the casino a couple weeks back and she was there going ham on the dealer. She's a tough one." Seven looked down at the coffee table and smiled. There was a nice sized pile of weed, along with two swishers, and a lighter, all perfectly aligned. "You went and got the party favors, huh?"

"Well you're a pothead so I figured I should look out for you. If I knew you liked Minute Maid, I would have a glass of orange juice waiting for you."

"I wish you had, because I'm thirsty as hell."

"Really, you want something to drink." Bobbi stood up and went to the kitchen.

"Yeah, you got some Jack Daniels?"

Bobbi's eyebrows raised. "Oh you're trying to get turned up already huh?"

"Believe it or not alcohol chills me out."

Bobbi checked the cabinet to see what they had. "Will Vodka give you the same effect?"

"I don't usually do the light, but I'll take it if that's all you got." It was hotter in the house than Seven thought it would be. He pulled his sweatshirt off just as Bobbi came back in the room with the bottle and two glasses.

"I'm not usually a drinker but..." Bobbi stopped when she noticed Seven's heavily bandaged arm. "Oh my God, what happened?"

"With what?" Seven asked, then remembered his arm.

He had gotten used to the bandages and forgot they were there.

"I got shot a couple days ago," he said, reaching forward to pick up one of the swishers.

He was so nonchalant about it; you would have thought he had just told her he had broken a nail.

"You got shot?" Bobbi asked in disbelief. "Are you okay? Why the hell aren't you in a hospital right now?"

"It wasn't that bad. Just a flesh wound. I put a Band-Aid on it," Seven joked but Bobbi didn't laugh.

Instead she sat the bottle and glasses on the table and looked at him seriously.

"I'm worried about you Seven," she started.

"For what?" Seven asked, playing dumb.

"You know for what. I've been hearing about you being out here in the streets since we were in sixth grade. You've always done your thing but we both know it can't last."

"I don't intend it to," Seven replied. "But me stopping to go get a regular job and squaring up isn't an option either. This is who I am, B."

"No its not, you are so much more, Seven. You're just letting this street shit block you from it all. I believe you can do a lot more than you are though."

Seven nodded as he looked at Bobbi. "You're right, I could but I need help being pushed in the right direction. I need you there with me."

Bobbi's face twitched as a small smile formed on her lips. She turned away from him and prepared to pour the drinks.

"You're just talking right now."

"Nah, I'm serious. I've been thinking about you a lot lately, and..." Seven tried to find the right words. "I don't know, I want us to try and form something. Something real."

Bobbi looked up to see if Seven was serious. His face was blank but there was a look in his eyes that screamed sincerity.

"I don't think I'm ready for that," Bobbi told him. "I just broke up with Xavier."

"Fuck that nigga," Seven said, almost angrily. "That was a waste of time. You gave your all to a nigga that didn't deserve one percent of it. I'm not going to lie, I've never been in a real relationship before..."

"Then how do you know this is what you really want?" Bobbi asked anxiously.

"I don't know, it's hard to explain." Seven hesitated as he tried to get his words together. "When I'm not talking to you I'm thinking about you. When I finally go to sleep at night I'm thinking about you.

Ever since that day I gave you a ride from across town, you've been on my mind. I find myself thinking about having you to myself." Seven moved closer and Bobbi found herself staring into his pale gray eyes. "I really care about you," he said softly.

A rush of emotion flooded through Bobbi at that simple sentence. The way he said it meant more to her, than if anyone else had told it to her. Bobbi liked Seven and had considered a relationship with him, but after seeing how serious he just was it was pretty much confirmed that she wanted him.

"Seven, I..."

She was interrupted by Seven as he planted a tender kiss on her lips. Bobbi closed her eyes as her heart began to race. They kissed for a few seconds before Bobbi pulled away.

Standing slowly, she grabbed Seven's hand and pulled him up. No words needed to be spoken. They both knew what time it was. Leading the way Bobbi took Seven up to her room where he stayed for the remainder of the night.

22

Calvin Cole sat in the diner, eating his deli sandwich and skimming through the newspaper he had laid on the counter.

A couple of his goons were situated in the nearby booths, involved in their own discussions. They were all waiting for the arrival of Johnny, who was nearby taking care of business with a potential associate.

Since he was an outsider who had just moved up there from Florida, Johnny suggested he go by himself to meet the guy just in case the dude tried to bust a move.

Polo came from the restroom, drying his hands. He tossed the paper towels at his homies and exchanged playful chatter before reaching Calvin's table.

"I see why you like this diner so much," he said, munching on the remainder of his fries. "That bathroom is nice as hell. It's the first public one I actually sat my ass on."

Calvin looked up from his paper and frowned.

"Did you really think I wanted to hear that shit?"

Polo shrugged. "Just keeping it real." he announced as he chewed his fries.

His eyes wondered to the television screen.

"They been talking about this shit for like a week," he said nodding towards the news story.

Calvin reluctantly looked up from his newspaper to see a picture of Lil Banger being shown.

"What's this? That shit that happened at the club the other night?" he asked, listening to the story coverage.

"Yep yep, I was right there when it happened."

Calvin shook his head. "You don't listen about going to all these fucking events, huh?"

"No sir," Polo grinned. "But even if it had turned bigger than it already was, I would have been straight. That was my nigga who put the hands on that buster."

"Who?"

"Junnie, you wouldn't really know too much about him. He's underground, tries to stay off everyone's radar. We go back to free lunch though."

"Yeah, well your free lunch buddy has me explaining to niggas how they could get touched even after I gave my word they would be unharmed while out here."

"What you mean?" Polo asked confused.

"That little nigga Banger's uncle Manny reached out to me before the show and I told him as long as he was out here on business, then I'd make sure that no harm came to them. Your best pal made my word look like shit," Calvin said calmly.

"You can't put all of the blame on Junnie though," Polo said sticking up for his old friend. "Word is, Bangers was coming at his girl on some real disrespectful shit."

Calvin gave Polo a stupid look. "So this muthafucka Junnie made me look bad over a bitch?" Calvin shook his head. "That's what's wrong with you little niggas today. More concerned about pussy than anything else. I might need to have Wolf go holler a this li'l dude."

"Hell no, that's my guy," Polo argued. "Believe me when I say he wasn't trying to step on your toes. Junnie ain't that type of nigga, big homie."

"Yeah, I hope not."

The door to the restaurant opened and Johnny strode in. Even though the streets were experiencing a heat wave, he was still dressed in all black, from his shades down to his boots. He nodded at the soldiers as he passed their table but didn't say anything until he reached Calvin.

"How'd it go?" Calvin asked, setting the newspaper to the side.

"It was decent. Ol' boy was talking like he had some sense. When I let him know how much he stands to profit working with us he let it be known he wasn't trying to come muscle anybody out the way. He just wanted a piece of the pie."

"That is smart on his part," Calvin agreed. "Was his shit any good?"

"You know I don't do that shit, but luckily that fool Earl was walking past," Johnny said, referring to a notorious crack head. "He tasted the shit and really didn't have too much to say."

"It was that bad?" Polo asked.

"Nah, it was that good. Dude couldn't say anything. As soon as he sniffed it he started having a fit, sneezing and having spasms. When he did calm down he couldn't do much but give me a thumbs up."

Calvin grinned, hearing about the next product that would be added to his income.

"That's what the fuck I'm talking about. Looks like we're going to get them foreign bitches you like sooner than you think."

"Shonuff," Johnny nodded. "But ol' boy invited us to a little event he's throwing together later tonight. He said he's never been to a sideshow so he had some of his people put one together as soon as he got in town. He wants us to come through as his special guests."

Calvin frowned. "C'mon J, you know I don't be out here like that."

"Nigga, you know I already know that, but for the deal this nigga is throwing at us for the coke I figured the least we could do is show up to his little party. I'll be there, I know Polo's ass is gonna come."

"If there's music and weed then you already know I'm there," Polo said, performing a dance. Johnny stared at him before turning back to Calvin.

"And we'll take some of the young boys out with us," he finished. "So we'll be good for a couple hours."

Calvin pondered on it for a second. It had been a while since he had been out to a function, and it wouldn't hurt to get out and see what the event had to offer. In the worst case he could at least snatch up some bitches to bring back to the crib.

"Alright, let's do it," Calvin agreed, going back to his newspaper. "Oh, by the way, we just finished closing a deal with this new dude and I don't even know his name."

"It's some goofy shit. 'Shake 'Em Up'."

****

Ace stood in the dark den of a house, flicking his lighter open and close, staring out the window. Across the room, West was hitting push-ups, concentrating on the task they were preparing for.

They received the call they had been waiting on all day, now they were waiting for the person to show up.

Ace would be lying if he were to say he wasn't a little nervous, but you could never tell from his facial expression. His eyes remained calm as he watched the evening sky grow darker and darker as night drew near.

West finished his workout and stood to is feet. He had various scars across his body from different enemies who had attempted to take him out, but it was evident that none of them had succeeded.

He looked over to his best friend and felt the tension coming from him. Ace might have been good at hiding his feelings but West had known him almost all his life.

"You good, bro?" he asked, going to stand beside him.

"Of course I am," Ace responded calmly.

He was getting ready to attempt something that no one before him had ever succeeded at doing. Just that thought alone was enough to spook someone out of doing it, but Ace wasn't so easily swayed.

"Just preparing myself mentally."

"Don't even trip. We've planned this shit down to the T," West encouraged him. "Other people might have tried, but they don't have the heart that we got. That's what sets us apart from these faggot ass niggas. We're built Ford tough, through and through, feel me? And once we're running this shit this won't be shit but our success story."

Ace looked over at his best friend and seen the conviction in his eyes. West was ready to ride until the end, just as he had always been.

Before Ace could respond they heard footsteps leading down the stairs to where they were at. Rowdy walked inside the room, closely followed by three men.

"We made it, dun dun," Rowdy greeted, his wild dreads swinging every which way. Behind him was an old friend of Ace's that he hadn't seen in years.

When he was a kid, Ace's mom had sent him to live with his father for a few years in Florida, and it was during that rough patch of his life that Ace met Quintin.

Quintin had always been a special case, with a knack for violence you usually didn't find in an eleven-year-old, and as he gotten older it got worse. Now he was grown, with the physique of a body builder, and the killing skills of a trained mercenary. He also changed his name.

"My nigga Quintin." Ace walked over to greet him. "I see you made it safely."

"No doubt, you thought I wouldn't," Quintin drawled in his southern accent. "But don't start off our reunion but fucking up my name, family."

"Oh yeah, my bad." Ace grinned. "Shake 'Em Up, right?"

"Just Shake 'Em, if you're pressed for time." Shake 'Em motioned towards the two hard faced men behind him. "These are my extra muscle."

"You need extra?" West challenged, eyeing Shake 'Em's large arms.

"Can't be too safe," Shake 'Em grinned, showing his gold tooth.

"Wassup with y'all?" Ace nodded at them and the two men muttered responses. "How's shit been going in Dade County since I left? You still wearing the crown?"

"You thought I wouldn't be? Me and my squad been holding shit down for a minute, doing what we need to. Same ol' shit since you left."

"I'm glad to hear it, cuddy. Well I'm already knowing we need to catch up on old times but we should get a start on what I paid you to come out here and do."

Shake 'Em held up his hand. "You're too late, family. I already met up with your boy."

Ace's eyebrows raised in surprise as he and West exchanged similar expressions of surprise.

"You met with Calvin Cole already? Your plane just landed two hours ago."

"Aye, you offered me some bread to come out here and do some work, so that's what I intend to do. As soon as you called me I got the skinny on your boy Cole from my mans and them. They connected me with him and I hit him when I was on the plane. By the time I landed I had a meeting already set up with this cat Johnny.'"

"Damn," Ace said, impressed with Shake 'Em's efficiency. "Did they go for it?"

Shake 'Em snickered. "Not only am I doing business with them, but Calvin Cole's coming to my party I'm hosting later on tonight. If I were you, that's when I would make my move."

"That soon?" Ace frowned.

He had been planning on mapping out a more solid plan. He had the basis of how he wanted to execute his plot but he wanted more time to work out the finer details. Shake 'Em could sense his hesitation.

"Dawg if there's one thing I know from experience it's that sooners always better than later. If you really want this thing to happen I would do it first chance I got, which is tonight."

Ace rubbed his chin as he thought it over. He knew he was really hesitating because he didn't know whether or not they would succeed in their mission, but he had already set the wheels in motion by having all of them gathered together, ready to follow his orders.

Looking up he found every eye in the room focused on him, waiting on his reply.

"Fuck it," he said finally. "Let's do it. Calvin Cole dies tonight."

23

Junnie was in the middle of getting changed when Essence made it home. She came into the room, sniffing suspiciously.

"Allah was just here huh?" she asked, knowing where the strong scent had come from.

"About an hour ago." Junnie walked over and gave her a kiss. "They'll be back in a little bit to pick me up."

"Oh you're finally getting out of the house? Is that Li'l Banger crap still on TV?"

"A li'l bit, but that shit'll blow over," Junnie told her confidently.

He knew Essence was still worried about the situation with Lil Banger but, Junnie was used to it. Lil Banger was just another person added to the long list of people that would be more than happy to see him dead.

"We're about to go hit up this little shin-dig over on the east side. Nothing major."

"Okay, I'm probably going to stay in tonight. I've been feeling real shitty lately," she told him, laying down on the mattress.

"What's wrong?" Junnie asked, pulling his Dickies on. "Your head hurt?"

"Yeah, a little. I've just been feeling real nauseas lately. Like, I ate a sandwich earlier at work and threw it right back up. Plus, I've been feeling dizzy."

"Damn, you need some Advil baby?" Junnie tightened his belt before going to sit next to Essence on the bed. He rubbed her thigh as he looked at her with concern.

"No, you know I don't take medicine," Essence replied softly. "I'll probably just sleep it off."

"Want me to stay home? I don't have to go out tonight."

Essence looked at Junnie and smiled. "No you go ahead baby. You've been in this house for days. Go with your friends. Just don't be out too late. I need my special cuddle time."

Junnie laughed. "I wouldn't miss it for the world," he told her, planting a kiss on her forehead. Standing up he headed towards the bathroom. "Hey, maybe you're pregnant," he told her before shutting the bathroom.

Essence false smile slowly faded as she turned over on her side. She was feeling extremely ill, she had let on to Junnie, but she didn't want to ruin his night by having him worry about her. Without giving it a conscious thought, her hand slowly moved towards her belly and began to rub it.

"Pregnant?" she whispered to herself.

****

Seven sat in the passenger seat of the car, thoughtlessly rubbing his chin and staring across the street. His hood was pulled over his head, as he blew cigarette smoke from his nostrils. His objective was in the building only a few yards away, but his mind was completely somewhere else.

Beside him Angel was slouched in the driver's seat, staring intently at the apartment's entrance. He was quieter than usual as he waited patiently to make their move.

Angel had waited for as long as he could take to enact revenge and now their chance was here. He looked at his partner and noticed the troubled look on his face.

"You wanna talk about it?"

Seven looked over to find Angel looking at him. "Nah, I'm good," he said turning his attention back out the window.

"Sev, bruh, you know we go back to tag football on the playground. You can keep it funky with me." The sincerity in Angel's voice made Seven look at him again.

He searched for any sign of a smile or a wise crack forming but there were none. He finally decided to say something.

"Remember the other night when you asked me who I was fucking with?" Seven started. Angel nodded. "Well I have been fucking with someone and its getting kind of heavy. She got me in my feelings dawg, and I can't even front, I'm thinking about fucking with her on some deep shit."

"Ain't nothing wrong with that. You see I cuffed Shawna's crazy ass. So why you looking all depressed and shit?"

"I want to fuck with her but I don't think I can," Seven said what had been bothering him. "This chick deserves the best, you feel me, and what do I have to offer her? I'm a hood nigga, with a gun and a pocket full of money I snatched off some dude. No chick with a solid future wants that."

"Yeah, you might be right but, who's saying this?"

"What you mean?"

"Is she saying she don't want you because you're a hood nigga or are you saying what you think about yourself?"

"Well nah, she said she doesn't want me doing it anymore because she's worried about me but, she didn't say the other shit. It's just how I feel."

"So it sounds like to me you got a girl who's willing to ride with you, even if you ain't shit." Angel nudged his arm and they both chuckled. "Nah fa'real though, if she's still willing to try things out with you even when you're up to no good then she's going to ride with you through the good and bad, trust me. In the meantime, we'll stay out of trouble."

"Yeah, good luck with that," Seven grumbled, gripping his gun.

At that moment the apartment door across the street opened and a face poked out. The man looked around to make sure everything was clear before stepping out completely and heading on his way.

"Once we get this out the way you can ask for forgiveness," Angel told him, grabbing his shotgun from the backseat. "Let's wet this nigga first."

Together the two crept from out the car and edged along the sidewalk making sure they stayed out of the view of their target.

****

By the time Junnie and his crew made it to the 60th and Dewey the streets were packed and traffic was at a complete stop. It wasn't as crowded as it was at The Dawg House but, a lot of people had still come out to enjoy the festivities.

For those who didn't know, a sideshow was an event that was made up of people pulling off stunts with their vehicles or simply coming out to meet up and chill like a party.

Music, weed, and females were a must when throwing one. A lot of the times, rappers would come and set the shit off but, they weren't needed to make it a good time.

Allah and Harlem made their way through the crowd, speaking to everyone they came encounter with.

Junnie played the background, just checking out the different faces. None of them were hostile, but still, Junnie kept his hand close to his gun just in case.

"Damn, this shit is live," Allah commented, adjusting his beanie over his dreads.

"Nah fuck that. You didn't want to come remember?" Harlem reminded him, while he looked around.

He had smoked the whole car ride and was feeling his self. His shades where resting on the tip of his nose as he observed the scene from over the frames. He held a cranberry juice bottle in his hand that he had mixed with vodka before they had left the house.

"Don't worry about me nigga," Allah told him, nodding at a female he recognized. "You good June?"

"Always," Junnie replied.

They found an empty bench that held a front row seat to all the action and took a seat. The night sky was filled with the loud noises of wild thugs and laughing females, while different stereo systems played the latest hits as loud as their car volume would allow.

Junnie looked at the rowdy bunch of people assembled and couldn't help but think how uncomfortable white people would be in the presence of so many wild goons.

"Yo, y'all fucked up my plans at the club the other night but, I'm snagging one of these bitches tonight," Harlem told them, winking at a group of girls walking past.

"Don't put that on us. Just work on your game nigga," Junnie told him, while Allah laughed.

Before Harlem could snap on him there was a commotion as someone broke their way through the crowd.

"I thought that was you," Deray said, walking up to them. He shook all of their hands. "What's good with you niggas?"

"Just chilling," Allah answered coolly.

"Yeah me too. Its crazy out here, right? Aye, what happened at the meeting the other day?" Deray asked curiously. "When I got back Ace and them niggas seemed agitated."

"Nothing really, just a disagreement between parties," Junnie replied.

He was cool with Deray but Deray worked for somebody he wasn't cool with, so he didn't give too much information.

Deray nodded. "Yeah I figured it was something like that. Ace my dude but he be tripping sometimes."

Junnie made an approving noise but nothing else. Deray didn't seem to catch the hint because he continued talking.

"Yeah, I heard about that shit at the club. I was like damn. Everybody's been talking about that shit."

"What shit?" Junnie asked, playing dumb.

"That shit with Lil Banger," Deray replied like it should have been obvious.

Junnie looked at his crew. "Y'all know what he's talking about?"

"Nope," Allah said.

"Who's Little Banger?" Harlem asked, glaring at Deray.

Deray looked at all their faces and nodded in understanding.

"Oh my bad homie, I wasn't trying to be all in the business, my nigga. I was just saying."

"It's straight, homie. I'm just chilling right now so I don't really feel like discussing politics."

"I feel it, I feel it. I'll leave you alone gangster. See y'all around." Deray turned to leave and as he did, his smile vanished from his face.

As he pushed his way through the crowd he hurried to tell his boss who had turned up for the show.

Shake 'Em sat behind the wheel of the old Cadillac, Ace had lent him. He looked around at all the people gathered. In just a few minutes he had sent a text to his people and told them he wanted to set up a party, and they gladly obliged.

They contacted some people, their people contacted some people and pretty soon a full fledge block party had been created.

His boy Frosty was in the passenger seat, scowling and smoking a blunt while he watched the people crowding the block across the street. His hood was pulled on tight, only showing his red slanted eyes and nose.

"You already know. Dade County has the baddest bitches, hands down, but Cali ain't slacking when it comes to pussy," Omar drawled from the backseat.

He was peering through the tinted windows at the buffet line of women walking past.

"Aye Shake, I know we said we were going to be out here for a couple days but we might need to extend it for a li'l bit."

Shake 'Em looked in the rear view mirror at his younger comrade. "This ain't fucking spring break nigga. We got a job to do, and once we do it we don't have time to be sitting around here waiting for you to be getting some pussy."

"Waiting on that, we would be in Cali the next two months," Frosty snickered.

"Fuck you, nigga. When's the last time you even smelled pussy?" Omar shot back.

"When we went to that meeting with this nigga Johnny Welcome, or whatever his name is."

"Right on to that." Omar laughed and gave his homie dap. "If we lived out here that pussy ass boy or his man wouldn't be running this shit. We could shut this shit down if we brought the whole squad up here with us, Shake!"

"Omar, shut your dumb ass up," Shake 'Em told him. "We already got our own thing to take care of back home. Only reason we're up here is because Ace offered us a pretty dime to get at this nigga Calvin, so that's what we're going to do."

At that moment Shake 'Em's phone rang.

"Yeah?" he answered.

Listening for a second, he nodded before hanging up. Tossing the phone to the side he leaned forward in his seat and pulled his gun from his jeans.

Cocking the slide back, he narrowed his eyes as he scanned the crowded street for the red Impala the caller had told him to look out for. After a second he saw it coasting in his direction.

"Was that the call?" Frosty asked him.

"Yep, y'all get ready. It's about to go down," Shake 'Em told them, staring hungrily as the red Impala parked and the occupants stepped out.

24

Holly walked quickly, with his hands shoved deep in his pockets. He looked around the street as he walked, keeping his eyes open and aware of his surroundings. There was already a number of murders occurring and he had placed himself in the eyes of a killer. Needless to say he was on edge.

After the botched hit on Seven and Angel, Holly had decided to lay low. He knew that they had seen his face and he wasn't prepared for them to see it again anytime soon.

He had been hesitant in trying to kill the two boys in the first place and now he had good reason to. Seven and Angel were maniacs and everyone knew it.

Holly had been peeking around every corner he turned and he wouldn't relax until Seven was taken care of for good. Looking behind him Holly thought he saw something, He stopped walking and stared in the direction, but he decided it must have just been a shadow shifting from the trees.

He was relieved when he reached the corner store. Nodding at the man behind the counter Holly went inside the cooler and grabbed a six pack of beer.

He was deciding on which chips he wanted when he heard the chime of the bell over the stores entrance. He looked up in time to find two men rushing in. They both wore hoodies and had black bandanas wrapped around their faces.

"Get the fuck down!" the one with the shotgun yelled at the store clerk.

The store clerk instantly raised his hands and got down on his knees. The second masked man walked over to Holly and shoved his gun in his face.

"Holly, Holly, Holly," the man taunted. Holly stared into his cold gray eyes and knew what time it was. "Lesson one; when you run up on a nigga this is how you do it." Seven slapped him across the face with the butt of his gun.

Holly cried out as he crashed back into the shelves. Before he could fall, Seven grabbed him and began to drag him outside. Angel backed away, tossing a few hundred dollar bills on the counter top. Placing his fingers to his lips he signaled for the clerk to stay quiet before following Seven out.

Seven dragged Holly around the building and into a nearby alley. Holly tried to squirm away but Seven had a firm grip.

"Hold on, hold on, Seven." Holly began but a vicious slap to his face made him shut up.

"We're past talking, my nigga." Seven said calmly. Shoving him against the wall of the building Seven gave Holly another slap. "So you thought you would grow some balls huh?"

"It ain't even like that Seven." Holly quickly tried to explain. "After you ran up on Rango he told me he wanted to take care of y'all. I wasn't even trying to get into it with you, I swear. That was Rango's ass. Come on Sev, don't do me like this."

Seven couldn't help but laugh. Lowering the bandana from his face, he looked at Holly in the eyes.

"There's no use in begging. I'm not in the best of moods today." Seven raised his gun to Holly's face.

"Hold up, Seven! Hold up!" Holly covered his face with his hands terrified to meet his end. "I can—"

That's as far as he got before the first shot rang out. The bullet tore through Holly's cheekbone and the next two splattered his face. Seven stood over his fallen body and continued to empty the clip in Holly. Satisfied with his work Seven and Angel ran off into the dark.

****

Ace stood near the entrance of an alley watching the festivities. He leaned against the concrete wall with his arms crossed over his chest. His shades hid his eyes as he watched the local dread-heads stand on top of an escalade as it did donuts on the deserted street. People were cheering loudly as everyone got hype to an old E-40 joint. It was going to be the perfect cover.

West slowly walked up and stood next to him. They stood quietly for a minute, just taking in the event.

"I got word from Rowdy. Calvin Cole's already on the scene."

"Who he with?"

"Johnny, the young boy Polo, and a few other cats I can't name."

"They all in one car?"

"Johnny and Calvin are. A red Impala. The young boys are in a truck not that far behind. Rowdy said they just left a gas station on Fifty-Ninth, and are heading here."

"Good, that means they should be coming down this street," Ace said, glad that everything was working out so far.

Deray came up to them, grinning from ear to ear. Ace and West watched him come up quietly.

"Fucks so funny?" West asked once Deray had reached them.

"Guess who came out to the festivities?"

"I'm not in the mood for guessing games, Deray," Ace snapped, irritated.

"Your boy, Junnie."

"Really? I thought he was laying low after that club incident."

"Don't look like it. That niggas over there flossing with his boys right now."

Ace rubbed his chin thoughtfully. True, he was still feeling some type of way about Junnie's disrespect, but he was much more willing to enact his revenge on Calvin Cole and would meet up with Junnie another day.

West tapped his arm and Ace looked up to find a red Impala in the distance, slowly driving in their direction.

"What we do now?" West asked, watching Calvin Cole's vehicle drawing nearer.

"Now we do what we came here to do," Ace said, taking out his phone and placing a call.

25

Calvin Cole observed the crowd of people going wild at the outside show. People were running through the street, getting turned up as if they were at the club.

Even though their windows were rolled up the strong scent of weed still managed to find its way inside the vehicle.

"Yeah, these niggas got shit jumping off tonight," Johnny said, trying his best to drive through the crowd without hitting anyone.

"Yeah, it's popping off," Calvin said, looking out the window.

Before they had left his house he had had second thoughts about going to the sideshow. Sideshows were main events for drama to pop off at and Calvin Cole wasn't exactly a favorite name in everyone's household.

There were people that weren't too fond of him, which was why he made sure he had his Berretta tucked in his jeans.

"Don't trip bruh. All we're going to do is show our faces for a minute, show our respect towards this business deal, and we'll split. I'm trying to grab a bite to eat over at that restaurant on the eastside."

"Did that chick Tanisha ever hit you back?" Calvin asked, lighting a Newport.

"Oh I forgot about her bruh. I got something way better set up for us."

"Who?" he asked, turning towards Johnny.

Johnny smirked. "Don't trip, my nigga, just know that the chicks I got lined up will make you forget all about Tanisha and her raggedy ass sister. Trust me."

"You're crazy as hell, bruh," Calvin laughed.

The streets were packed so it took them awhile, but Johnny finally found a parking spot not that far from an alleyway. He pulled in and parked the car and they got out.

Polo and his crew pulled up in their black Tahoe alongside the car. The passenger window rolled down and Polo stuck his head out.

"Damn, big homie, you couldn't find somewhere that had enough room for all of us?"

"Lil nigga, do you not see how packed it is out here? You muthafuckas better drive up the block and see if they got anything."

Polo frowned and looked up and down the street.

"You sure? There's more muthafuckas out here than I thought. We should stick together."

"We're only going to be right here," Calvin said, smoking his cigarette. "We'll be good. Just park and bring your monkey ass on. No stopping to talk to these bitches out here."

"Don't trip, we'll be right back." he laughed.

He tapped the hood of the car and his driver drove forward.

"That kid loves the glamour life," Johnny shook his head.

"That kid is the future of this family," Calvin replied. "Polo has a good head on his shoulders, it's just weighed down with the immatureness of age."

"You ain't never lied," Johnny said, and they both laughed.

Walking across the street they headed towards the center of the event. A group of nearby girls seen Calvin approaching and their expressions were similar to seeing a celebrity.

They said his name and everyone standing near them turned around. Within seconds people were turning to see the young man who was known as a legend around town.

Johnny turned and grinned. "Looks like your fans came out today."

"You could say that."

Calvin wondered how many numbers he would be able to pull before they left, and that's when he suddenly remembered he left his phone in the car.

He had needed to charge it and had left it in the ashtray.

"Hold up bruh, I forgot my fucking phone." He jogged back towards the car.

"This nigga.' Johnny shook his head.

He turned towards the crowd but froze when he noticed something. The smile slid off of his face as he watched three men with Halloween masks running in their direction.

Before Johnny could pull his gun from his holster the man leading the pack lifted his gun and opened fire.

"Calvin!" Johnny yelled.

****

Harlem stood in his own zone, cap tilted, and rapping along with the lyrics to Mac Dre's song "California Bear".

"This that shit!" he yelled to his comrades, while he danced in an unsteady beat.

"Yeah, that shit do go hard," Junnie agreed, nodding his head as he sat perched on the park bench.

So far no one seemed to recognize him from the shaky cellphone footage that was being shown everywhere. He had relaxed a lot since they had first arrived, and was even sipping a drink from a plastic cup that Harlem had handed him.

"I would never whip my car out here for a show," Allah said, watching as a group of men hopped on a parked car and began to wildly swing their dreads to the music. "These fools be wildin' out."

"You ain't lying but, at least they're not being as bad as they were last time. Remember when we went to the one in Frisco?"

"Yeah and this nigga pushed the bitch down the stairs at the train station?" Allah shook his head.

Harlem abruptly stopped his dancing and started laughing.

"Nah, fuck that shit. That bitch was popping off, talking about she'll get her brother from Seminary to run up. That's why she took a trip down the fuck..."

Harlem's words were cut off as loud gunfire suddenly erupted through the air. The three jumped up, each reaching for their own weapon. Junnie watched as people began to run, looks of terror etched across their faces.

"What the fucks going on?" Harlem asked, sober within seconds.

"I don't know, but I doubt we want to stick around and find out," Allah said, tucking his gun beneath his shirt.

As soon as the words were out his mouth there was a fresh round of bullets, as a full shootout took place.

The crowd scattered and ran as far away from the danger as possible. Junnie tried his best to see what was going on but people were knocking him back as he tried to get a good look.

The only thing he could make out was men with hoods over their heads and masks on.

"Jun, let's roll before the bulls get here!"

Junnie looked back to find his friends already jogging away with everyone else. Glancing back at the commotion one last time, Junnie turned and took off at a brisk walk as people pushed around him to get away.

26

Calvin had almost made it to the curb when he heard Johnny shout his name. Looking up he noticed the three men in the middle of street.

The shot whizzed past Calvin's head but, the second one knocked him back into the car.

In an instant, bullets were surrounding him, as he grabbed his side where he had been hit. Just as the shooters drew closer they were forced to retreat as Johnny ran across the street, twin 9mms out and blazing as he charged on their attackers.

"Muthafuckas!" he yelled, not giving his triggers a break as he continued firing.

One of the shooters raised from his hiding place and let off with an AK. Wood splintered and glass shattered as the bullets ripped through parked cars and every tree surrounding the area. Johnny had no choice but to take cover behind a car as the shooter let loose on everything moving.

Seeing that his protector was momentarily distracted Omar crept towards Calvin's hiding place, prepared to pop his top but he was surprised when the man jumped up from the ground, Berretta at the ready.

"What's up nigga," Calvin spat before squeezing the trigger.

The bullet hit Omar in the center of his forehead, snapping his neck back and dropping him from the equation. Calvin looked for Johnny but didn't see him in the crowd of people.

With two more shooters on him, and no sign of backup Calvin turned and ran into a nearby alley, just as Shake 'Em and Frost opened a new attack.

Holding onto his side, Calvin ducked into the alley and began to speed down the empty runway. Even though he had been shot, his adrenaline still seemed to be functioning properly.

He was thinking of stopping to call Polo and the crew when something in his path caused him to trip and crash to the pavement.

Laying on the ground to catch his breath for a moment, Calvin looked up to find Ace step from the shadows. He wore a blank expression on his face as he stood over Calvin.

"You can't pay people to do anything right," he said softly, shaking his head.

Reaching in his jeans he pulled out his revolver and pointed it down at the kingpin.

"If you want something done right..."

Calvin glared up at him defiantly.

"You know your ass is done if you pull that trigger," he croaked.

"You think so?" Ace asked. "Guess you won't be around to find out."

He pulled the trigger, hitting Calvin Cole in the face. The next two shots made his face almost unrecognizable. Basking in what he had just done for a moment Ace stuck his gun in his pocket, before slowly jogging out of the alley.

****

Johnny continued shooting it out with the remaining two men. They exchanged shots back and forth, no one hitting anything. Just as Johnny was switching his clip a new round of gunfire started, loud enough to vibrate the concrete.

He looked behind him to find Polo and the rest of the gang running towards the altercation, guns out and blasting.

Realizing that they were outgunned, the two shooters sent a few more shots before turning and ducking into the sea of people.

Polo ordered for his boys to follow them, which they did without hesitation. Johnny on the other hand was far more interested in his comrade.

"O.G., what the fuck just happened? Are you hit?" he asked approaching Johnny.

"I'm fine, we need to find Calvin," Johnny demanded.

He ran to the place he had last seen Calvin. He found blood smeared on the door of a parked car, and the sprawled out body of one of the shooters.

Thinking that his friend simply made a run for it Johnny took off, searching the faces of everyone he passed, while Polo followed close behind.

Johnny glanced down an alley they were passing and seen something a few yards away. Skidding to a stop, he turned and ran down the alleyway, his stomach slowly sinking as he got closer to the large object on the ground.

As he drew near and seen the color of Calvin's shoes Johnny almost felt his heart stop beating.

"What the fuck!" Polo said, coming to an abrupt stop.

Recognizing the body sprawled out in front of him. His jaw dropped as he looked down at his leader, someone who had been like a big brother to him, obviously gone now.

Calvin looked up to the sky with unseeing eyes as Johnny slowly approached his best friend.

"Go get help, Polo," Johnny said, kneeling besides Calvin.

"But Johnny, let me…"

"I said go get fucking help!" Johnny yelled, a crazed look in his eyes.

Without another word Polo turned and ran as fast as he could back out the alley.

****

West stood on the sidewalk in front of the park, as he watched an ambulance and countless police cars arrive on the scene.

At least twenty minutes had passed since the first shot had been fired and after it was all said and done there were two bodies left to be picked up.

The first body was a young man that no one gathered around could identify. They had never seen him around before. But the second body was the one being talked about the most.

A gurney came wheeling through the crowd, with a sheet covering the whole body of whoever was underneath.

People wept and hugged each other as it was confirmed that Calvin Cole had been murdered in the shootout. It was going to be a sad day in history, but West could do nothing more than smile.

"My nigga really pulled it off," he mumbled to himself

Pulling his hood on tighter, West turned and prepared to go meet his friend at the rendezvous spot.

27

Rango was sitting in his house, chain smoking and nervously glancing at his watch. He had been sitting in the house waiting for Holly to show up but his partner hadn't been answering his phone and he was an hour late.

In the pit of his stomach, Rango knew something was wrong but, he wanted to hope for the best. He hadn't seen a hint of Seven or Angel since the shootout and he was thinking that they had decided to let the attempted murder go without retaliation.

He knew he was hoping but there was nothing wrong with that. With everything going on in the streets right now, Rango knew he was going to have to wait to try again on Seven's life. Rango was losing out on a lot of sleep while knowing that the young demon was out there somewhere.

"Yo, when we leaving?" Lynx asked, chomping on a turkey sandwich. He was seated on the couch, with his feet propped up on the glass table, dropping chips on his shirt as he stuffed his mouth.

"You wanna quit spilling shit on my fucking couch?" Rango snapped.

Lynx had been there all morning and had been working his nerves. He would feel a lot better when Holly came through.

"Shit man, I'm fucking hungry. I'm trying to go to the steakhouse and you got me in here eating ham sandwiches and shit."

"I don't got you doing shit. You can go where the fuck you want nigga, you're a grown ass man."

"Whatever man, you been on that emotional shit all day," Lynx told him angrily. "You want to act like a bitch then go ahead on your own time." Lynx took one more giant bite of the sandwich before tossing the rest on the table. "I'm out." Walking over to the front door Lynx prepared to leave. That's when a giant boom rocked the apartment.

Rango watched in horror as Lynx was blasted backwards and sent sailing through the air as the front door was blasted off the hinges.

A man stepped inside, dreads hanging and a bandana wrapped around the lower half of his face. It didn't take a rocket scientist to guess who it was.

Moving off instinct Rango grabbed his gun from the table and fired two shots at the intruder. Angel ducked and avoided the shots but that gave Rango a chance to run to the back room.

Slamming the bedroom door shut, Rango made it to the window and opened it up. He took one look behind him to make sure that Angel wasn't coming before crawling out the window and leaping down to the small platform.

He shimmied down the side of the building and jumped a few feet to the ground. As soon as his sneakers hit the pavement, Rango took off running.

He took another look behind him to make sure Angel wasn't coming and ended up crashing into something. His heart almost dropped when he realized that that 'something' was in the form of Seven, who was glaring at Rango.

"Going somewhere?" he asked coldly.

Rango tried to raise his gun, but Seven slapped it away with one hand and punched him in the face with the other. Rango stumbled, but came back with a swing of his own. Seven ducked and came up with a hard uppercut, which dropped Rango and took the fight out of him.

Angel caught up with them, breathing hard and looking around to make sure no one was watching. Rango stared up at them from the ground, breathing heavily. His gun was a few feet away where Seven had slapped it. As he looked at the two menacing faces staring at him, Rango knew it wasn't going to end nicely.

"I thought you was a killa but, you make a good track star too," Seven taunted, crossing his arms over his chest.

Angel kicked Rango across the face, causing the man to cry out.

"I thought you would be happy to see us. You were looking for us a few days ago, right."

"You niggas ran up on me first," Rango tried to reason. His nose was bleeding heavily, and his breathing was hard and ragged. "You know how it is."

"Yeah I know how it is." Angel kicked him in the face again. "You tried to play the role, now it's time to prove that shit. You came on our block."

Kick!

"Tried to dead us..."

Kick!

"And you think we give a fuck what you're talking about?"

"Come on, blood. Come on!" Rango tried to plead.

He jumped and tried to rush Angel but Seven hit him in the back of the head with the butt of the gun. Rango crumpled back to the ground, blood covering his face and almost out of consciousness.

"You know there's no use in talking about it," Seven told him calmly. "I've went head to head with harder niggas than you, so this isn't much of a victory."

"Seven man, I'm sorry." Rango pleaded, knowing his life was coming to an end. "I'll leave! I'll leave town, I promise! Just don't kill me!"

Seven stared at him, his face emotionless. "You could have just paid us the money we requested but you wanted to act on some G shit, so this is how this movie plays out. You came for my life nigga, so your tears don't phase me. Ask Jehovah what you could have done different."

Standing up straight Seven raised his gun and fired twice, both shots to the head. The terrified look on Rango's face gradually slipped away into a peaceful expression as his life drained from his body. The sound of police sirens could be heard in the distance. Seven stared at Rango for a minute more, until Angel tapped his arm.

"Let's get it," he said, holding his shotgun down at his side before jogging off. Seven gave Rango one more glance before following after him.

****

Seven and Angel walked down the street, trying to remain unsuspicious from the police that were patrolling the streets. They had dumped the car they've been driving in an empty lot. After setting the car on fire, they left on foot, satisfied that nothing incriminating would be connected to them.

It seemed as if there was more activity going on than usual in the hood. Seven wasn't worried about it. He had done his dirt and was ready to lay low like he did whenever he had finished putting in work. It wasn't one of the worst beefs he had ever been involved in, but dead bodies were dead bodies. It would be wise to let things blow over before he started making moves again.

"You think we need to go hit the rest of his crew?" Angel asked. Seven knew he was referring to Rango's remaining boys.

"Nah, I don't think so." Seven replied.

"You know that nigga was running his mouth about us to them. Some of them might come around on some hot shit," Angel warned.

He had had his fair share of people coming up to him on some revenge type drama and though he had granted them their death wishes that didn't mean one of them might happen to get lucky one day.

"I don't doubt it, but it's too hot right now," Seven reasoned. "We need to chill out for now and when we come back out here if they want the beef we can give 'em a full course meal, feel me?"

"A'ight bruh," Angel shrugged. "So what about ol' girl?"

"Who?"

"The one you were talking about earlier? You going to stick it out with her?"

Seven thought on it. "Well after tonight, I think I'ma have a lot more free time to see if things are going to work. I'ma just be real with her."

"Yeah, don't keep it too real though." They stopped once they got to the bus stop. Angel pulled out a cigarette and lit it. "I don't think Bobbi's going to be too understanding about you killing a few niggas tonight."

Sevens head snapped towards him. "How you—"

Angel smirked. "Like I told you, we go back to the playground days, my nigga."

Seven couldn't help but grin. "Yeah, well we still going to see how it's going to work out." He looked up when he heard the bus coming. "You heading to the house?"

"Yep, guess I'll lay-up with Shawna's punk ass for a while. I got a couple g's to sit on for a good minute. Might get out of town for a while and go see my cuddy in Cleveland."

"Exactly, take a vacation bruh. We deserve some time off. Get well rested because when we do get back out here we're going to come harder than we were before."

"I feel it." They exchanged handshakes. "Where you about to go, to the house?" Angel asked, as Seven boarded the bus.

"Nah, I have one more piece of business to handle for the night," Seven told him before the doors closed.

****

"What the fuck was that about?" Harlem asked from the passenger seat.

He was smoking and switching the radio stations to see if he could find out what had happened.

"I don't know, but it sounded like someone had really pissed someone off," Allah gave his input. "Them niggas came out with the choppers. You only ride with those if you're really planning on killing a niggas whole squad."

"Well shit, it sounds like they got the job done," Junnie said.

As soon as he had heard the gun shots, he had assumed someone was coming for him and had prepared to get it popping.

Just looking at the situation made Junnie wonder if Essence was right about the street life taking a toll on him.

"Whoever did that shit was incredibly brave or incredibly stupid. The police station was only two blocks away from where it went down at," Allah said. "I wonder how many niggas got killed."

At that moment Junnie's cellphone rang. He recognized the house number. "Wassup baby?" he answered.

"Oh thank God baby!" Essence's worried voice came through the speaker. "I thought you might have been hurt! Are you guys okay?"

"Yeah we're good. You heard about what happened already?" Junnie asked, not too surprised. Word usually spread through the hood quickly.

"Yes, when I heard there was a shooting I just knew you were involved. I was so worried."

Junnie chuckled. "I'm not the only one with a gun in this city, Essie. I don't always have to be involved."

"Yeah I know but still."

Hearing that her man was okay and safe calmed Essence greatly, but she wouldn't be satisfied until he was home and in her arms.

"Baby are you almost home? I want you to hurry up. You know niggas are going to be going wild over Calvin Cole getting killed..."

"Wait, what?" Junnie interrupted, completely thrown off. "He's dead?"

"Yeah, weren't you there?"

"Yeah, but we didn't see what happened. We got out of dodge soon as the rounds start letting off." Junnie ran his hand over his face. "Damn, shits about to get crazy out here."

"I know, that's what I'm saying. Come home baby," Essence pleaded.

"Don't worry I'm on my way right now. Stay up for me ma."

"I will. I love Junnie. Be safe baby."

"Love you too."

"What's wrong?" Harlem asked, taking a swig from his bottle.

"Calvin Cole just got killed at the sideshow," Junnie told them, still stunned by the news.

"What?

Both Allah and Harlem expressed their surprise at the news.

"Aww shit, it's about to go down tonight," Harlem said shaking his head. "Niggas are 'bout to burn this city down."

"Exactly, that's why I'm trying to get to the house." Junnie told them, checking his phone for any new messages. "This shit has nothing to do with us."

"You ain't lying," Allah said, shaking his head. "It's a wrap for anybody that's out in these streets tonight. Whoever managed to get at Calvin Cole wrote their own death certificate."

"Shit, they got brass balls to go against the Family," Harlem said, stretching out in the backseat. "I feel sorry for their own families because once Johnny and them niggas get a hold of them it's a done deal."

"Yeah, I wonder who pulled it off," Junnie wondered aloud, glancing out the window.

"Aye, before we go to the house can we stop over on Central really quick?" Harlem suddenly asked, sitting up straight. "I gotta grab something."

Allah looked in the rearview mirror. "What the fuck, Harlem? It's about to be the sequel to the 'The Purge' out here, and you trying to make pit stops."

"Man, quit acting all scared and shit, B," Harlem sucked his teeth. "Since we're out here I need to stop by this bitch Gina's house. Last time I was out here I left my burner on her table."

"You got us making detours to grab a gun?" Junnie asked irritated. "You got two on you right now. Fuck that gun."

"Yo this ain't just any gun, my nigga. This is the first Glock I ever owned, its sentimental. Just stop by her house, damn. It's like five minutes away."

Allah sighed heavily. "You better come up out your pockets for this gas money, dawg."

"Shut your crybaby ass up, nigga, I'm good for it,"

The two began to argue, as Allah drove in the direction of Gina's house. Junnie sat back and thought about the war that was surely about to start in the hood and how much he wanted to be at home with his lady.

28

By the time the bus got back to town Seven was starting to feel nervous. He was heading into a new territory and he wasn't sure if he was ready for it. He would rather face Rango and a thousand of his goons single handedly than finish the mission he was currently on.

Seven stepped off the bus and headed down the familiar street, his mind filled with thoughts. When he reached Bobbi's house he actually began to feel himself calm down. Walking to the front door he knocked softly and waited. A few seconds went by before he heard footsteps from the other side and the scrap of the lock being turned.

Bobbi opened the door and peeked out in confusion. She opened it wider when she seen Seven on the porch.

"What you doing here Sev?" she asked, stepping out. "Are you--?"

"I love you," he blurted out nervously. "I want us to make it happen."

Bobbi's facial expression turned to surprise. "You want us to make what happen?" she asked softly.

Seven stared into her eyes. "Me and you. I want us to be together. Fa'real."

Bobbi couldn't contain the smile that crept on her face at his words. There was a sincerity to Seven's words that made her believe everything he says. Stepping forward she wrapped her arms around him and he grabbed her waist.

"I don't know if I want us to be in a serious relationship yet, Seven," she responded honestly. "I do care about you a lot, and you're the only dude I'm interested in, believe me, but your lifestyle scares me. You're out here too heavy Seven, and if I worry about you now, then I already know I'd lose my mind if we were together."

"Nah, I'm giving that shit up, B." Seven pushed away from her slightly so that he could look her in the face. "I'ma chill out for a while on the running wild."

Bobbi looked at him skeptically. "You want me to believe that?"

"I want you to believe, that I really love you and I'm willing to switch my life up to make something real with you."

"I believe that part just fine but, if we're really going to give it a try I'ma need a promise; I'ma need you to promise never to leave me if I decide to give my heart to you. I'm not up for being a widow before I hit me twenties."

Seven grinned. "Then you don't have to worry about that, red bone. I ain't never going anywhere and I promise you that."

"That's what I like to hear." Bobbi gladly accepted the kiss that Seven gave her.

Feeling victorious, like a lion claiming his territory, Seven stepped back and smiled cockily.

"Now how about we go upstairs and make them bed springs squeak again."

Bobbi shook her head. "You nasty," she said, but turned around and led the way into the house with no further objections.

****

Dark clouds rolled through the sky, bringing a steady down pour which had been casting down for the good part of the night.

Johnny stared down at the street below from the large penthouse window. The room was completely dark, except for the orange glow emitting from the tip of the blunt he held pinched in between his fingers.

Thick smoke circulated around his head as he turned his red rimmed eyes towards the city in the distance. He briefly wondered if his brother's soul could see how much chaos his death had caused in the hood.

Even though he couldn't hear or see it from his current location Johnny already knew that the wolves were running through the neighborhood tearing it apart.

Calvin Cole's death had spread through the whole Bay Area like wildfire and everyone knew that one of the hood's most legendary drug lords was now laid to rest.

Once it had been confirmed the cities underworld had erupted. It had been only a few hours and there had already been a dozen known murders documented on the evening news, and those were only the ones that the media knew about.

As many people that were getting clapped since his best friend's murder, Johnny knew that is was unlikely that Calvin's murderers were in the body count.

As soon as he had offered the reward for the ones responsible, he should've known that that would send most of the hoods grimiest players out into the wild ready to kill anyone they thought responsible.

But at that point Johnny didn't care. All he wanted was the life of those that took his best friend's.

There was a light knock on the door and then came a beep from a card key being used. Light spilled into the dark apartment as someone stepped inside. Johnny didn't bother turning around, there was only one other person with access to his crib.

"What you got for me, Polo?" Johnny asked softly, still staring into the distance.

"Nothing but everything." Polo switched on a lamp and walked over to his boss. "You might have caused a new genocide, my nigga. These niggas are out here wildin' out. These fools don't give a fuck about anything but collecting that bread or just riding for the big homie.

"Most these little niggas running around ain't even old enough to fully understand who Cal was but, they claim they're busting for him. They're using it as an excuse to pop off. And everybody from heavyweights to crack-heads is out trying to cash in on the cash. It's crazy." Polo shook his head as he dug out his pack of cigarettes and sparked one.

"I've been in the streets since a shorty and I ain't never seen any tension like this. What you got planned?" Polo asked.

Johnny was quiet for a minute as he thought about the destruction that was coming about.

"No matter what, someone really knows what happened to Calvin," he finally said. "Whoever it was wasn't a basic nigga to pull off something like this, so that eliminates half of these simple minded niggas.

"Send some more of the crew out. Have them lay into these muthafuckas. I don't give a fuck how they do it. Break these niggas down until somebody talks. All that code of conduct shit is out the window right now."

The weed had calmed him down momentarily, but now all the anger and hate he felt came back full force and Johnny suddenly felt like he needed to kill something.

He turned to look at Polo, who was looking nervous. He had never heard Johnny so upset before.

"My brother is laid up in a morgue right now, and that shit ain't gonna be let go easy. Show these muthafuckas the hand of God, my nigga. Flush out any body that smells like they had something to do with it. We still run this city!"

Polo hesitated slightly before speaking. "That's another thing. When I was out asking around I got word from a few people that a lot of niggas been talking sideways."

"What you mean?" Johnny asked, turning towards him.

"Some of these niggas are fighting for the big homie but, there's more trying to capitalize on his death. They're running around talking about it's a wrap for the Cole family.

They're plotting to overthrow us, Johnny. The way they see it, with Cal gone then the thrones open for whoever wants to claim it. There's fools arming up right now to come take us out."

Johnny cursed and turned back to look outside the window. He had been so blinded by his rage over his best friend's death he didn't stop to consider this possibility.

True, a lot of people had loved the drug lord, but there were just as many that would have loved to see him buried. With him out of the way now it was only logical that the goons would try and take over everything.

Johnny shook his head. There was so much to do, that a normal general might have folded under pressure, but Johnny Welcome lived for his namesake.

He had been a soldier long before he had been a right hand man to an empire. If the streets wanted to come for him and his, they had best been ready to die trying.

He turned back to Polo who looked tired but still ready to take care of whatever his boss asked of him. Johnny's affection towards the youngster made him beam inside with pride.

"Remember when I found you on the streets all those years ago and I told you if you roll with us there might come a time where it might be too much to handle?" Johnny asked seriously.

"Yeah I remember."

"This might be that time little brother. We're about to go head first into a storm that you might not be ready for. I want you to sit this one out."

Polo's face went blank. "What?"

"There's about to be a lot of people coming for this empire and I'm number one on their hit list. When it comes to greed, anybody could be the enemy. Shit, our own people might be playing in somebody's pocket. You're the only one I have left to trust." Johnny placed his hand on his shoulder. "I don't wanna see anything happen to you little brother. Doesn't make sense for both of us to go out on some G shit."

Polo's face slowly shifted from confused to anger.

"Are you serious? Johnny, you looked out for me when I wasn't shit but a little nigga stealing out of grocery stores just so I could eat. If it wasn't for you I would've been dead a long ass time ago, and you really think I'ma leave you now that you need me? With all respect fam, fuck that. If they come for you they're gonna have to body both of us," he said with conviction.

A slight smile crossed Johnny's face as he looked at his little homie.

"Spoken like the soldier I trained you to be," he said playfully putting him in the headlock. "This shits gonna get real out here though. You really think you can handle it?"

Before Polo could respond there was a knock at the door. The smile vanished from Johnny's face as he looked up, drawing his gun at the same time. Polo pulled out his own weapon and slowly turned towards the door.

"Did anybody follow you?" Johnny asked quietly.

Polo shook his head with uncertainty. Creeping across the plush carpet as silent as a cat, Johnny eased to the door and peeked out the hole.

He relaxed slightly when he seen the familiar face. Turning the bolt, he pulled the door open.

"Fuck you doing here?"

"Damn, don't shoot killer."

Wesley stepped inside with his hands raised. Behind him was Bone and two cats Johnny didn't recognize.

Johnny's face turned to stone when he seen the two men.

"Who the fuck was you expecting, the boogey... yo what you doing Johnny?" Wesley asked in panic as Johnny raised his gun at the two strangers.

"Wesley, I didn't think you were as stupid as you really are," Johnny said with an edge in his voice.

He was talking to Wesley but his eyes were trained on the men.

"You know what the fucks going down right now, and you're gonna bring two unknown muthafuckas to where I'm at? Somebody better start talking before my hammer does."

"Be easy fam," Ace said, raising his hands slightly. "Your man Wes...."

"Nah, ain't no 'be easy' nigga." Polo interrupted from the sidelines, his own gun trained on Ace and West. "Not when y'all stepping through our domain."

"Yo, y'all bugging." Wesley stepped in front of his team. "This the nigga Ace from Acorn. This who Calvin had the meeting with the other day."

Johnny remembered the day. He had been handling some business with Queenie when Calvin and Ace had had their meeting. Still, he made no move to lower his gun until Wesley spoke again.

"They know who killed the big homie."

Johnny looked at Wesley, then to Bone who nodded in confirmation. Hesitantly lowering his gun, Johnny took Ace in for the first time. Just giving the man a quick look over he could tell that he wasn't too fond of him but if Ace had the name of the person that took his brother from him then he would tolerate him.

"You do huh? And how you know that?" Johnny asked suspiciously.

Ace smirked. "I got my ways, but before I start giving up all the secrets maybe we should discuss my grand prize."

Johnny's face scrunched into a scowl as he glared at Ace.

"Nigga you'll get your bread when I get a name. Until then you're still in threat of getting pushed back by my little homie over here."

"Haven't we had enough violence for one night?" Ace asked sarcastically. "But you're in grieving, so it's cool. I understand. Besides I don't want any money. I want something else for what I'm about to lay on you."

"What the fuck else could you want?"

"Well, now that the king is slain niggas are starting to think that it's a wrap for this whole company y'all have going on here, but I don't think it is. Not when they have someone just as solid to take over now."

Ace nodded respectively toward Johnny, who continued to stare. "I'm thinking maybe me and my team can be down for the cause. We're a small time clique just trying to make it out here, but if we're backed by the realest then we could be good from now on."

"No disrespect, my dude, but I would have to get up with you on that later. I got a lot on my plate right now to be thinking about anything else but what my objective is. Let's see how solid your word is on this and we'll talk about business in the future."

West looked as if he wanted to say something but a look from Ace stopped him. Ace turned to Johnny and smiled.

"Fair enough," he said. "But trust me, you might want a little extra gun power for this nigga. Him and his crew aren't known for going down quietly."

"Who?" Polo demanded.

"You familiar with a young cat named Junnie? If not, you should be. He's been in the news all week for slapping that nigga, Lil Banger at the club."

Instantly Johnny's mental rolodex began to spin before the name connected with a face. Junnie and his crew was a small gang from 54th who weren't known for their size but for their viciousness. Johnny had met the young boy a few years back with Calvin while a mutual friend of theirs conducted business with Polo.

At the time, Junnie had been nothing more than a nappy headed teen selling weed on the corner, but his reputation had become much more since then. Either way, it didn't matter to Johnny. It was a reputation that was surely about to be spoken about in the past tense.

"Junnie?" Polo asked in disbelief. "Are you sure? I know dude, and he's a wild muthafucka but he ain't dumb enough to do something like this."

Ace gave Polo a look which was equivalent to a grown up looking at a child that had spoken out of turn.

"Look, y'all wanted the information that led to your leader's death and I gave it to you. I got my sources out here, and this is the name I got for you. You can either check it out or not, but I'm sure Calvin Cole is a name Junnie would be glad to add to his resume'."

Johnny rubbed his chin thoughtfully as he took in Ace's words, he stared the man in his eyes to try and find any hint of deceit but could find none. This cat Ace was a hard dude to read.

"Yo Johnny, can I holler at you for a minute?" Polo spoke up, nodding to the side.

Johnny followed him to the corner, with Wesley and Bones close behind.

"What's good Polo?" Johnny asked.

"Aye, I hear what ol' boy is saying, but I think he's wrong," Polo objected. "I know Junnie. He wouldn't pull off something like this. Last time I seen him we were just chopping it up about putting him on with the team. He didn't do it."

Johnny stared at Polo for a second. "Are you telling me you're vouching for this li'l nigga?"

"Without a doubt,"

Johnny slowly nodded as he seen the certainty written on Polo's face.

"Okay, let's say your boy is innocent. Why is this nigga in my house saying he's the shooter?"

Polo shrugged. "I don't know, but how can we take his word? We don't even know dude like that. I actually know Junnie."

"Was Junnie at the sideshow?" Bones asked.

Polo hesitated before answering. "I did see him there while we were parking the car. He was across the street with his people smoking. But Johnny trust me, it wasn't him."

Johnny considered what was being said to him.

"I hear what you're saying Po, but as of now this nigga Junnie is the only lead I've had for the past few hours. I have to take it."

"Well let me go to him," Polo offered. "I can bring him back so you can talk to him, he trusts me. Just talk to him Johnny and see what he has to say."

Johnny nodded. "A'ight, I'ma let you go holler at this nigga, but I'ma warn you right now Po, if he's spitting some shit I don't like I'm splitting his cabbage, then paying a visit to anyone who shares his DNA."

"I'll bring him back, I promise," Polo vowed.

"Take Wesley with you," Johnny demanded. "Bones, I want you to come with me to rally some of the troops. We need to defend the throne from whoever has the balls to try and come take it.

"I'm also sending word that I want this nigga Junnie brought to me. Alive," Johnny added as he seen Polo's mouth open to argue. "Just in case he is guilty and tried to skip town before you find him."

"Alright," Polo said, knowing it was no use in arguing at this point.

Johnny nodded before turning back to Ace and West, who were trying to act as if they weren't eavesdropping on the conversation. "So check it, we're going to look into the information that you gave us, and if it checks out I'll have somebody come through the hood to drop your bread off."

"That's considerate of you, but I'm more concerned with the seat at the table of the Family," Ace told him evenly. "That was my main interest in the terms of me giving you this information."

"And like I told you, I have a lot on my plate right now. Besides a few stories regarding your business you're running, I've never heard of you, homie.

"My team is built from the best, so once I get at these niggas about my brother, then I'll do my research on you and make a decision. You understand?"

"All the hostility ain't necessary," West spoke up, not liking Johnny's tone.

"Nigga, for you to be rolling up to my spot unannounced, you better be glad all I'm giving you is hostility," Johnny told him. "Now you two are good to go."

"That means get to stepping," Polo told them, his gun still held at his side.

Realizing that any more conversation would be pointless, Ace nodded and left the condo without another word. West followed him out, giving Johnny a dark look, which he gladly returned.

"I don't like them niggas," Polo said, as the door closed behind them.

"Me neither, but they gave me the information I needed." Johnny walked to the closet across the room and opened the door.

Where an average person might have hung their coats or possibly stored Christmas decorations, Johnny had rifles, and ammunition tucked away nicely inside. Grabbing a shotgun from the rack he cocked the slide and prepared to go on the biggest battle of his life.

"Find me this nigga Junnie."

29

"After this shit blows over, I might have to come pay this nigga a visit," West said as they got off the elevator in the lobby. They walked out the building and headed towards the car. "He got a bigger mouth than that nigga Calvin."

"I noticed. But don't worry, Johnny's gonna get his soon enough. Being down with the Family will serve its purpose before we decide to roll with the next plan. But before we open that can of worms, we need to finish this one."

"What's gonna happen if they find out the truth?" West questioned as they got into the car. "You heard what the young boy upstairs said. They're bringing Junnie in alive. What if he manages to convince them he's innocent?"

"I doubt it, I'm sure that somebody is gonna snatch him up before the rescue squad could save him. If someone approaches him, Junnie ain't going quietly, so someone bound to rock him. In the meantime, we need to set some shit in motion."

"Like what?"

"Call up everyone you know and let them know Johnny put a bounty out on that whole squad. Tell them Junnie played a part in the death of the city's hero."

"Everyone in the hoods gonna try to cash in on that," West said pulling out his phone.

"That's what I'm banking on," Ace snickered, starting the car up and pulling out of the parking lot. "My bet is Junnie won't make it through the night.

****

Gibbs was your definition of the average, grimy hustler always looking for a come up. He was a dark skinned older dude who just looked like somebody you wouldn't want to run across in a dark alleyway.

His profile screamed trouble, and the young thugs he ran with were just as wild and ruthless. On this particular night they were gathered on Gibbs' porch smoking and drinking the night away.

"Yo yo, this is for Calvin Cole, one of the realest niggas this hood done seen in a while," Gibbs said, pouring liquor from his Ole English can.

"Damn, I still can't believe someone finally got at homie," Laquan, the youngest of the group, said. He shook his head. "Honestly I figured someone might try one day, but I didn't think they would succeed."

"I ain't gonna lie, I thought about it once or twice, but that army is thick," someone else spoke up. "Looks like it could be accomplished though."

"Yeah, they got at Calvin, but now they gotta worry about Johnny Welcome coming for that ass." Gibbs nodded wisely. "I know dude from way back. He might even be more solid than Calvin and he ain't going to let that shit ride out about his man Cal."

"You damn right. Word is Johnny put a ten grand bounty on whoever bring in the shooters," Laquan informed them. Everyone let out their similar responses of approval.

"That makes a nigga want to go out here and do some detective work. I could use that bread, my nigga," Gibbs thought hungrily of the money he could have.

He was just a small time hustler who made money here and there but he had never had ten grand. Just thinking about that much money made his mouth water.

"We should go out here and hit the pavement," another thug from the group declared.

He was a large man with a beard that hung to his chest.

"Somebody knows who did this shit."

Just as he finished his sentence, Gibbs cellphone rang. Looking down at the screen, he was pleased to see the name 'Gina' flashing across.

"What's good, shorty?" he answered, taking a gulp from his can.

He was smiling at first but as Gina began to talk his smile vanished. He sat up straight as he listened intently to what she was saying.

"Alright, alright, check it. Me and my niggas are about to be on our way. Aye, keep those niggas there until we get there. I'll be there in a few." Gibbs hung up, stunned at what had just been placed in his lap.

"What's good cuddy?" Laquan asked, noticing the look on his face.

"That was my bitch that stay over on Central. She said the niggas that everyone is claiming killed Calvin are on the way to her house right now."

"You're lying!" All the goons said simultaneously.

Gibbs held up his hands to calm them down.

"Chill out, niggas! Grab your straps and let's get the fuck over there!"

Gibbs pulled his gun from his jeans and checked the clip. Leading the way off the porch, with his pack of wolves following close behind he couldn't help but thank God, or the devil in this case, for the ten grand he was easily about to snag.

****

Even though Harlem had said his girl's apartment was ten minutes away, it ended up being at least a twenty-minute drive from the freeway entrance.

Harlem had called the chick in advance to let her know that they were on their way, which she gladly agreed.

"I'ma let you know right now, Harlem. You're on my bad side right now for having me out in the boonies like this," Allah said, driving the car down the dark street which Gina lived on. "If you're planning on staying in this bitch more than thirty seconds I'm leaving you over here without a second thought about it."

"Man, if you don't calm your ass down, my nigga," Harlem warned, looking out the window towards Gina's apartment. "I'ma be in and out, chill out. Park right here," he pointed to an empty spot by the curb.

Allah parked the car and killed the engine. Junnie looked around the dark street. He never really been this far out of the city, but he could feel the tension from inside the car.

There were only a couple people on the street but Junnie knew the familiar feeling of death in the air. Allah was looking around too, with the same expression that Junnie wore.

"Where the fuck are we at?" he asked, watching an old man pushing a shopping cart cross the street.

"The boonies, remember?" Harlem retorted sarcastically. "Look, I'ma be right back. Y'all chill for like two minutes."

"You better be back in two minutes, nigga," Junnie demanded. "I'm trying to get home to my wife."

Harlem growled, irritated. "Do you niggas want to come up with me?"

"Yeah, I actually do need to piss," Allah said, pulling his key from the ignition.

Harlem gave him a look before exiting the car and slamming the door shut. Not exactly too happy about sitting in the hot car Junnie reluctantly got out and followed the other two to the apartment.

They went up the stairs and walked down the balcony until they got to door 3A. Harlem knocked heavily, the kind which would annoy most people.

They waited for a few seconds before the door swung open and a pretty light skinned girl answered. She smiled widely when she seen Harlem's face.

"Long time no see," she greeted brightly.

Taking one look it was easy to see why Harlem would talk to her. The shorts she wore hugged to her wide hips letting you know that you were in for a treat when she turned around.

"You know me," Harlem shrugged. "I be making moves ma."

"I know, and none of them with me," Gina replied slyly, her wide grin still intact. She looked at the other two. "Hello," she greeted politely.

"These my brothers," Harlem introduced before pushing past Gina and into the house. "Who you got up in here?" he asked, looking around the living room.

"Does it look like anybody is in here, nigga?" Gina replied, shutting the door once Junnie and Allah had stepped in. She turned the deadbolt and latched the chain. "You got a lot of nerve coming in here questioning me about what I got going on when you haven't called me in fucking weeks."

"I just told you, I've been making moves." Harlem continued to look around. "Remember last time I was over here?"

"Yeah because it was so special," Gina rolled her eyes.

Walking into the kitchen, it was confirmed that her ass was stretching the limits of her tiny shorts. It jiggled with each step she took and Harlem couldn't help but stare.

"Well, I left my piece over here. What you do with it?"

Gina stopped and gave him a look. "I haven't seen you all this time and you just came over here for a fucking gun?"

"Hell yeah, I didn't come for a fucking picnic." Harlem barked. "Don't start all that sensitive shit, Regina, I just need my piece. I gotta get back across town."

Gina looked as if she wanted to flash on him but thought better of it.

"I don't know, go check the bedroom. I think I threw it in the closet or something. Don't be leaving that shit over here, lord knows how many bodies are on it. You trying to get me locked up?"

"Shut the hell up," Harlem mumbled, walking to the back room.

"Excuse me, can I use your bathroom?" Allah asked. "I've been holding it for a fat minute and my bladder on its last stretch."

"Yeah, it's just down the hallway. First door on your left."

Allah nodded and went to the bathroom, leaving just Junnie and Gina. She looked at him and smiled.

Junnie gave her a small smile back and moved across the living room to the window. Looking out he could see the street below where they had parked.

"Why don't you clean up this fucking room every once in a while, with your stank ass?" Harlem's harsh voice came from the back. Gina shook her head and rolled her eyes.

"I don't see how you deal with him every day," she said to Junnie.

"I do a lot of drugs,"

Even though he didn't say it with humor Gina laughed as if it was the funniest thing she had ever heard.

"I heard that. You wanna smoke? I just loaded a bowl before you guys called." she said, motioning to the container of weed she had on the coffee table, next to the weed pipe.

"Nah, I'm good." Junnie replied politely, still staring out of the window.

He was trying to sit in his thoughts but Gina seemed intent on starting a conversation.

"Did you go to Jefferson High? You look familiar?"

"Nah, I'm not from out here," Junnie told her, starting to wish he had stayed in the car.

"You sure? Do you ever go to the club on the east side? Like, Chocolate Room, or the Cabana?"

"Nah, can't say that I have."

"Oh, maybe it was someone else." Gina came from out the kitchen and set down closer, now only a few feet away from Junnie. "Oh my God, did you hear about what happened over at the sideshow on Sixty-first a few hours ago?"

"No what happened?" Junnie asked playing dumb.

"There was a shootout and Calvin Cole got killed."

Junnie's eyebrows raised. "Word? Calvin Cole?"

"Yeah, it's crazy. They shot him in the head like three times. It's been all over the news."

"That's fucked up." Junnie turned his attention back outside the window. "Hopefully they catch whoever did it. Cole was a good dude from what I heard."

"Yeah, I have a good feeling their going to catch the person," Gina said smirking.

Junnie nodded but didn't respond. His thoughts turned to the big event that had probably already reached every corner of northern California.

"Yo, I can't find my shit," Harlem said, coming back in the living room.

He was now munching on a bag of Doritos he'd come across.

"Nigga, who told you to go back there and touch my chips!" Gina exclaimed, jumping from the couch as if Harlem had taken a precious diamond.

As they began to argue over the potato chips, Junnie turned back out to the window. He was looking up the street when he seen a car turn onto the block and speed towards the apartment building. The car parked next to Allah's and sat for a minute.

After a while the back doors opened up and three men climbed out. Junnie's eyes narrowed as he watched them glance around the street to see who was watching. His suspicions were confirmed when the passenger got out the vehicle with a gun held tightly in his hand.

The men exchanged words for a moment before heading for the apartments stairs. Junnie didn't recognize any of them but somewhere deep in the pit of his stomach, he knew the men were coming to the apartment they were currently in.

"June dawg, want some chips?" Harlem grinned as Gina began to cuss him out.

He was holding the chips away from her as she tried to grab them from him.

"We need to shake from out of here." Junnie moved from the window, drawing his gun as he did so.

Harlem's grin faded as he noticed the serious look on his friends face.

"What's wrong with you?" Harlem asked, dropping the bag of chips.

Before Junnie could answer there was a hard knock on the door

"Who the fuck is that?" Harlem asked, pulling his gun from his pants.

In response, the front door burst open as it was kicked off its hinges and three men rushed in.

Gina screamed and dived to the floor, but Junnie and Harlem had other ideas. Without bothering to ask for names, they both opened fire on the intruders just as they lifted their own weapons and began to fire.

Glass shattered and plaster tore apart as bullets ripped through the living room. Harlem was forced to backpedal down the hallway as the shooters tried to take him out.

Junnie ducked behind the couch and returned fire, not having time to register that he was really involved in a full-fledged shootout in a matter of seconds.

One thought that did cross his mind was how Calvin Cole had been in a shootout only a few hours previously and had lost. Junnie knew that wouldn't be him. Letting out a war cry he aimed at the men and continued shooting.

One of the men managed to avoid Junnie's fire and chased Harlem down the hallway, leaving Junnie to take on the remaining two.

They had heavier firepower, but their aim was off as they continued to hit inanimate objects.

Junnie aimed at Gibbs and gave the trigger three quick taps. The first missed, but the next two, tore into his face, ripping his cheek off and sending blood splattering on the wall behind him. He spun in a complete circle before hitting the carpet.

Laquan seen his leader get hit and it scared a new sense in him. He wanted to run back outside to where one of their guys still had the car running, but that gave Junnie a clear shot at him.

Instead he chose to duck into the bathroom next to him. Opening the door, he attempted to make a dash inside but froze when he realized someone was on the other side. Before he could get a good look at the man, Allah had raised his gun and tapped the trigger. The young boy crashed to the bathroom floor, his brains vacating the back of his head.

Junnie raised from behind the couch, gun still aiming at the front door. No more intruders came running in as he slowly backed towards the hallway. Allah stepped over Laquan and met Junnie halfway.

"What the fuck just happened?" Allah asked, looking around the destroyed living room and Gibbs sprawled out body.

"An ambush," Junnie replied. "Harlem!"

He ran into the bedroom to find that it too had been destroyed from bullets. One of the men who had come into the house was on the floor, bleeding from his neck and gasping for breath. Harlem was standing over him with his gun trained at the man's head.

"Got the nerve to run up on me and mine, pussy?" Harlem sneered, gold teeth shining. "Nigga I ain't Calvin. Nighty night," Harlem's finger tightened on the trigger.

"Hold up!" Junnie walked over and lowered Harlem's gun.

Harlem protested but Junnie ignored him. Leaning down he looked the man in his eyes and seen nothing but pure terror. Junnie knew he could get the information he need.

"Who the fuck are you, homie?" he demanded, slapping the man's face.

"James man, just James," the man cried, wincing in pain as he held his gunshot wound.

"What the fuck you and your people come here for, Just James? I peeped y'all out the window when you first pulled up. You came here specifically nigga, so don't even think about lying, or I might just let this ratty ring off." Junnie lowered his gun to James privates.

"Hold up man, we just wanted the money! It wasn't nothing personal!" he shouted hurriedly.

"What money?" Allah demanded, frowning.

"Johnny's money. Word is y'all killed Calvin Cole at the sideshow earlier. Johnny and his squad put a green light on you. Ten g's for whoever can bring you to him alive. We weren't trying to kill you, we just wanted to turn you in!"

Junnie's heart dropped as he listened to James. His mind began to whirl so fast he got light headed. Looking up at his comrades he could tell they were just as confused as he was at the information they had just been given.

"What the fuck do you mean? Who told you we killed Calvin?" Junnie demanded, slapping James viciously.

"It's all over the hood! Everyone's saying you three pulled off the job, and now that there's a bounty on you. There's probably more niggas looking for you. That bitch in the kitchen told Gibbs you guys were here so we came to pick you up. I'm sorry!" James pleaded, crying like a five-year-old who knew he was about to get a whooping.

Harlem looked at him in disgust. "Yeah, you're the sorriest muthafucka I've ever seen. But you tried to get me and my brothers killed so I don't have any sympathy for you. Tell Jehovah how sorry you are, bitch ass nigga." And with that Harlem raised his gun and put an end to James whimpering.

The room was quiet as the gunshot rang through it. The three men looked at each other still shocked by what they had heard. Junnie stood to his feet, trying his best to put together everything.

"Everyone thinks we killed Calvin Cole," Allah said his tone low.

The seriousness of the situation seemed to sink in more when he said it aloud.

"Fuck that shit." Harlem angrily shook his head. "I don't know what kinda crack this nigga Johnny is smoking but I'm about to go pay that nigga a visit right now."

"Chill out Harlem," Junnie told him. "We need to think this shit out, but first thing we need to do is get the fuck out of here before the boys pull up and we're really in some shit."

No one argued with that and the three of them rushed out of the room and for the front door. Gina was still cowering on the floor but, when she saw that they were still alive a new wave of tears started.

"I'm so sorry Harlem, I didn't think they were going to do this!" she cried, shakily standing to her feet. "They just told me they wanted to come talk to you, and offered to pay me some cash if I let you come over. My mom's sick and I have her doctor bills to pay, I'm sorry, I swear I am."

Harlem stared at her with a curious expression on his face.

"You guys go ahead. I'll be down in a minute."

"Harlem…" Junnie started, but Harlem gave him a dark glare.

"I got this."

Giving him a look, Junnie tapped Allah's arm and they hurried out of the apartment.

No one was outside now, but Junnie seen people peeking from behind their curtains as he and Allah ran down the stairs to the car.

Allah unlocked the doors and they hopped inside, waiting for Harlem. A couple minutes later he came down the steps and climbed into the backseat.

There was fresh blood on his shirt, and stained the front of his jeans but he appeared extremely calm as he shut the car door.

"Let's get the fuck out of here," he said, wiping blood from his cheek.

Allah started the car and skirted away from the curb and away from the massacre they had left upstairs.

30

Rabbit sat back on the sofa, blunt in one hand and his eyes focused on the television screen. Beside him, Chucky and Hasaan flicked the controls to the PS3 and talked shit as they controlled their football players.

Yanni was seated at the table, rolling another blunt and talking away on her phone. His team had been in the house for a majority of the evening and Rabbit was starting to get irritated.

By this time everybody in town had heard about the money that was up for grabs in the form of the young thug named Junnie, but instead of being out in the streets trying to cash in on it, everybody in the small apartment were content with their current activities.

"Bitch ass nigga, I could've sworn I told you that that shit ain't flying in my domain." Chucky laughed, before tilting back the rest of his beer. "The Eagles ain't doing shit in real life and yo' mark ass can't make them move in fantasy either."

"Man, fuck you nigga. You stuck me with this raggedy ass controller," Hasaan complained, examining his controller.

"Yeah, that shit sounds good," Chucky brushed him off. "You got next Rabbit? This niggas about to be off real soon."

Rabbit turned his gaze to his partners. "Do it look like I want to play some damn video games? There's ten grand out there being offered to us and you niggas rather be up in here jerkin off and getting high."

"Who the fucks been jerkin off?" Chucky asked, turning to look at Hasaan who shrugged.

"Whatever nigga, you get my point." Rabbit jumped to his feet and began pacing. "Did you hear what this nigga Johnny announced? Ten Gs for this nigga Junnie's head. Five for his boys. Now I don't know about you niggas, but twenty grand would be looking real nice in my pocket right now and you can best believe every killer in this city is thinking the same thing."

"Yeah but, I heard he wants Junnie alive," Hasaan announced, cracking open another can of beer.

Rabbit made a face. "So the fuck what? Alive or dead, at least he's getting the muthafucka. I say we get up off our asses and go make this happen. Do you niggas know what this could mean if we pull this off?"

"Hell yeah, I'm copping that new Cadi from Kahlil's mark ass." Chucky laughed, while Hasaan nodded in agreement. Rabbit stared at them while they exchanged dap.

"If you niggas were any slower you'd be moving backwards," he said, shaking his head. "If we're the ones to grab Calvin Cole's killers we'll automatically move up in the ranks out here.

"Calvin might be gone but you already know his nigga Johnny was second in command. Think about it. Not only would we have enough money to finally make some real moves but we'll also be in good with The Family. How much more solid could it get?" Rabbit's mind began to fast forward to the look on everyone's faces when he delivered Junnie and his crew.

He would be considered the hero who defeated Calvin Cole's killer. The streets would always remember his name and he would be set on the path to his criminal career. It all made sense.

"Yeah, that sounds good but that would mean we would have to kill Junnie," Chucky said, interrupting his thoughts. "It might sound easy enough but this nigga has a track record that stretches out, my nigga. Plus, don't you think he would have gotten up out of dodge already? If I had killed the city's most influential nigga, I would have been on the next thing smoking up out this bitch."

As much as he hated to admit it Rabbit knew Chucky was right. Junnie was already a phantom in the normal state of things, so finding him when he wouldn't want to be found would prove even harder than usual. There was also the worry of somebody else getting to him before they did. Rabbit looked at the clock on the wall and began to instantly work out a plan.

"Junnie might have ducked off, but what about the rest of his niggas?" he asked. "Harlem and Allah could still be around here somewhere, and they have a price on their dome too."

"Yeah, but they wouldn't tell us where Junnie is. He's the one Johnny really wants," Hasaan pointed out.

"Oh, they'll tell us where he's at," Rabbit said confidently. "Niggas can play tough but I bet you if I break their legs, they'll start talkin'."

"I know where that nigga Allah be at too," Chucky said, twisting one of his dreads. "One of the bitches he fucks with stays in my cousins building over on Seventy-Fourth."

Rabbit nodded. "A'ight, we could start by looking over there. We're already behind though. These other muthafuckas been out here hunting for these niggas all night. That means we need to move quick on these pussies."

"Will y'all shut the fuck up, you don't see me on the phone?" Yanni shouted.

She was a dark skinned beauty, with a body that guaranteed you looked twice, and an attitude that made you want more. Rabbit fucked with her from time to time but they were more friends than anything else.

"Shut the fuck up bitch, we over here talking money." Hasaan shouted back.

Yanni gave him the look of death.

"Hold on, let me call you back real quick. These niggas over here done drank some courage and think they 'bout that shit. Yeah, alright."

Yanni hung up the phone and tossed it on the table. She stood to her feet and walked over to Hasaan who was looking her up and down. Without a word she slapped him.

"Who the fucks a bitch now, nigga?" she said, following with another slap to the face. Hasaan tried to back away and ended up tripping over the rug.

"Man, go on Yanni before I fuck you up. Ain't nobody playing with your ass!" Hasaan threatened from the floor, while Yanni stood over him in a fighting position.

"Yeah, go somewhere. We got shit to do while you over here playing," Rabbit told her, not too interested in their drama.

"You niggas ain't got shit to do but go out here and get killed," she snorted. "I know about Junnie, Allah and all them niggas and y'all tripping if you think you can just go out and kidnap them. Last time I checked they weren't eight-year-old boys. You stick with that plan and I might as well go shopping for my dress to your funeral right now."

"Shut the fuck up. What do you know?" Chucky said, snatching the blunt from her hand and sparking it.

Yanni smirked. "I know that if it was me I wouldn't go out here trying to find Junnie. I would make him come to me."

"I doubt that nigga would want your washed up pussy," Rabbit said, causing Chucky and Hasaan to roll with laughter. Yanni just nodded in agreement.

"Probably not, that's why I would snatch the pussy that's his already," she said matter-of-fact.

"What?"

Yanni rolled her eyes. "His girl, you retard. Snatch his girl and he would come to you. Don't you niggas watch movies? That's the first move you're supposed to make."

Rabbit's mouth opened in surprise. Yanni was right. Why go out there and try to snatch Junnie when he could snatch something much easier, that would guarantee that Junnie surrendered without a fight. He grabbed Yanni and planted a kiss on her forehead.

"You might not be so useless after all,"

"Sick," Yanni backed out of his reach and wiped the kiss away. "I don't need pussy juice on my forehead for you to show your appreciation."

"Yeah, I hear that hot shit." Rabbit walked over to the couch and moved the cushions aside. Smiling triumphantly, he grabbed the pistol that had fallen down the cracks earlier.

Chucky was looking at him in awe. "So you're serious about this huh?"

"Oh, I'ma show you how serious I am, my nigga." Rabbit assured. Tucking the gun beneath his hoodie as he headed for the front door. "Y'all coming or not?"

Chucky and Hasaan exchanged brief glances before grabbing their hoodies and following after Rabbit.

****

Allah drove them on the backstreets to avoid the police. He stuck to the speed limit the whole time and respected every street regulation in the driver's handbook. After a few minutes of aimless driving, they pulled to a stop on an empty road behind an old factory.

They got out the car, and stood around it. Dark clouds were rolling across the sky but the air was still warm as it had been that afternoon. It felt like a storm was coming and it seemed to fit the situation perfectly.

Junnie pulled out a cigarette and sparked it as he stared up in the sky. Allah leaned against the bumper of the car, arms crossed and apparently deep in thought. Harlem however was pacing back and forth, cigarette dangling from between his fingers.

"So word around town is we killed Calvin Cole," he said, shaking his head. Suddenly he let out a loud, hyena-similar laugh. "That shits crazy, kid!"

"Did any of y'all tell anybody you did it?" Junnie joked softly, rubbing his beard.

"Yeah, I alerted the press as soon as we got in the car," Allah responded. "How the fuck did our names get involved in this? Like, what made people say we did it?"

"Hell, they needed somebody to pin it on, why not three niggas known for putting in work?" Harlem stated sarcastically, kicking an empty bottle into the street.

"But there's plenty of niggas known for that out here, we're not the only ones," Allah pointed out. "They named us specifically for killing him. There has to be a reason why."

Junnie thought as hard as he could. When they had been at the sideshow he hadn't known that Calvin Cole was there, let alone seen him anywhere.

When the shooting happened, they weren't even near the commotion. How could anyone mistake them for the shooters?

"Why don't we just go to the Hills and ask Johnny himself?" Harlem suggested, angrily clenching his jaw. "He's the one who has muthafuckas out here looking to get on our heads. Let's just see him head up about it."

"Because not only would that have gotten us killed in the normal state of things, but now that the cities on high alert I'm pretty sure that would get us killed faster," Junnie pointed out.

"That's what we thought before but I see Calvin Cole is on a slab in the coroner's office now," Harlem shot back. "How do we know that Johnny didn't set this shit up himself?"

"Why would Johnny kill his best friend just to set us up?" Allah asked.

"These hoes ain't loyal."

"Look, I can't imagine why Johnny would want to set us up, nor do I think he would kill his homie to do it," Junnie to told them, taking a drag from his cigarette. "But I do think someone is setting us up, so we need to think of someone that has a beef with us."

Instantly, all three of them knew a whole list of people that wouldn't mind pulling a stunt like this. Their individual lists were full length so combined it could be anyone.

"Let's think about the most recent beefs," Allah said, coming with a new tactic.

"That's easy. Let's just ask Sir Smack-a-lot," Harlem jerked his thumb towards Junnie. "This nigga just publicly slapped the most popular rapper out."

"Yeah, but does Banger have muscle to pull something like this off?" Allah frowned.

"It doesn't have to be him. Anybody that fucks with that nigga could have done this."

"Nah it has to be more personal than that," Junnie said, finally getting his brain to work. "Think, why would they kill Calvin just to set us up. Being able to just get to him was risky enough as it is. If they really wanted to handle some old score, why didn't they just try to kill us directly?"

"What you saying, someone had beef with you and Calvin?"

"Hell yeah, that's the only reason why they would risk their lives to kill him. Setting us up must have just been a second part of it."

"So someone who would want you, a notorious stick-up kid, and Calvin Cole, a king pen, dead." Harlem gave them a look. "That doesn't really shorten the list, dawg."

"Well we need to get somewhere where we can figure it out. Going back to the city isn't an option right now," Allah told them, uncrossing his arms. "Everyone within a fifty mile radius is looking to cash in on our blood. Niggas will do anything to try and get some bread. We need to drive to another city and lay low until we figure this shit out."

"You right, I'm glad my momma lives across the country," Harlem snickered. "The first thing niggas do for ransom is grab your momma, daughter or girl."

"Yeah that sounds like a plan," Junnie agreed. "We just need to..." his voice trailed off as he suddenly remembered something extremely important. "Essence!"

Allah's face shifted as he realized what Junnie was talking about. "Aw shit."

"We need to go," Junnie told them, heart racing. He envisioned Essence lying in bed, waiting for him to come home, but receiving his enemies instead as they come looking for him.

"Junnie stay calm bro, we're going to get Essence and get out of here. She's fine, don't trip. But we need to get some gas before we get on the freeway, we're almost out."

"Man, fuck!" Harlem yelled, rubbing his hand over his head. "We don't be in this much shit even when we really do kill a nigga. If we're going to lay low, we need to swing by my crib first."

"Why?" Junnie demanded, his sole focus on getting to his own house.

"We're going to need some money if we're leaving the city, and I don't have nearly enough on me. I need to go get my stash, and I want to get more ammunition just in case these niggas get to us."

"Fuck that shit dawg, I need to get to Essence!" Junnie yelled. "They could be on their way to my house right this second.

Harlem rubbed his chin. "A'ight listen. When we cross the bridge to the city you guys are gonna let me out so I can run to the crib and grab everything we'll need. I can grab my whip when I'm done and meet back up with y'all afterwards."

"Hell no, we ain't splitting up," Allah told him sternly.

"I'm not saying I want you to run off on your own, Harlem," Junnie explained trying to get him to understand. "I just need to get to my wife, and we need to go together. Once we're all together, that's when we can worry about all the extra shit."

"That's wasting time, B. By the time I got the money and heat y'all could be meeting back up with me so we can dip out." Harlem placed his hands on both their shoulders. "Trust me y'all, we'll be good."

"Don't you think they'll be waiting at your house?" Allah asked.

Harlem grinned and lifted his cannon. "I hope they are," he said confidently.

31

Essence sat in bed, watching the news coverage on the shooting that had taken place a few hours earlier. The reporter was outside the hospital that Calvin Cole had been taken to.

There was a sea of people standing outside with candles as they cried and wept over the loss of one of the most influential criminals to touch the hood in a decade.

Like most people that weren't involved with criminal activities Essence had never met Calvin Cole, but she had heard that he was a generous man who was all about his people.

It was sad that a life as young as his had to be taken and it just made Essence more worried about Junnie as it became clear to everyone that anyone was touchable.

Essence continued watching the news for a few more minutes before turning it to the HBO movie channel.

A movie she was familiar with was on and she planned to get into it, when her stomach began to growl. Rubbing her stomach, she had forgotten to make herself something to eat.

Thinking about what might be in the refrigerator, Essence remembered she was supposed to go grocery shopping the day before and had never got around to it. Sighing, Essence got out of the bed before she could change her mind.

Throwing on her sweats and one of Junnie's t-shirts, Essence prepared to run to the corner store. There wasn't many food selections at the corner store but they made good deli sandwiches. Grabbing her wallet and keys Essence left the apartment. Once outside she was surprised that it was as warm as it had been. Despite the current events of things, the streets were empty.

Usually there were people surrounding their block, which usually stopped Essence from doing any nighttime walks to the store, but there was no one out except the usual crack head here and there.

Essence was almost to the store when she realized that she had left her phone on the bed. Putting a pep in her step just in case Junnie called her, Essence got to the corner store and rushed inside.

Across the street two armed men sat in the darkness, looking at the girl who had walked inside the store to the photo they had on their phones. They exchanged looks of confirmation. Nodding, the younger one of the group exited the car and headed towards the store.

****

Junnie hung up the phone angrily as the call went to the voicemail. He had been calling Essence since they first left the warehouse and had gotten no answer. It was ringing so it wasn't dead, he couldn't understand why she would not be answering.

He tried to convince himself Essence was just sleep, but the worst kept popping into his head. Allah got them across town in no time, ignoring the law enforcement this time around. Getting them across the Bay Bridge in half the time it would have taken if they had been driving normally. As they got closer to the exit, Harlem sat up from the backseat, his red rimmed eyes scanning outside the window.

"Drop me off in front of Jack London," he demanded, blowing cigarette smoke into the air.

"Listen, Harlem, you sure you want to do this?" Junnie asked again, as Allah followed Harlem's directions. "We can just stop by your house after we pick up Essence."

"Nah, that's wasting time," Harlem answered.

His face showed no worry as he finished his cigarette and flicked the butt outside the window. Checking the clip to his twin 9mms he tucked them at his side and prepared for any opposition he might meet.

"Where do you want us to meet you at?" Allah asked, pulling in front of Jack London Square.

There were a few people wondering the courtyard but no one that stuck out suspiciously.

"We can rendezvous at Lee John's. He shut it down for a week while he went to Chicago so no one should be over there this time of night."

"Alright, how long you need?"

"Give me about twenty minutes, tops. I'm gonna be in and out so it shouldn't be that long." Harlem opened the back door. "If I don't make it by then, I'll just call you and we can meet somewhere else."

"Yo, Harlem..." Junnie started but didn't know what to say.

He had a bad feeling about everything, but he knew telling Harlem wouldn't get any results. Harlem was a soldier and knew no other way to be.

"You better be there in twenty. I don't want to have to come looking for you, nigga."

Harlem smirked as he stood outside the car. "Just make sure you clown ass niggas are there," he said, slamming the door shut.

"You sure you want to leave him?" Allah asked, not wanting to leave one of his closest friends behind.

"You know Harlem would never listen to us," Junnie answered, looking out the back window to see Harlem already disappearing across the street. "Let's just hurry up and get Essence so we can come back for him."

Reluctantly, Allah pulled the car from the curb and sped to Junnie's house. They were both silent as they drove, each in their own thoughts. Junnie's thoughts were on Essence and wondering if she might be in trouble because of him. Though Junnie hadn't done anything wrong this time, he knew Essence would be in grave danger.

"Don't trip, bro. Essence is good," Allah told him, reading his facial expression.

"What if she's hurt and it's my fault?" Junnie asked, a little more emotional then he intended. "I can't live with that shit, Lah."

"I know, fam, I know. But that's why we're about to pick her up. Once she's with us you'll quit worrying. We'll meet up with Harlem's busted ass and we'll go get a hotel somewhere. It's going to be good, trust me."

"Lah, everyone in the Bay is out looking for us. There's a chance this might not end good for us." he said looking at his partner.

"Yeah, this shit is pretty fucked up," Allah admitted. "But if this happens to be the last battle we fight side by side, we're gonna go down swinging."

"Oh, you already know that's a must."

They exchanged dap as Allah exited the highway and turned onto the main street.

As they pulled onto Junnie's block at first glance everything appeared okay. No one was out, which was unusual, but Junnie was okay with that. Placing his gun in his lap, he looked towards his apartment for any sign of trouble.

"Are you going to call her again?" Allah asked, looking for a spot to park.

Before Junnie could respond, the silence erupted into loud gunfire. Bright light flashed as guns rang off from what seemed like every direction.

Junnie thought they were being ambushed again, but that was quickly expelled when he seen Essence run into the middle of the street, with two men on her tail.

****

Essence stepped inside the store, heading towards the back where they made the deli sandwiches. She was disappointed when she seen that they had closed early. Settling for a cup of Ramen, and a cranberry juice, Essence paid for her items and walked out the store.

She was sorting out her change, seeing what she had left when she bumped into someone. She looked up to find a pleasant faced young man standing in front of her looking embarrassed.

"My bad, I didn't see you coming out," he said politely, bending down to pick up the bills Essence had dropped.

"It's okay, I guess I should have been looking too," she said just as embarrassed. "Are you alright?"

"Yeah, you didn't hurt me too bad," the young man responded as he handed Essence her money.

"Pretty woman like you shouldn't be out here like that anyway. If I was your nigga, I'd have you in the house all the time."

"Yeah, well mine usually does but luckily he's not home," Essence joked, sticking her money in her bra.

The young man nodded. "You're right. That is lucky."

Without warning he punched Essence in the face, sending her crashing to the ground, dazed. Looking up in pain and confusion Essence watched as the young man's face changed, and he was suddenly glaring at her dangerously.

"What are you doing?" Essence cried, grabbing her forehead.

"Cashing in on the grand prize," the young man said, producing a gun from his jacket. "The price is on your niggas head but I'm more than sure Johnny will cash out a pretty penny for your fine ass. Get the fuck up bitch!" he barked, aiming the gun at her.

Head throbbing and heart beating a mile a minute Essence stood to her feet, being sure to keep her hands in plain sight. The young man grabbed her roughly and began to direct her towards a car that was waiting nearby.

Essence couldn't believe what was happening to her as she walked on shaky legs towards the vehicle. She was just thinking of what she could do to escape when a gunshot suddenly rang out.

The young man turned towards the sudden noise with his gun drawn, but a few seconds later cried out in pain when a bullet ripped through his shoulder. He fell to the ground, withering in pain.

"What's up muthafucka!" Horace barked, running towards them from the apartment building.

His shirt was off and his khaki shorts were sagging, but that didn't stop him from sprinting across the parking lot.

"Essence, you good?" he asked, reaching her and pulling her close to him.

"I don't fucking know! He just came from nowhere and hit me, I don't know what's going on!" Essence yelled hysterically.

"Where's Junnie?" Horace asked, looking around the dark street.

"On his way home now, I just talked to him before I left!"

"A'ight, we need to get you out of here. There's a lot of shit going on right now and you don't need to be..."

Horace words were cut off as the sound of a Mac-11 being sprayed interrupted him. Horace let out a yelp of pain as bullets hit him in his arm and shoulder. His gun flew from his hand and skidded across the pavement, underneath car.

The young man's accomplice had exited the car and quickly approached the two.

"Don't move bitch!" he demanded, aiming the semi-automatic at Essence, who was crying and holding her hands to her head.

The man approached the wounded thug who had shot his partner. He didn't recognize the thug as Junnie or one of his homeboys so he decided to kill him. Raising the gun, he prepared to finish the job when bright headlights bearing down on him caused him to hesitate.

Looking up, he only had time to yell as Allah hit him with the Monte Carlo. The man flew across the street, and went rolling across the sidewalk.

Junnie hopped out of the car before it could come to a complete stop. His gun was out and he scanned the area for anymore enemies, before approaching Essence who was crouched over Horace.

"Are you okay?" Junnie asked her, wrapping his arms around her.

"Yeah, but Horace got shot," she said, sobbing into his shoulder.

Junnie quickly broke away from her and scooted over to Horace who was already climbing to his feet.

"Watch out, li'l homie, I'm good," Horace swung his arm from Junnie's grasp. "This ain't shit but a scratch, cuz. You need to take your old lady and get the fuck from around here. We both know there's about to be way more than these two coming for you, not to mention one-time. Shake out this spot, homie."

"Horace, you looked out for my wife, dawg. Is there anything I can do to pay you back for that?"

"You can roll the fuck from out here and stay alive so I don't get these bullets in vain," Horace motioned towards his shirt which was soaked with blood already.

"Stay safe, cuz."

"You too, fam."

Junnie gave him dap again, and pulled Essence towards the car. They were at the door when Essence suddenly ran back and gave Horace a hug.

"Thank you," she told him, tears streaming down her face.

"Don't mention it. Now get the fuck out of here," he told her.

Without another word she turned and jumped into the backseat of the car. Allah burned rubber peeling down the street. Horace watched them go, wincing from the pain that was numbing his side. The wounds hurt a lot more than he had let on to them, and the pain was starting to come full force. Across the street, the young man he shot was slowly climbing to his feet, grunting in pain and holding his arm.

Never one to leave a job undone Horace pulled his knife from his pocket and flicked it open, stalking over to the young man who was about to meet his maker. Rabbit and his crew watched the man who had just saved Essence life, walk over to the wounded shooter and plunge his knife into the man's neck.

After the shooter fell to the ground the man took off into the night, disappearing in the shadows.

Hasaan looked at his boys in shock.

"Did you just see the same shit I just seen?"

"Hell yeah."

Rabbit had driven them to Junnie's street just in time to find someone else coming to do the job.

They watched the whole scene, from Horace's rescue, to Junnie's arrival, to their escape. It let him know that snatching Junnie was going to be just as hard as they had thought.

"What we do now?" Chucky asked.

Rabbit was quiet for a moment. "We follow them, then attack at the right moment," he answered.

Starting the car, he slowly drove in the direction that Allah's car had gone.

32

Harlem made it to his block in about ten minutes, giving him only ten more to grab what they needed and meet back up with the crew.

Looking around suspiciously, he didn't notice anything out of the ordinary as he walked towards his house, as he turned the corner that led to his street he bumped into a large man who was just stepping from the corner store.

He was a stocky man with a hideous face, and a lazy eye, with a scar running across it. Harlem's first thought was how the man looked like an animal. A wolf to be exact.

"Damn nigga, you can't watch where you're going?" Harlem barked at the man, not caring that the man was giving him a hard look.

"My bad, gangster. Didn't see you," the man replied in a gruff voice.

"Open your fucking eye, ugly, and maybe you would've." Harlem continued on his way, more important things on his mind than slapping the dude.

Crossing the street, he jogged the rest of the way to his house. He opened the gate and hopped onto the porch, unlocking his front door cautiously.

Kicking the door open, Harlem poked his gun inside the house and peeked inside. The house was completely dark, providing shelter for anyone that might be lurking in the shadows waiting for him to step inside. After waiting for a moment Harlem stepped inside and flipped the light switch.

Everything seemed to be exactly how he had left it, but he wouldn't take any chances. Harlem checked every room in the house and once he concluded that the house was empty he went inside his bedroom and straight to the closet. Pulling open the door, he grabbed his backpack and a trash bag that was inside. Taking them to his bed he emptied the trash bag, spilling stacks of cash onto the mattress.

Unzipping the backpack, he filled it up with as much money as he could, choosing to leave the rest. Once he was satisfied, Harlem pulled the backpack over his shoulder and headed to the living room where he kept his guns put up at. He checked his watch to find that he only had a few minutes left to meet the others.

Stepping in the living room, Harlem froze as he realized he had company. Standing across the living room was the man he had just ran into outside the store. Harlem reached for his gun and remembered that he had left it on the bed as he had been filling his backpack up.

His stash of weapons was in the kitchen, tucked away in the pantry, but he would have to get past the man to reach them. Harlem grinned.

"I shoulda known you would be one after me," Harlem told him. "You look like you could use the money, fat boy."

"Trust me, I'm not doing this for some fucking scraps of money," Wolf told him, loosening his shoulders. "Calvin was like a brother to me. I'ma feel good ripping your arms from their sockets."

"That's a new one, but you're gonna need more than threats to come at me, homie. You got the drop on me. Bet your niggas are waiting for your word to come running up in here next, huh?"

"Oh no, my nigga. This is all me. I rather have your boy Junnie's head on a stick, but you'll make an excellent consolation prize."

Wolf took his shirt off, showing his chiseled form. Harlem dropped his backpack to the floor and kicked it to the side.

"However you wanna do it, but I'ma warn you now. I only have five minutes to meet my people, so sorry if I rush this," Harlem told him.

"Don't worry, I'll be done by then," Wolf shot back.

Without another word the two men ran at each other, clashing in the center of the living room.

****

Seven and Bobbi had just left the movie theatre and were still laughing over what they had seen. Seven was usually too busy running the streets to go and enjoy something as relaxed as a movie but Bobbi had been really set on seeing the new Ice Cube flick. It was a warm night and Bobbi insisted on stopping for ice cream.

As they walked, Seven felt as if something was off. To a normal civilian such as Bobbi it might have gone unnoticed but Seven could feel that something was not right. He paid extra attention to the street cats they passed as they walked.

"You hear me?"

"Huh?"

He hadn't heard Bobbi talking. His attention had been on a group of young cats across the street. They were gathered together talking excitedly about something.

"I said, are you coming back over to spend the night?" Bobbi repeated.

"Yeah, you know I am, ma." Seven responded distractedly. Bobbi followed his gaze to the group of young men. She smacked her lips.

"Seven I know you're not over here plotting while we're together," Bobbi hissed angrily.

"No, are you crazy?" Seven gave her his attention again. "I would never put you in harm's way. I just feel like somethings off."

"Like what?" Bobbi asked frowning.

Seven shrugged. "Just a feeling I have in my stomach."

"Want to just head straight to the house?"

"Nah, because I don't want you complaining in an hour about how you didn't get your damn ice cream," Seven laughed.

"Shut up." Bobbi slapped his arm before grabbing his hand in hers. They walked and talked about the movie, but Seven made sure he kept his eyes open to what was going on around them.

They had just reached Cold Stone when Seven spotted Scarecrow walking briskly in their direction. He looked anxious and was mumbling to himself. He had yet to see Seven.

"Crow!"

Scarecrow looked up at the sound of Seven's voice. A look of relief crossed his face as he rushed over to his friend.

"Bro, I been looking all over for you!" Scarecrow called as he got closer. "It's going down tonight. Calvin Cole just got killed!"

Seven's eyebrows raised in surprise. "Word?" he asked, genuinely shocked. There weren't too many people that Seven gave respect to but Calvin Cole was one of them.

"Oh my God!" Bobbi covered her mouth.

"Someone managed to touch him?" Seven asked, not believing it.

"Yeah, a couple hours ago at the sideshow. Some shooters came through and had the whole block shaking. But that ain't the worst part. People are saying your brother was the shooter."

"Junnie?" Seven was at a loss for words, which was uncommon for him.

Everyone knew Junnie did his dirt but killing Calvin Cole wouldn't be on his list of risks. Even Seven knew better than trying to take on the king of the Bay Area.

"You sure?"

"I don't know if he really did it or not but that's the word around town," Scarecrow told him. "Johnny Welcome put a price on his head. Niggas are out hunting for him right now."

If Junnie really did play a part in Calvin Coles death Seven knew this night wasn't going to end well. As of right now, Junnie was one of the most wanted men in the state, but if they were coming for his brother they were going to have to take Seven out too.

"You see Angel?" Seven asked Scarecrow.

"No, I've been searching for both of you. He's probably on the block though."

Seven turned to Bobbi. There was almost a pleading look in his eyes. Not for her permission, but for her understanding about what he had to do.

"Please be careful baby." Bobbi told him before he could even say anything.

Seven gave her a deep kiss. "I'll call you as soon as I can, I promise. Scarecrow, take Bobbi home for me."

"I'll get her home safe, Sev." Scarecrow vowed. Seven nodded then took off running across the street.

"Come back to me," Bobbi whispered as Seven disappeared around the corner.

****

"We have about five minutes left to meet Harlem," Allah announced as he tore away from the crime scene at Junnie's apartments.

"Step on it then!" Junnie commanded. He turned to Essence who looked as if she was on the verge of a nervous breakdown. "Baby are you okay? Are you hurt?"

"What the fuck is going on Junnie?" Essence demanded hysterically. "Who were those men?"

"You have to calm down baby. You're okay now," Junnie tried to comfort. "I don't know who those dudes were, but they won't be the only ones after us. For some reason people think we were responsible for Calvin Cole getting killed."

"Oh my God!" Essence cried, placing her head in her hands.

Her worst fear had been confirmed as she took in the seriousness of the situation they were all in.

"Did you do it?" Essence asked, looking up at Junnie.

"Hell no, I have no reason to kill Calvin Cole. I've never even met dude. We were set up."

Essence couldn't believe what she was now involved in. She had always worried about Junnie being hurt in all the chaos that he was involved in but now it looked as if she might be going along for the ride.

She was scared out of her mind but she knew that she wasn't going to leave Junnie, no matter what.

"So what do we do now?" she asked, tears sprinkling down her cheeks. "Go to the police?"

Junnie gave her a look. He knew she was more on the square side, so he didn't go too hard on her.

"We don't talk to the police ma. And even if we did, most of them were in Calvin's Cole pockets. We wouldn't make it in front of a judge."

"Harlem went to his house to get some cash, then we're all going to lay low for a few days," Allah informed her. "We just need to get out of the city and we'll be okay for the time being. Speaking of, we still need to get some gas. I'm surprised how we're still driving honestly."

"Alright pull over to this Arco," Junnie pointed to the closest gas station.

Allah obeyed and pulled into the station. He parked at a pump and cut the car off.

"I'll be right out," he said quickly exiting the car.

Junnie also got out the car and motioned for Essence to do the same. She stepped out into the light and Junnie seen her good for the first time that night. Her hair was all over her head, and her eyes were red and puffy from crying, but Junnie was more concerned with the purplish bruise forming on her forehead.

"I should have been there," he told her gently, wiping the tears away from her face.

"I was so scared baby,' Essence told him, sobbing as she realized how close to death she had been.

The thought had shaken her to the core and she couldn't get rid of it.

"You're safe now baby. I promise," Junnie whispered as he hugged her. "I'm gonna protect you no matter what. No matter what."

They stood and hugged each other waiting for Allah to hurry and come back. Junnie felt Essence shaking in his arms as he tried to soothe her. Looking over her head his eyes narrowed as he watched a black Tahoe pull into the gas station's parking lot.

Junnie gently shifted Essence to the side as he grabbed the handle of his gun. He watched as the doors opened up and men began to file out. Junnie prepared to make a move when he recognized one of the faces walking towards him.

Polo's expression was grim as he approached Allah's car, followed by Wesley and two more goons.

He had almost got to the pump when Junnie raised his gun, aiming at Polo's head. Instantly Wesley and his men also produced their guns, ready to shoot but Polo motioned for them to stand down.

"You know we go back like cornrows Po, but in the current state of things I'd prefer if you stayed right there," Junnie cautioned. There was no hostility in his voice but his eyes said he wouldn't hesitate to shoot.

Polo raised his hands in the air. "There's a lot of people out here searching for you June," he called out. "I'm here to help."

Junnie smirked at that one. "Help huh? Didn't you hear? I killed your boss. And you want to help me? Forgive me if I don't jump and skip for joy. I'm not too trusting these days."

"I know you didn't do it Junnie," Polo told him. "I told all of my people you didn't have anything to do with it."

Junnie looked at him suspiciously. They used to be close back in the day, but times changed and so did people. The fact that Junnie was said to have killed Polo's boss gave Junnie doubt that Polo wasn't here to kill him.

"Look Junnie, Johnny's willing to listen to what you and your people have to say, but I'ma need you to come with me," Polo continued. Junnie laughed aloud at that one.

"Po, you've known me long enough to know better than that," he told him, keeping his eyes on Polo's men just in case they made a move.

Essence was beside him, looking at the men with terror in her eyes.

"Junnie, just trust me fam," Polo pleaded. "I'm trying to look out for you. Just come with me and I'll make sure none of these niggas bust a move."

As Polo was talking he didn't notice the group of young thugs coming from the side of the store. They were behind Polo and his crew, with their eyes trained on Junnie.

The kid in the front turned his attention to the back of Polo's head and seemed to decide to shoot him just because he was standing there.

As he raised his gun and prepared to knock Polo's head off, Junnie knew he didn't have a choice. Letting out a roar, Junnie raised his gun and fired. That's when all hell broke loose.

33

Harlem swung and connected with Wolf's jaw. He followed with a right, but Wolf grabbed his arm with one hand and delivered a crushing blow to his rib with his other.

Harlem cocked his free arm back and rammed his elbow down on the back of Wolf's head. The man stumbled but refused to fall to the floor.

The two struggled, throwing punches here and there before finally breaking apart.

"I'ma fuck you up, dawg," Wolf growled, breathing heavily.

"You better hit harder than that then," Harlem taunted, resuming his fighting stance.

All he needed was enough time to reach his pantry but Wolf seemed determined not to let him across the room. Wolf growled and ran forward. Harlem back peddled, throwing punch after punch but they seemed to bounce off of the muscular man.

Wolf wrapped his large arms around Harlem and lifted him in the air. Letting out a roar he slammed Harlem through the coffee table, sending glass flying everywhere.

Dazed Harlem tried to jump back to his feet but Wolf grabbed the back of his neck and pulled him up. Harlem came with an uppercut, catching Wolf off guard.

Wolf stumbled from the blow and Harlem was on him like white on rice. He rushed forward with a barricade of punches, that caused Wolf to back up and try to block as many as he could.

Harlem picked up a vodka bottle he had on the nightstand and smashed it across Wolf's face, momentarily blinding him. Seeing his chance, he ran into the kitchen to grab his guns.

Ripping open the pantry he grabbed the first thing his hand touched which was his .22.

It was a small gun but it was powerful enough to get someone off of you when needed. Not checking to see if it was loaded Harlem turned and aimed at Wolf who was staggering towards the kitchen.

Keeping his arm perfectly steady Harlem pulled the trigger. The shot hit Wolf in the stomach but he kept coming as if it had no effect on him.

Harlem fired two more times, each finding their mark but Wolf launched forward and wrapped his hand around Harlem's throat.

Feeling the nails digging into his flesh, Harlem gasped as he raised the gun again, this time at Wolf's head.

It was hard to get a straight shot while the life was being choked out of him but that didn't stop him from trying.

Aiming the gun around Wolf's arms Harlem fired again, grazing the side of his head. Almost losing consciousness Harlem gave all his effort to shoot just one more time.

This time the bullet entered Wolf's skull, dropping him to the carpet. Harlem leaned against the wall, gasping for air as he looked down at the large man he had shot five times.

Checking his watch Harlem seen that he was five minutes late from getting to the meeting spot.

Limping to the living room Harlem picked up the backpack with the money, and swung it over his shoulder. Looking down he noticed a shard of glass sticking from his side.

It must have lodged in when he was slammed through the table. Stopping, Harlem winced as he pulled the blade of glass from his body and tossed it to the side. The pain was bad, that, combined with the other cuts he had received were enough to make him move slower than normal. Holding onto his backpack strap with one hand, and his gun with the other Harlem limped from the house.

Once outside he took a deep breath before stepping down the porch. He was just digging in his phone to call Junnie when a shot rang out and Harlem felt the pain in his back.

Stumbling forward he turned around only to get hit two more times to the chest, knocking him off his feet and onto his back. He dropped his gun and the backpack as he hit the sidewalk hard. Looking up Harlem was shocked to find Wolf standing over him, gun in hand.

"You got skills, li'l nigga, I'll give you that," Wolf croaked as he stumbled down the porch. "But I'm a beast out here." Reaching Harlem, he shakily raised his gun. "Die knowing you tried."

Knowing when the curtain was about close, Harlem closed his eyes, and thought about all the times he had been on the opposite end of the gun in these situations. Now it was his turn to face the music.

He heard the bang of the gun and felt the heat from the bullet before everything turned to darkness. Wolf looked down at Harlem's body, satisfied that he had at least got one of the men responsible for Calvin's death. Taking two steps forward he fell face first to the sidewalk, overcome from his injuries. He died only a few seconds after Harlem took his last breath.

****

Junnie's bullet hit the man in the head, putting an end to whatever he had planned. Polo's crew, who still hadn't noticed the men behind them, opened fire as soon as Junnie's gun went off.

Ducking behind the car, Junnie pulled Essence down with him as she began a whole new round of screaming. Having been watching the drama from inside the store Allah ran outside, shooting at Polo's men, as well as the hit man who had come for him and Junnie.

He seemed to move in slow motion as he sprinted through the hail of gunfire, firing relentlessly. Miraculously he made it to the car without getting hit by the bullets.

"How come every time I leave and come back somebody's shooting at you?" Allah demanded as bullets continued to strike the side of the car.

****

Polo ducked as Allah came from out the store opening fire on him and his crew. He had come to bring Junnie back with him but now it looked as if he had no choice but to take him and his people out.

Just as he prepared to join the battle, Polo happened to look over his shoulder and his eyes opened in shock at the gang of men standing behind them. They were all armed and coming towards them with murder written on their faces.

"Shooters!" he yelled to Wesley, who turned and was just as surprised as he was to find a row of dudes coming towards them.

Polo had thought that Junnie had been firing at him but as he looked and seen one of the men sprawled out on the cement with a gun next to his hand Polo suddenly knew what time it was.

"Stop shooting!" he tried to tell his team but the battle was already on.

The hit men had their guns raised but didn't seem to know who they were supposed to be grabbing, so instead they chose to fire on everyone.

Polo focused his attention on the men and began to slowly advance towards them as he let his hammer spark. He managed to drop one, but the guy's partner was just as lucky. His bullet struck Polo in the neck, putting him out the fight.

"No!" Junnie yelled seeing his old homeboy collapse after being struck.

He wanted to run to him, but bullets were flying from everywhere and he knew he would never make it. Anger coursing through every pore in his body, Junnie jumped up and let off an assault of gunfire.

The viciousness of the attack sent Wesley and his thugs ducking for cover. Allah leaned around the side of his car and let off his own shots, dropping a man who had been trying to inch his way closer to them.

"We need to get the fuck out of here June!" he yelled to his friend, while they both continued to lay fire. "They keep shooting at these pumps we're all going to blow up!"

"You won't get any argument from me!" Junnie yelled back.

He turned to check on Essence and noticed she was gone. Ceasing his fire, Junnie looked up to see her being dragged across the street by three young cats in hoodies.

"Essence!" he yelled, forgetting about everything else.

He took off running towards the car they were throwing Essence in but he was too late. By the time he reached the street, they had already burned rubber on the pavement and was zooming into the night.

Junnie raised his gun and prepared to shoot but stopped. He didn't want to risk hitting Essence. Staring helplessly, he watched as the car made it a few blocks before disappearing around a corner, and out of sight. Gunshots still rang out and men were shouting and running through the parking lot but Junnie didn't care. He stood in the middle of the street, gun dangling at his side. A car pulled up next to him and screeched to a stop.

"Junnie, get in nigga. Let's go!" Allah demanded. He checked his rearview to find men running in their direction, guns blazing. "Let's go, let's go."

Junnie climbed in the passenger seat, and before he could close the door Allah had taken off, leaving the chaos behind.

"Drive Lah, drive! Maybe we can still catch them!" Junnie demanded, leaning forward in his seat and scanning the streets for the beat up Chevy that had his girl in it.

Allah turned onto the street that the car had gone. They drove around the block and every other one in the vicinity but there was no sign of the car.

After a few minutes, Junnie yelled and slammed his fist into the dashboard. Again and again.

He had told Essence he would protect her and she had been snatched right underneath his nose. If something happened to her because of him, Junnie knew he could never live with that. The car began to slow down as they drove past a dead end street. Junnie looked around to see where they were at.

"Why you stopping?" he asked.

"We're out of gas," Allah sighed, parking the car next to the corner. "I never got the chance to get any."

"We need to go, we need to find Essence!" he shouted angrily.

Throwing open the car door Junnie could feel the tears starting to form in the corner of his eyes.

Thoughts of Essence being beaten and tortured was spinning through his head, it was too much for him.

He didn't know where she was, or who had her. Their car was out of gas, and they were low on ammo. And to top it off they hadn't heard from Harlem.

Allah walked over to him and placed his arm around his shoulder.

"Look bro, we're gonna get Essence back. I don't know how, but we will. Trust me. Tonight will not be the end for us, dawg. We're gonna get through this."

"Yeah bro, I feel you, it's just..."

Junnie stopped as he happened to look at Allah's shirt. There was a dark red stain that seemed to be spreading even as Junnie looked at it.

"You're hit!"

"This ain't shit. Just a flesh wound," Allah replied, but the sweat pouring from his face said otherwise.

Junnie helped him lean against the car as he examined the wound. It was leaking blood down Allah's side and down the side of his jeans.

"We need to get you to the hospital now!" Junnie said, taking off his t-shirt. He placed it against the bullet wound and applied pressure.

"Nah, we need to find Essence and we still need to meet up with Harlem," Allah winced as the pressure sent pain up his side. "Call that nigga and see where he's at. He can pick us up if he got his car."

Junnie pulled out his phone just as it began to ring. Looking at the screen it was a blocked number, Junnie's heart jumped hoping it was Essence's captors.

"Baby?"

"Baby, We haven't even gone on a date yet, my nigga," a male's voice taunted from the other end.

"Where the fucks my girl at?" Junnie barked into the receiver.

"Don't trip nigga, she's good for the time being," Rabbit announced. "How long she stays that way is up to you, homie."

"Nigga you lay one finger on her and I promise..."

"This really isn't the best time to be making threats is it?" Rabbit asked.

There was a smack from the other end and Junnie heard Essence cry out.

"Essence!" Junnie yelled. "Alright, what do you want?"

"Glad to hear that bass out your voice, faggot ass nigga." Rabbit was feeling more powerful than he ever had in his life and he was enjoying it. "If you want this bitch back you can come get her. She'll be here with us at the old firehouse on Jefferson.

"If I was you I would hurry up my nigga. My boys ain't had a bitch this bad around them for a while so they don't know how to act."

There was howling in the background then laughter. The last thing Junnie heard was Essence begging them to stop, before the phone cut off.

"Essence!" Junnie yelled, almost feeling his throat tear apart.

Allah was looking at him with an anxious expression on his face. He was in a world of pain but ignored it for the time being seeing that his best friend still needed him.

"What's the deal?" he asked, already having a good idea of what was going on.

"They got her," Junnie said numb, thinking back to Essence's screams. "They want me to meet them over on Jefferson.

"You know it's a trap right?" Allah told him.

Junnie was quiet for a moment. It was obviously a trap, which now brought up the question; could Junnie exchange his life for the life of the women who had taught him how to live in the first place?

"I need to get to Jefferson," he said, moving into action.

Checking the clip to his .40, Junnie quickly began to launch a plan on how to get his lady back.

"Fuck you mean homie? We both need to get to Jefferson," Allah clarified, pushing himself off of the car.

"Not on this one, Lah," Junnie replied seriously. "I'm going all in on this one bro and odds are I might not make it back. If that's the case I need someone to take care of Essence."

"Then you'll be good, my nigga because we're both going to be around to look after her yellow ass," Allah said sternly. "We're in this shit until the end bro. If we fight, we fight together. And if we die we die together."

Junnie smiled weakly. "You know this might be the end of the road for us."

Allah shrugged, wrapping Junnie's t-shirt around his waist to cover the wound.

"Who wants to live forever anyway?"

34

Horace's head snapped back from the force of the slap. Blood was pouring down his face and his eye had swollen shut, but the men holding his arms down prevented him from doing anything. As he felt himself losing consciousness he cursed for allowing himself to get caught slipping.

After helping save Essence, and taking out her attackers Horace had wobbled his way upstairs to check on his injuries, change, and leave before the police came to respond to the shooting.

There was so much chaos going on through the city he knew it would take them a while. Once inside the house he found out that neither of the bullets had pierced him.

They had grazed his side, taking a chunk from his flesh but nothing too serious. After dressing the gash with gauze, Horace was changing his clothes when someone busted in his front door.

Horace went for his gun, but they were too quick. In no time they were beating the life out of him without saying a word. That was ten minutes before. Now they surrounded him as he laid on the floor, bleeding from his fresh injuries.

"That's enough," the leader of the pack called out.

The men stopped stomping Horace and moved aside for the man to step through. Johnny Welcome glared down at Horace, with no ounce of pity for him.

"Where is he, nigga?"

Horace spit out a mouthful of blood before glaring up at him.

"Who?"

"Junnie, I heard there was an altercation outside not too long ago and you participated in his escape. Now, where the fuck is he?"

"Junnie? Who's that?"

Johnny shook his head.

"Dawg, usually I applaud loyalty, but tonight's not the night to test my patience. Where is he?"

"Did you check your Mommas crib?" Horace suggested, laughing. Johnny just stared at the man until his cell phone rang.

"What you got for me?" Johnny answered.

"They shot Polo fam! They shot po..." Wesley's panicking voice came from the other end.

For the first time that Johnny could remember, a pang of fear hit his heart. A pang that his little homie might be dead.

"What you mean?" Johnny asked hurriedly. "Who did?"

"I don't know, I think it was this nigga Junnie's people!"

"What the fuck do you mean you 'think'? Was it his people or not?" Johnny demanded.

"I don't know, cuddy, I don't know! We were going to pick up Junnie like you said then all of a sudden..."

"Hold up, chill out with what you say on the jack," Johnny warned remembering they were on an open line. "Meet me at the HQ. I'll be there in five."

Hanging up the phone Johnny glared down at Horace who was wheezing and chuckling.

"Was that your boyfriend?" he asked.

"I'ma ask you one last time," Johnny pulled his gun from his jeans. "Where's Junnie?"

Horace looked at him defiantly. "Nigga, you can ask me ten more times and I'm not gonna answer you. I'ma soldier until the end, cuz. I won't ever fold, so suck my…"

Johnny's bullet hit Horace in the temple cutting his sentence short. Looking at the men assembled in the apartment he pointed at the door with his gun.

"Keep looking for this nigga!"

As they all ran out of the door Johnny's phone rang again. The number calling was unknown.

"Who the fuck is this?"

"I got who you want. Meet us at the old fire station on Jefferson in twenty minutes."

****

Luckily Jefferson wasn't far from where they were, so Junnie and Allah decided to make a jog for it.

They had to take it slower than usual with Allah's injury, but they still made it within fifteen minutes.

On the way they tried calling Harlem, but got no answer. Junnie hoped for the best but he began to fear the worst for his comrade. Promising to search every street for his friend as soon as they got Essence, Junnie prepared to meet his enemies.

Once they reached Jefferson they made their way to the fire house. The building had been abandoned years ago but the city was too lazy to tear it down. It usually served as a shelter to the homeless or a rock house for crack heads but tonight it would serve as a burial ground for whoever had touched Junnie's wife.

"You ready?" Allah asked quietly as they walked around the side of the building.

There were no lights back there, so it was almost impossible to see. Every step they took Junnie expected someone to leap out and shoot them in the head.

"As ready as I'll ever be, compadre," Junnie mumbled back, gun at the ready.

They got to the back of the building and looked for a back entrance to get inside. Luckily the latch was already broken off the door, meaning that Essence and her captors must already be inside.

Giving Allah a nod, Junnie crept in first.

All the lights were on, but it was eerily silent inside. Creeping down the hallway, both men looked for the first sign of trouble, or Essence. Making it down the hallway without trouble, they walked through the doorway and into the main entrance. It was then that Junnie found Essence lying on the floor tied to a metal beam that resembled a stripper's pole.

"Essence."

Forgetting everything else, Junnie ran towards her. She had a new bruise beneath her eye but other than that she appeared to be okay.

"Junnie," she mumbled groggily.

"I'm here baby, I'm here."

Junnie kissed her forehead repeatedly as Allah made his way to join them. Suddenly there was a wave of commotion as people entered the warehouse.

It was packed with men, all armed with guns, and wearing facial expressions that meant business. The last man to walk in was a cat that Junnie had heard stories about since he was younger.

"I've been looking for you all night, nigga," Johnny told him, as he approached the trio. Allah aimed his gun at him, and all ten of Johnny's men raised theirs. They were surrounded.

Junnie stood to his feet and looked at Johnny.

"And you just happened to look here huh?" he retorted. He was holding his gun but he knew he would never be able to shoot them all before they managed to kill him, with Essence and Allah too. "You're just as good as people give you credit for, homie."

"Nah, just happened to get word that you were here," Johnny replied coldly. "I think it'll be best if you come with us."

"After you let my people go," Junnie demanded.

Johnny snared. "You're not really in the position to bargain, nigga."

"They don't have anything to do with this," Junnie replied evenly, as he tightened his grip on his gun.

"You killed my brother muthafucka," Johnny spit angrily. "You're lucky I don't make you watch my niggas gang rape this bitch and post it on YouTube."

"I didn't kill Calvin Cole or have anything to do with it. I was set up, homie."

"Yeah, I hear that hot shit," Johnny waved him off. "Drop your hammer and come take a walk with us, nigga."

"Let my girl go," Junnie repeated, his mind racing as he tried to come up with a plan.

"I got a better idea." Johnny pulled his gun out. "Drop your piece or we chop down all three of you right now."

At that moment, Johnny's men raised their weapons, all muttering agreements as they aimed at the trio.

Junnie looked at them before turning to his family. Essence was holding his arm, and sobbing softly as she looked at the men.

As Junnie looked into her wet eyes he thought about the first time he had saw her. She had been crying then too and he had tried his best to prevent those tears from ever having to fall again. He had failed.

Looking at Allah he found his partner giving him a look that said they both realized the same thing. They wouldn't be going home that night. Giving each other a knowing nod everything suddenly seemed to go in slow motion.

Junnie grabbed Essence and threw her to the ground just as Allah opened fire on Johnny and his crew.

Back peddling, he aimed to take out every last one of them as they began to return fire. As Essence hit the ground Junnie lifted his cannon and began sending shots of his own.

Standing side by side they went toe to toe with the Family, fighting a losing battle. A bullet whizzed past Junnie's ear.

"We have to get the fuck out of here!" he yelled to his comrade.

"You're right. Go!" Allah commanded, holding onto his wound with one hand and shooting with the other. "I'll cover you and Essence."

"You must still be high from earlier! I'm not leaving you muthafucka!" Junnie yelled back.

Stopping his assault, Allah pulled Junnie down behind the crate of barrels in front of them. He winced as he knelt down.

"Bro, you have to go," he said seriously, being sure to keep his head low.

"So you can get killed?" Junnie asked, hoping Allah realized how stupid it sounded.

"If we sit here trying to shoot it out with them we're all going to die!" Allah told him.

He moved his hand from his side and showed Junnie all the blood he had lost. It was worse than Junnie had first realized.

"This is it for me, bro. This is my day of reckoning. At least you two can make it out. You got something to live for, my nigga. Go!"

Junnie stared at his best friend. The same best friend who had been their when his parents had died and had been there to back him up in his first fist fight against the neighborhood bully. The same friend who was willing to give his life in exchange for Junnie's.

Junnie wrapped Allah in a hug.

"You're my brother, Lah."

"Why the fuck you think I'm doing this," Allah laughed. Pushing Junnie off him he adjusted his shirt. "Fuck out of here with all that mushy shit. I'ma see you in a few minutes. Now go."

Junnie grabbed Essence hand and they both crept behind a stack of wooden crates towards the side exit.

Junnie opened the door for Essence but before he followed Junnie looked back at Allah. Knowing it was the last time he would ever see him he nodded, which Allah returned with an encouraging smile.

Once Junnie was gone Allah's smile faded. Leaning against the crate Allah pulled the joint he had in his pocket out and sparked it up.

"Flush these niggas out!" Johnny commanded to his team. Leading the way, he crept towards the barrels, with his team of thugs following close behind.

Allah took a deep pull from the joint as a small grin crossed his face. His fingers had long ago gone numb as the coldness spread through his body. He had never imagined that he would die as young as he was but he knew the rules when he had signed up for the game and he was ready to face the consequences.

Taking another deep pull from the joint Allah wiped his face with the back of his arm. When he heard the first footstep reach the barrel he leapt up and put a bullet in Johnny, sending him flying back.

"C'mon muthafuckas!" he yelled, squeezing the trigger so hard his knuckles began to hurt.

****

Junnie pulled Essence through the dark back way of the building, bobbing and weaving through the huge debris in the back yard.

There was a series of gunshots from inside but Junnie didn't want to think about what was taking place inside.

Clenching Essence's hand tight in one hand and his gun in the other Junnie led them to freedom.

"Hold on baby my ankle hurts," Essence complained.

They stopped as she bent down to rub her leg. Junnie kept looking behind them to make sure they weren't being followed.

"C'mon Essie, we have to go before they come," Junnie told her. "I won't have enough bullets if they catch up."

"I'm sorry Junnie, I'm sorry," Essence sobbed, on the brink of losing her sanity. "This is crazy, we left Allah!"

Junnie grabbed Essence and turned her to face him. He stared into her eyes. "I know you're scared baby, trust me. I know you are. But we have to get out of here. We need to put distance between us and them before we break down. Allah just risked his life so we could get away. It'll be in vain if we let them catch up with us ten seconds later, okay?"

"Okay," Essence agreed, taking deep breaths.

"Okay," Junnie quickly wiped the tears away from her eyes with his thumb. "Okay, now we have to keep going. Can you walk?"

When Essence nodded Junnie gave her a slight pull to get her going, and then held his gun at the ready as he led them back towards the main street.

Junnie could see the street lights up ahead as they ran, both breathing heavily. Junnie turned to see if Essence was close behind and that's when his heart literally stopped.

A man had stepped from the shadows and was aiming a shotgun in their direction. Essence was running towards Junnie and hadn't heard the man sneak up behind her.

Before Junnie could open his mouth to yell Chucky had lifted the shotgun and let it roar out. The blast hit Essence in her back and sent her flying forward.

Junnie watched as her facial expression slowly turned to fear as she flew towards him with her arms outstretched.

Junnie yelled at the top of his lungs as he raised his gun and shot at Chucky. The first bullet hit him and the next three dropped him to the ground before he could fire the shotgun again.

Junnie ran over to Essence and turned her over. Blood was leaking from her mouth and her eyes were wide and terrified. Her lips were quivering but no words were coming out as she stared up at Junnie.

"Shhh baby, don't talk. Don't talk," Junnie whispered, smoothing her hair back. "Fight it Essence, fight it. I'ma get you to the hospital. I'ma get you out of here." Junnie tried to lift her but Essence let out a whimper of pain so he stopped immediately.

"Help!" Junnie yelled as loud as he could.

At that point he didn't care if anyone heard him. He didn't care if Johnny came and got him. He didn't care whether he lived or died.

All he cared about was the hole in Essences back and the blood pouring from her mouth. Tears rained down Junnie's face as he told Essence it would be okay.

After a while he didn't hear her gurgling breathing, or feel her trembling anymore. Looking down at her face Junnie stopped rocking back and forth.

Even though she had blood everywhere Essence's face was peaceful as her eyes stared up into the empty sky.

She had gone to a place that Junnie couldn't call her back from. Lowering his head Junnie placed a tender kiss to Essence's forehead and gently closed her eyelids. Time seemed to freeze, sound seemed to be obliterated, and everything was spinning as Junnie sat in silence, not wanting to leave Essence behind even though she had already left.

Junnie was so hurt he never heard the footsteps creep up behind him, but he did hear the click of a round being chambered as a pistol was pressed to the back of his skull.

"If it was me I wouldn't have killed your bitch," Rabbit told him. "Wasn't no paper in that." Looking over at Chucky's sprawled out corpse, Rabbit sadly focused his attention back on Junnie.

"You'll be with her soon enough, nigga. This for my cousin, Sammy."

Junnie didn't say anything. He didn't reach for his gun. Welcoming death, Junnie closed his eyes and waited for it to come. Rabbit pulled the trigger. Junnie's body slumped to the side as his brains exited the side of his head. He crumpled beside Essence, as his life ended.

Barely able to believe what he had done, Rabbit looked down at Junnie's dead body, unsure of what to do next. He thought of running in the building where he knew Johnny was at but the sound of police sirens in the distance quickly dispelled that idea.

Giving Junnie one last look, Rabbit turned and began to jog back to the idling car where Hasaan was waiting behind the wheel. They would meet up with Johnny to collect their money another day.

EPILOGUE

Over the next few weeks, the sun glowed brightly everyday as the summer came to an end, but the events that had taken place over the time overshadowed the good weather. The night Calvin Cole was murdered, was followed by dozens of murders. The night was known as one of the bloodiest in Bay Area history. Many funerals took place in the months following, with family and friends busily attending them.

The day of Junnie and Essence's funeral brought gray skies. It was the first time it had rained all summer, which seemed to fit the mood just right as the two lovers were buried by loved ones.

Their ceremony was held together, with the outcome being larger than anyone expected. It seemed that everyone that had come in contact with Essence had been affected by her bright smile and cheerful nature. Everyone from coworkers to people she had grown up with her whole life came to mourn the loss.

For as many enemies as Junnie had made in the short years he had been alive, he had made just as many allies. In the last few hours of his life, Junnie had turned into the cities bad guy and had had more than a fair share of people looking to cash in on him, but he also had people who didn't believe in his involvement with Calvin's death.

Young drug dealers, old pimps, and even a few neighborhood bums came to pay their last respects to a young man who had shown a lot of promise. But just like most boys in the street, his eyes had been closed too early.

No one was exactly sure who had pulled the trigger, or who was directly the cause of Junnie and his squads deaths, but there was someone who planned to get to the bottom of it. Seven's face was blank of emotion, but for those that knew the young boy, it was obvious that Junnie's death would not go unsolved for very long. He remained silent, with Angel and Wiz flanking him on either side.

Ace stood near the exit of the church, trying his best to conceal his smirk. From behind his shades, he watched the people cry and pray for Junnie and Essence's soul. It was the most entertaining thing he had seen in a long time. When he had first had the thought to kill Calvin Cole there was no way he could have planned for the outcome that would follow the murder.

Not only had he killed his enemy, but his scapegoat had actually been murdered as the result of it. The only people that knew the truth was West, Rowdy and himself.

Shake 'Em had flown back home the day after Calvin Cole's murder so he wasn't anything to worry about. Now that he had taken care of the largest part of his plan, Ace had to launch into the next phase.

As the pastor stood to his feet to begin speaking Ace turned to leave, almost bumping into someone. A gang of hard faced men were also preparing to leave and leading the pack was none other than Johnny Welcome. He too wore shades and like Ace, it didn't seem like he came to pay Junnie a farewell.

"Let me get that for you, big dawg," Ace grinned, standing to side as he held the door open. Johnny nodded, but didn't speak as he led his entourage outside. Ace followed them out and tried to walk with Johnny but the men flanking him blocked Ace's path. Johnny motioned to let Ace through and they stood away as Ace approached.

"You need something?" Johnny said rudely, his voice sounding hoarse and tired.

The night after Calvin's murder Johnny Welcome and his crew made their way through the city putting the hurt on any and every one that threatened to come for the throne that The Family occupied. It took a few weeks, but Johnny managed to get a firm grasp on the dynasty that was threatening to slip away from him.

"Nah, nothing besides making sure I'm still good on what we talked about a few weeks ago,"

"Last I checked, my li'l niggas came through the hood and dropped your bread off to you," Johnny replied.

"Yeah, they did, and good looking on that. My pockets never been fatter." Ace tapped his pants for emphasis. "But if you recall, that wasn't the only terms of my payment. It wasn't even my first priority of payment. I wanted a seat at your table, and if I do say so myself, I think I'm worth it." Ace motioned towards the church where Junnie's service was taking place.

Johnny's face remained solid. "Check it, you did good by pointing me to where I needed to get to, but a seat at my table costs a lot more than a name being dropped on my lap. Me and my niggas grind hard for this shit. Blood and sweat, dawg, so we're not exactly in the habit of just taking anyone's application. And even more importantly, I'm not feeling the way you're trying to capitalize on my brother's death."

At Johnny's last statement his crew seemed to tense up as they expected violence. Ace was outgunned and outmanned but he hadn't come this far to be scared off now.

"Yo, my dude, I grew up trying to be like Calvin Cole," Ace started, his face turning serious. "He paved the way for niggas like me coming up and I would never disrespect his memory by trying to use him. I just want to be a part of the legacy he created, which is why I gave you his killer. You and him were leaders and even though I view myself as a leader too, I wouldn't mind taking a few lessons from Johnny Welcome."

Johnny looked into Ace's eyes, and just like the first time he had met the man, his eyes were hard to read. If there were any hint of lying in his speech, it went unnoticed in his facial expression. Johnny was quiet as he considered it than slowly nodded.

"Come by tomorrow at twelve sharp, nigga. If you're going to be late don't bother coming," Johnny said. "I want one of my people to check you out and see how you operate. If they say you're good, then you're good."

"Thank you, Johnny. Trust me fam, you won't regret this." He said as his lips split into a wide grin.

Nodding at the group, Ace turned to walk away. His grin grew wider as he thought about the day that the streets would mourn over the death of Johnny Welcome. It was a day that was going to come sooner than anyone would expect, and when the dust cleared, Ace would be there to save the day again.

Johnny watched Ace cross the street and head for his car before turning to leave. He had only made it a few feet when he heard someone call his name.

Turning around he was slightly surprised to find two young boys coming his way. The one with the dreads was glaring at him but the one wearing the hoodie was giving him a look of pure hatred. It was so deep, Johnny tapped his hip to make sure his gun was at the ready as the boys approached.

"Johnny, right?" Seven asked as he reached the gang of men. "I've been looking to meet you for the past few weeks."

"I know you?" Johnny asked rudely, looking at the boy and his disgruntled face. "You have a run in with one of my li'l homies or something?"

Seven snickered at that. "Dawg, none of the pussies you run with could fuck with me on my worst day," Seven said boldly.

One of Johnnies men moved to step forward but Johnny held him back. Seven glared at Johnny, who was several inches taller than him.

"But you are the reason I'm here today, and the reason my brothers laid out in a pine box."

Johnny finally understood. Looking closer at Seven he was surprised to find how he could have missed the resemblance between him and Junnie.

"So you're Seven. Yeah, I know about you. You've been giving some of our young boys a hard time for a while now. Calvin used to talk about putting you down with us, but he wanted to wait until you got older. Looks like he won't get the chance to because as we all know your brother killed my brother, nigga. So don't come crying to me about his life, or his death for that matter."

"So that's what your first act of power?" Seven could feel his blood began to boil but he played it cool. "Killing a man you only heard had something to do with your boy's murder? What happened to innocent until proven guilty?"

"That's the country's way of order, not mine," Johnny said coldly.

"Well, I've got my own way of order too, and mine says blood will answer for blood," Seven said not backing down.

People who were standing near the altercation began to slowly move away as the tension began to build between the two parties. Johnny's men began to fidget, and Angel tensed as he prepared to make a move. Johnny slowly took his shades off as he stepped closer to Seven.

"If you want to live longer than your brother did, I suggest you chop this one up to the game, little dude," he said softly. "I've been laying niggas out for many years now, and best believe I won't miss any sleep if I leave you out here for the trash man to pick up when he makes his rounds. I run this city, nigga, and I can have your life stomped out with a clap of my hands. Don't fuck with me."

Seven nodded slowly. "I hear that hot shit, my nigga, but I figure it would be kinda hard for your team to stop what they don't see coming."

""Is that a threat?" Johnny asked, his eyes narrowing.

"Nah, that was a straight fact." Seven motioned at Angel that it was time to go. "See you soon, King of the Bay." Seven called before heading back to the church.

"Yo J, you don't want me to bang this nigga right here?" one of Johnny's men asked, putting his hand beneath his jacket.

"Nah, let him be." Johnny said softly. "That little nigga got heart, you can't help but respect that. If he ever decides to try to grow a pair, then we'll take it to that level."

Signaling to his entourage, Johnny got in the backseat of his Maybach and he and his family drove off.